FIRE

BY

STEPHANIE HUDSON

Wraith of Fire
The Transfusion Saga #11
Copyright © 2021 Stephanie Hudson
Published by Hudson Indie Ink
www.hudsonindieink.com

Wraith of Fire/Stephanie Hudson – 1st ed.
ISBN-13 - 978-1-913904-84-5

*I would like to dedicate this book to all my wonderful fans,
those who are both new to the Afterlife and Transfusion world
and those who have support me for years.
I cannot thank you enough for keeping my dreams alive for so
long and I will be forever and always eternally grateful.
All my love,
Steph and family.*

WARNING

This book contains explicit sexual content, some graphic language and a highly additive dominate Vampire King.

This book has been written by an UK Author with a mad sense of humour. Which means the following story contains a mixture of Northern English slang, dialect, regional colloquialisms and other quirky spellings that have been intentionally included to make the story and dialogue more realistic for modern day characters.

Thanks for reading x

PROLOGUE

AMELIA

F*ear.*
Stone cold fear.
That was all I felt now.

It had become my life. Because I had faced Hell and beaten my way through it to survive. I had stepped into a war with demons, and I had survived dungeons and hexes. I had even fought harpies and Hellhounds and lived to fight another day. I had lived through every one of the witch's attacks and everything that had been thrown at me, I had survived. Then being pushed into a new realm to be faced with bandits, a fae army and their Dragon King. I felt as though I had faced it all in Hell and yet no matter how scary, I had never let that fear consume me to a point where I could not go on. No, what I had done was conquered that fear and turned it into something I could use to fuel anger, retaliation and revenge. I had channelled every frightening moment into my greatest weapon, my determination to never give up fighting.

Yet this… well,
This was different.

This was fear on a whole other level.

It was paralysing at best and at its worst, it felt as if I could not breathe. It felt as if it was suffocating and something that had the power to drag me under and simply drown me. A fear I was constantly running from and even now, as I sat huddled against some dark wall praying for the shadows to be enough to blanket me from view, I knew…

He would eventually find me.

He haunted me and terrified me to my core. This never-ending hunt he was on to capture me, the one that had broken in and infiltrated his Hellish world. Gods, but it felt as if there was nowhere I could hide, for he would always find me. That rage was like a wave of terror flowing over my body and leaving chills in its wake. My only warning became how my own body reacted to him when nearby. A rage so pliable, you could almost taste its bitterness in the air. Like breathing in smoke from a fire, where it actually had the power to burn you from inside out. A rage that had been nothing compared to what my own had once been.

I had questioned what this place was, but then the puzzle pieces of the true horror started to slot into place and soon a picture started to emerge. This wasn't just my new Hell, it was also his chosen torture, one he must endure for all eternity. His punishment for his crimes. The one I had fallen into and the reason he needed to capture me was becoming clear. As he not only wanted his revenge for what had been done to him, but he also wanted to ensure that I did not survive. A survival he couldn't chance. Because if I did, if I survived this place, it would only mean one thing.

He would die in my place.

So, this is what I had to do. I had to keep running and hiding for what was left of my life. The last spark I had in me, no matter how lost I seemed in the darkness. I had to hold on. I had to hope that I would be rescued, and that Lucius would find a way to save me.

Save me against what seemed like an unbeatable force that I had so little in me left to fight against. It was like watching a horror movie, only through a dead person's eyes and unfortunately, they were my own. Sometimes the sounds of thousands of screams were enough to drown out that of my frightened beating heart. Enough to mask my own screams lost to the echoing horror that surrounded me.

This insane world that I seemed to be imprisoned in, one that was half his and half mine. We were connected somehow and unless I discovered a way to break it, I would be forced to relive this horror over and over again until my body withered away and died.

I would often call out to him, the one man that I knew could save me, but it was as if he couldn't hear me. As if he thought I was already lost to the underworld. As if I was already lost to death, like some real-life Snow White.

Lost to this crazy place. this world of nightmares and darkness. A soulless place where phantoms were locked away in cages then used and abused by their captor.

The Wraith Master.

A cursed King.

One who was coming for me.

Coming for me to...

Finish the job.

CHAPTER ONE

LUCIUS

CRACKED HEARTS

F*ear.*

Stone cold fear.

That was all I felt now.

Since my rebirth I had never been afraid of anything. Well, that wasn't strictly true as every fear I'd ever known, ever experienced had all been centred around losing Amelia. And now… fuck! I looked down at her still body, one that should have been smiling, laughing, teasing and kissing me, and I saw it as I never had before. Because I had not even a fucking heartbeat to prove this fear unnecessary.

It was a lie.

It was all a fucking lie!

She couldn't be dead, *it was impossible.*

"No." I couldn't be sure but I thought the whispered plea had made it through my dry lips, yet it didn't matter. Nothing mattered anymore. *I had nothing.* Only moments ago my mind had raced with all of the ways that I could save her, coming up with idea after idea and now, because her heart silenced for the very first time, I knew I had been too late. I had been too late to save her.

I had failed her… failed us both.

Fuck! But if there hadn't been an entire fucking race depending on my survival, I would have taken the same dagger that had inflicted her wound and hammered it into my own heart! A heart that felt fucking useless without her, for every beat felt like a fucking waste. Like an insult that mine got to beat whilst her's did not. I wanted to tear the fucking thing out and lay it at her feet! I wanted to lie down next to her and fucking die.

Something I would have done in hopes of finding her soul once more. So fucking tempting, had it not been for the weight of my world sat against my shoulders in the form of all those lives linked to my own, her mother's included. For the first time in my existence, I fucking hated what I was!

I loathed my very being.

Just looking down at her and I found myself screaming internally. Screaming out that this couldn't be it!

It just couldn't be!

Because this wasn't the way it was supposed to be. I was supposed to get my Chosen One. I was supposed to keep her… *keep her forever.* My mortal heart, one that would have been made immortal by my blood, that was the prophecy I'd waited for. One that for all of these years I had let fear hold me back from. Years… fuck, all those years I had fucking wasted! Waited like a fucking idiot, and for what? For it to come to this point in time where I was destined to lose her too soon? Why… how… Gods be damned for being this fucking cruel! Hadn't I given enough?! Hadn't I sacrificed enough, in both this life and in the first?!

Because I hadn't had enough time... we hadn't even been given a fucking chance to live! I hadn't yet had the chance to show her, to truly show her... how much I love her...

Loved her.

My face was wet... why was it so wet... these stupid fucking tears that wouldn't stop! I just wanted them to fucking stop! Yet they wouldn't. Wouldn't stop flowing, running down my cheeks, my neck and falling over her beautiful face. I had to stop them, but I didn't know how. I didn't know what to do with this pain. This fucking agony that ripped me down to my very soul. It tore me open and now I couldn't fucking stop the emotions from spilling out of me!

Fucking tears!

But she wouldn't like them dripping all over her. No, she wouldn't have liked that. Maybe she would have teased me about it, just opened her eyes and told me to man up. To stop being a pussy. Fuck, wake up and say that!

Please, My Khuba.

I reached out and wiped my tears away with my thumbs from over her cheeks, catching them and taking them away in case they had the power to burn. Just like they were burning me. Each one felt like acid running down my skin and soon I couldn't breathe... fuck, why couldn't I breathe? I was a fucking vampire for Gods' sake! A vampire that couldn't fucking breathe!

I just needed her to wake up call me an idiot, call me a foolish asshole, call me anything to drown out this fucking silence! This deafening emptiness I could hear from her chest as a heartbeat that should have been there. I had grown so used to hearing it, so used to feeling it. I just needed it to beat one more time, and then another... and then another, and then to just keep going and going and never fucking stop… *that's all I asked for.*

I couldn't cope with this madness, this fucking madness. I just needed the silence to end… I needed her heart to beat again.

I just needed her.

"I want you back… please come back to me, please don't go. Don't leave me, I can't do this without you," I admitted, whispering in her ear, hoping, praying, fucking ready to tear this place apart, anything just to get her to whisper back to me.

But it was useless.

She wasn't going to answer me.

She was gone.

Which meant there was only one being that had taken her from me! And now, *I was going to tear him to fucking pieces!* I was going to destroy him in every single way possible for what he had taken from me! Then, when I was done with him, I would take my rage and find the one who sent him. Him, and every single living being involved! I would hunt every single hand responsible for taking her from me, the start of a deathly mission I would never stop. I would carry on until I had tortured and killed every last one of them, making them suffer in ways even the fucking Devil would be impressed with. I would take everything from them, because they had taken everything from me! Then, when I was finished, I would find out where Amelia's soul had gone to and I would demand they give her back to me! Even if I had to go to Lucifer himself and get him to bring her back.

I would wage a war like no other!

Against Heaven, Hell and Earth, I would stop at nothing. I would become the next end of days, and watch as everything burned around me with a sadistic fucking grin on my face if she wasn't returned to me! I would become the destroyer of worlds and the bringer of death. Even if it meant overthrowing my own father from his Hellish throne.

I would become the next King of Kings, for my revenge would never stop. I knew I had it in me. I knew I had that untapped power of a fucking Titan God inside me, and it was one I was willing to fucking use if she wasn't given back to me!

I swore to fucking God himself and his precious *Jesus fucking Christ!*

The true betrayer of souls!

I lowered over her one more time and told her softly,

"I will bring you back, I will save you, I promise... I will get you back," I whispered as my voice broke with the pain, it was unimaginable. I had once believed nothing could be more horrific than the way that my mortal body had died. I believed nothing could be as painful as when I was then forged into this new body. When having Lucifer make me into what I am now. But I had been wrong. So, fucking wrong, for nothing was this painful. nothing broke me as this moment did. This loss...

It was killing me.

"My Lord, I'm so..."

"Don't fucking say it... not a single fucking person in this room gets to fucking say it!" I snapped, sitting back for the first time and taking in the room. All of these lives she had touched in such a short space of time, I found myself hating that they had taken that time from me! How dare they! SHE WAS MINE! But there was one still left in the room that had taken much more from me,

He had taken everything!

"WHERE IS HE!" I roared and even my demon sounded...

Raw. Ragged. Destroyed.

"He's here, my Lord." I rose to my feet, my demon rippling over me in a way that felt as though my skin was on fire. As if in my rage he had the power to consume me completely and, in that moment, I wouldn't have cared if he had. I felt as if I had nothing else to live for, even though I would have been reminded why by all those tied to me that indeed I had much to live for. Amelia would have been the first to do so. Which was why I couldn't look down at her again. I couldn't see her look of death. I couldn't do it any longer, it was simply more than I could bear. No, instead I focused on the one who had done this.

The Wraith Master.

The first life on my list I had to end. The first heart to destroy.

My movements became like one of the ghosts we had been fighting. I moved like a Wraith myself, barely even registering what I was doing as if I was having an out of body experience. A ridiculous notion for a vampire, yet it couldn't be denied as that was what it had felt like. As if there was only half of me doing this now and the other half of the me was sat slumped over Amelia's still form. As if the man in me was still crying over the death of who he considered as his wife, his soulmate. But the demon in me, he took control, letting that part of me still grieve. He took control of my revenge. The creature who wasn't allowed to get to breathe any longer, he had stolen her breath and then my own.

And now his last breath was mine.

"Lucius I wouldn't …"

"We dinnae ken enough, stop!"

"The souls he commands, Lucius, you don't understand!"

I ignored everything in the room. This echo of doubt was coming at me from all sides as I grabbed the Wraith Master by the neck, lifting him up and now strangling the life out of him.

"Stop him!"

"He cannae be allowed tae dae this!"

"All those souls, they will be released!"

That echoing continued and I threw my horned head back and roared, allowing my demon to tell them exactly what I thought of their words. I didn't care what horrors this would bring. I would kill every single last one of them! I would stop at nothing until it was finished. I lifted him higher and then slammed him down on the floor, making it crack beneath him as he began to writhe beneath my hand, trying to escape. My eyes went to the slice in his shoulder where my girl had thrown the dagger. She had saved us all.

She had saved my life.

I almost wanted to hate her for it because it had been an action that had taken her from me. Why hadn't she realised that I could have handled it all. I would have survived. She didn't have to save everybody… *my little fighter*. Gods in Hell, but why did she have to be a fighter! I had been so proud of her all those times before and now, it was so fucking foolish!

She had done this… he had done this…

I had done this!

"You will die for what you have taken from me!" I snarled down at him as I reached out for the dagger, making it fly into my hand.

"I will kill you with the same blade my Electus tried to kill you with, and this time… *you will die by it!"* I vowed as I lifted it high, ready to hammer it down into his face. Ready to slash, stab and tear into him until he was nothing but bloody pulp on the floor. I knew I should be making it last. I knew I needed to take my time and torture him. But the rage was rising within me, filling me up so there was nothing left of my heart but *Hell's fire.*

He tried to speak, but I wouldn't let him. Instead, I lowered my weapon and when it was but an inch from his face a hand clasped my wrist and stopped me. Whoever it was, was strong enough to achieve the task and I looked up to see Trice staring at me. His eyes full of pain and suffering, for he too had tears that had ran freely down the scar in his cheek, following the slice and tissue like a dried riverbed.

But he had no right to his tears.

No fucking right!

No one did. Not in that moment, for they were all mine. She had been all mine and now, *she was gone.*

"Let. Me. Go," I warned in a dangerous tone, one even he should have taken seriously, I didn't give a fuck how strong or powerful he was!

"Look! Lucius, fucking look at her wid ye… look at her heart!" The moment he said these words, my eyes shot to my girl to see that he was right. He was fucking right! The darkness around her skin, the infection, it was… *seeping away*. It was as if it was draining from her veins and going back to the cut at her shoulder.

"How… how is this possible?" I whispered in utter awe. Because nothing should have been moving on her body, especially not the blood in her veins, not after death. But that ink of an infection was flowing in them now. Was this just an after effect? Something that happened after her mortal body had died? Was this just something that happened naturally or did it mean something more.

"Put him closer tae her!" Trice barked the order at me, making me growl instantly,

"Fuck no, he doesn't get to…!"

"Dinnae be a fucking fool, King! Noo put him closer

tae her 'n' trust me!" I growled again but pushed back my demon and did as he asked, because if there was even the smallest chance, I was going to do it. I would not fail her again! And my reward was hope erupting as the second I put him closer, more of the infection seeped away as if it was drawn to the Wraith Master himself. I soon had him lying as close as possible and watched as the last of it drew completely away from her heart. I couldn't believe it.

It was really happening.

I got closer to her, the blade long gone, dropped to the floor after Trice had taken over, now holding the Wraith Master down and pinning him to the floor. This was so I was free to straddle my girl's waist.

"What are you…"

"What do you think I am doing!?" I snarled back and then I did something that in all my years I had never done before. However, I had lived long enough to know how to complete the act. So, I started compressions on her chest. Fingers interlaced I leant over her and found the area in the centre of her breast on the sternum. Then I pressed down about an inch with the heel of my hand, repeatedly trying to keep a steady pace.

"Come on!" I shouted down at her as I continued pushing, trying to get it to beat one more time. Just once more which would then give it a chance at beating twice and that would be followed by a third… and then I prayed it would never stop!

"Come on, Amelia, come on baby, just let it happen… just let it beat for me. Please. Gods, please just let it beat for me. Come on. Come on!" I screamed down at her, and I had to be careful not to crack her ribs or fuck, even break her sternum! I couldn't be too hard on her, or I knew I could puncture her lung and that would end up doing even more damage.

I just needed to be careful.

So, fucking careful.

"Hear me, Amelia... please hear me... wherever you are, hear me, come on, just follow my voice... *follow me... come back to me, sweetheart... reach for me...*" I sobbed out, then when it didn't work, I lowered over her and whispered over her lips,

"*Please don't leave me... I love you.*"

As for her reply, it was the best sound in the world...

Her first heartbeat.

CHAPTER TWO

AMELIA

RAIN OF TEARS

C *old.*

I was so cold.

But could I be surprised? Although I could honestly say I didn't know what to expect when dying. Especially not where I was, being so close to Hell. Had I been expecting to see a white light at the end of some tunnel? Or maybe some notion of Heaven that saved my soul from a darker fate. Like some Angel reaching out and grabbing me to stop me from plummeting down into some dark abyss before Hell greeted me. I mean, considering who my family was, then I would have at least thought they would have had the right connections to get me into the right places. But then this thought gave birth to another, one ultimately more painful, as I now questioned if my family knew? If my father had felt the connection with his daughter's soul severed? Had my Uncle Vincent, the King of Angels, been told there was a soul connected to him that needed retrieving? Or even my grandfather, had he been told of a reaper with his granddaughter's name written in his book of souls?

Did any of them know?

I could only imagine the pain it would cause them, and I hated that I hadn't yet been given the chance to make amends with my parents, *my mother especially.* The way we had left things between us, it was a cruelty I couldn't bear. So many things I hadn't had chance to do. So many things left unsaid. But then wasn't that the way with death? Most didn't get the gift of saying goodbye. Telling the ones they loved that they would never stop feeling that way, even in death.

I wished I had at least been granted that. Maybe like a free pass gifted by my grandmother, an Archangel... surely, she had the connections, right? But it was strange really, to think that I'd never wondered or questioned what it would be like, when most mortals do, even though there was no proof for them like there was for me. No proof that Heaven and Hell existed or knowing what the real Afterlife was like. Yet for me, I knew that it was real, without a shadow of a doubt, I had the proof of it every single day growing up with my own parents. Yet, I had never questioned what would happen to me when I died. Where would I end up or what would happen to me when I got there?

I admit to even feeling foolish.

But then again, I also knew that my mortality was a bit of a sore spot for my parents. I had heard them arguing about it few times when they didn't know that I was listening. Having a mortal daughter that they saw age each year, to the point where my own mother looked more like my sister. I knew it had been hard for them, I told myself that this was why I never questioned it myself. Because if I ever did, it would make it too real for them to face, too real for myself to face for that matter. But then, when I realised that Lucius was my Chosen One, I had simply allowed myself to believe that his blood would keep me immortal because after all, wasn't that the way it worked?

Well, not this time.

Then again, what was strange was finding that I wasn't faced with Heaven or even Hell. No, it was finding myself in what looked like someone else's void. Because, out of all the things I thought would have happened, being stood in a dark room looking around for anything that made sense was pretty much the last of them... well, perhaps finding myself in Pip's bedroom would have been top of the list of least expected places. Although, that would have been enough to convince anyone they hadn't died, they were just on an acid trip!

"It can't be my void," I whispered or at least I tried to, as it didn't seem like even a breath came out. But then my own question echoed around the room as if there were ten of me all saying it at the same time. Then, that's when I heard it...

The heartbeat.

Ba bump, ba bump, ba bump. It continued on, being steady at first and it was almost comforting, as if it was the beat of hope. As for the room, its greys walls looked as though they were covered in a thick layer of ash, as if I was stood in the room of a house that had once had a fire and what I saw now was all that remained. Pieces of the walls flaked like paper peeling away in the wind, yet they didn't float to the ground like they should have. No, instead they floated upwards as if some gentle force from below was blowing them that way.

I couldn't understand where I was, and I tried to make sense of the room once more... which was when things started to come to me. It started off as shadows, just fragments of a sight my mind used to know. Chairs were positioned around a beautiful fireplace, yet now all that remained was an ash covered stone, the carving beneath barely seen. There were empty frames and glass lay shattered on the floor, the paintings long since destroyed. Then even more shadows of my memory started to appear, a desk, a chair, a frame that once held a picture, but it too had floated away. I don't know how I knew but that painting, the one that used to be there, meant something to someone, but who that was… my mind couldn't remember. Because I wasn't just losing grip on reality, but it felt as though I was losing grip on my mind, as if the longer I spent here the more it took from me. From the place where I stored all my memories.

Whatever it was, whoever this void belonged to, they were trying to take back control and to do that was to tear down all I knew and all I remembered.

Yet, despite knowing this, I still had enough of my mind to question, what happened to this room? What had happened here enough to cling onto it? I opened my mouth to speak but stopped myself when I remembered what happened the last time. So instead, I reached up and touched my lips with my fingertips. They were so cold, just like the rest of me.

Everything was cold.

But why, was it because what I feared the most had come true… was I dead and this ash prison was now to be my Afterlife? Because it was as if my memories had been burned, touched by fire. But who had the power to do that? It was in that moment, I remembered. I remembered exactly who had that power and because of it, I looked towards where the windows once were. And it was there that I saw it, saw it in the darkness beyond. Those eyes. Eyes that were now on fire and I looked down, suddenly feeling something in my hand, something heavy. Then, without thinking about it, I threw it towards those eyes, using all my years of practice. Something in that moment I remembered all too easily.

However, as soon as it flew from my hand, it was the one time I wish that I'd missed. Because what came next was the result of my death... I was starting to remember it all. I knew this the second I saw it coming back at me, only this time... the second it hit me in my shoulder, I stepped back from the impact. As soon as it struck it was in that moment the room became whole again and I realised I was back in the King's office. My hand flew out as if trying to reach someone as I started to go down, now falling backwards and it was as if my body was floating in slow motion. This was because I didn't just land suddenly, not like the first time.

No, this time, my death was slow.

I fell and continued to fall through the floor, down into a dark hole with only one name leaving my lips,

"Lucius."

I sucked in a deep breath the second I landed, and suddenly I felt everything all at once. Burning sand against my skin turned to water and then to the freezing snow. The sand belonged to his first life, to Judas' death. Then the water from when I landed after jumping from the helicopter. And last in the snow from when I'd fallen in his winter garden. I looked down at the blood on my hand mixed with the pale white of the snow, reminding me of everything. The box, the witch and a ballroom full of raining ash. Every single piece that fell signified another rogue that had fallen. It was in that moment the snow turned to a blanket of ash before turning back again into the hard floor of the office.

But this was when I heard the pain. When I heard the heartache of so many. Trice fighting his brothers to get to me, crying out and roaring in anger, Vern and Gryph trying to contain him, their faces pained. but it was no use. They tried to convince him it would be okay, just give it time.

But I wasn't okay.

I never would be.

Because I was dying.

And know I knew that I hadn't gone to Heaven. No, this was my Hell, as I was being forced to witness the very moment I was to die. Because right in that moment I understood what this was. I was living my last moments trapped in the Wraith Master's void, now forced to witness myself as I took in my last breaths, echoing those same motions that were happening in real time.

That constant sound of my own heartbeat. I knew the moment the echoing thud around me started to slow down. I looked around the walls, and the once perfect office started to decay once again. Black veins like an infection crawled up the walls and turned it to ash in its wake. It had soon covered every inch of the office, the once beautiful furniture disintegrating just as the infected poison consumed everything in the room.

Including me.

Everyone was talking, yet there was only one sound I heard. It was Lucius as he was suddenly at my side. But for some reason I couldn't see him, I could only hear him. Yet he sounded so close, I forced myself to move, to sit up, and I kept moving until I was standing. This was when I realised that I had just stepped out of my body. My hands flew to my mouth in horror, asking myself if I should lie back down and try to get back in there.

I turned and looked to see the horrible truth as my pale form was now laid down like Snow White, as if I had only been cast under some spell. Only I knew that it wasn't one that could simply be broken by a true love's kiss.

Because fairy tales weren't real... *nightmares were.*

That's when I felt something wet touching my lips and I raised my hand up and found them wet, pulling my fingers back and seeing blood. I frowned. I had felt no pain. But that's when I heard the first panicked command,

"Drink, come on... come on, Amelia, I said drink!" After this I felt my body shake a little as if something was making me move against my will. I looked to the body on the floor, the one that looked so much like me, yet it didn't move. She was like a frozen doll. My eyes widened when I heard his pain... pain that now added to the heartbeat as it echoed around me. Then, just in the hope that I could help, I started swallowing knowing now that he wanted me to drink his blood.

Gods, but I hoped that it would bring me back. I hoped it was enough to bring me back to him. But then I felt an awful cramp in my stomach and reached down, fisting the material of my dress. This was when I felt the pain surging up in me at the same time as I felt his blood coming back up. Fuck, but why couldn't I keep it down? Why couldn't I just keep it down? I felt it coming out and I kept swallowing and swallowing but it was no use. I vomited, feeling it spirt over my lips and down my chin. I heard him shout, "no!" I heard the panic rising in him. I wanted to tell him how sorry I was. Sorry that I couldn't keep it down, that I obviously wasn't strong enough.

This was when I ran to him, wanting to cup his face and say anything so I may ease his pain. But then I found myself caught. I was trapped behind a glass wall, one that looked as if it wasn't even there. Like some invisible barrier that was now keeping me locked to this world. However, it didn't stop me from witnessing my own demise. It didn't stop me from hearing...

His heart breaking.

"Come on, Amelia, come on, baby, just swallow it down." I heard his desperate plea continue but it was no use. His soft coaxing words just weren't enough to get my body to do as he wanted. Not even when I felt a sharp tug by my shoulder, almost enough to make me feel as if I were there. I looked towards my injury to see now that my dress had been ripped. But that wasn't all, as now I could see the infection around the stab wound. I could see the way it was spreading out just like it was on the walls, consuming the space around me.

Once again, the heartbeat was slowing right down, and I opened my mouth trying to say anything to him. Trying so hard just so he might hear the last of my words. To hear how sorry I was. How this was all my fault. Coming to Hell, getting us both in this mess, not trusting him. I was sorry I wasn't strong enough, I was sorry for so many things. I wanted to tell him them all. But most of all I wanted to tell him… *how much I loved him.*

I wanted my goodbye.

"Come on now, Amelia, wake up, wake up for me… come on, open those pretty eyes for me… Gods, please… PLEASE!" I heard this and it broke my heart making me fall to my knees. I covered my ears with my hands trying to get it to stop. Trying to get the pain in my heart to stop… why wouldn't it stop!

Why wouldn't it just fucking stop!

Please! Oh please, I beg of you, I beg of the Gods for it to stop!

But it didn't stop. No, it just got worse. My heart breaking at the very same time his was, that was our fate.

"Amelia, come on, baby, come on now… don't you dare do this… don't you dare fucking leave me again… no, no… I do not allow this… I WILL NOT ALLOW IT!" I started shaking my head as his bellow of rage didn't have the power to bring me back, just as much his soft tender words hadn't. What I wouldn't have given to have been able to reach up and cup his cheek, to open my eyes so he could see the love in them one last time. For me to open my mouth and my last words be full of the love I had for him.

"Come on! Wake up, damn you! *Wake up... wake up... please wake up!*" His broken whisper was one I felt against my skin, my forehead tingling ice cold as his breath was right there. I reached out to try and touch it, but there was nothing.

I was alone in this nightmare world.

"...she will be fine... she just needs my blood, that's all... we just need to find a way for her to take my blood," he said and I tried to blank it all out, knowing what was coming. But this was torture. To witness his pain was fucking agony and I would have done anything to stop it. To stop this fucking chasm that was ripping open my chest!

My fucking heart!

My useless broken, infected heart.

I felt my hair moving, no doubt from when he was brushing it back from my face. I could hear people speaking to him, trying to get him to understand that it was too late... to understand that... *that I was gone.* I was already lost, and he was left all alone in the world without me. But he didn't want to admit it. He didn't want to believe it was true. I knew this when I heard him making excuses for me.

"She just needs time, just a little time as she's tired... yes, that is it, she is just tired is all, she just needs my blood and rest, don't you, sweetheart?" Finally, at this I opened my mouth, and a desperate sob tore out of it, one that echoed around me, as if it was the only way I was allowed to hear it. As if the real sound of agony was stolen from me by this horrific place. I just wanted to hear my own pain. I wanted to cry. No, I fucking needed to hear it! I wanted him to hear it, to know that his pain was not just his own but one we shared.

That was when I felt the rain. Tiny drops falling on my face and I looked up see if I could see where they were coming from. But there was nothing above me, no clouds, no sky, and no moon. Just darkness. One waiting to consume me. The heartbeat becoming a soft thud, barely heard over the sounds of Lucius' heart breaking. That's when I knew that it wasn't raining after all.

For a Vampire King was crying.

And then there was silence.

I opened my mouth to draw in one last breath, something my death had stolen from me. Then soon, as my heart finally stopped beating,

I felt the last of his tears.

Tears for his...

Fallen Queen.

CHAPTER THREE

ARMY OF ASH

After hearing the last beat of my heart, I started to sink into the floor, leaving the shell of whatever was left of me behind. And I did this to the echoing sounds of pain, as Lucius was forced to say... *goodbye.*

Even though it was clear he wasn't ready to let me go, just as I wasn't. I never would be. I knew that. I knew that despite wishing for the gift of those last moments to say all I could say, I knew now that even then I wouldn't have been ready to let him go. So, sat there on the floor, alone and scared, I held a fisted hand to my mouth just to stop myself from screaming his name. My body shook, and each breath felt like it was being dragged through jagged rocks before it finally reached my lungs. I held my knees to my chest and held myself tight, making me feel small and somewhat protected.

But then again, nothing could protect me from that pain. The one that tore through me like a lash. Over and over again with every word that came from his lips. The pain I was still being forced to witness despite my heart no longer beating. That's when I knew for sure, I had been right…

This was my Hell.

"I want you back…" I heard him say and as if unable to take anymore I fell forward intending to fall on my hands. However, once again I found myself falling through the floor, now making me wonder where I was to end up this time. I was crying out, only nothing but the sound of Lucius echoed around me. It should have been comforting as I was forced to leave the last of my world. But it was only a reminder of the pain my death had caused.

The whispered heartbreak that continued,

"Please come back to me…" he was begging for me not to go, yet here I was already falling. Plummeting through the dark clouds with not even the sound of my dress whipping around me from the force, and yet, that voice never left me.

"Please don't go… don't leave me…"

"Lucius," I whispered in return, even though I knew it was useless. Because, as I fell, the very last whisper I heard before another world was to become my own, was a desperate one.

One fraught and frantic.

One tortured and so alone.

It was one I barely even recognised, yet would know anywhere. It was Lucius as I had never heard him before.

He sounded terrified…

"I can't do this without you."

I cried out, reaching my arm up as if I could touch him. As if I still had the power to make it. As if he had the power to feel it…

But there was nothing.

However, what did come next was a sound I didn't expect. It sounded as though a war was happening beneath me. A raging battle where the clash of weapons echoed along the landscape, ricocheting off mountains and echoing in between valleys. The sounds of pain, roars of war cries, the bellowing of orders being made by generals. It was all there for me to hear and as I continued to fall, it was only getting louder and louder. As if at any moment I was going to plummet into the middle of the battle.

Then suddenly I heard Lucius' voice one last time, only now it wasn't a sound coming from above me or an echo from all around. No, this time it was whispered directly in my ear and I could almost feel the brush of his lips moving softly against my skin. It felt like a gift. One that made me close my eyes and absorb every single word, holding on to them like a prayer.

"I will bring you back, I will save you, I promise… I will get you back." It was a declaration. A vow made from someone who would never give up trying to get me back. Who would never give up from trying to save me from whatever Hell I was now plummeting towards.

It was enough to give me hope.

Hope that he would find a way because if anyone could… *it was Lucius.* But then when I thought it would never end, I finally landed and the moment I did, silence enveloped me. There was not a single sound other than that of my own erratic breathing.

After what felt like long moments of fear, I braved opening my eyes, now seeing the thunder clouds above me. The ones that I had fallen through. I swallowed hard, amazed by the fact that I could still feel everything as if my body was now whole again. This meant that I was not some ghost, as I had seemed to be when I left my body back in the room.

I sat up slowly, expecting to feel pain from my landing, but there was nothing. After a moment of shock, I looked around and that was when I noticed why the sounds of battle had suddenly stopped. I was right when I heard the battle beneath me. But now, it was one that was clearly over. Because I had dropped into the middle of a war that had now ended due to the immeasurable losses on both sides. Neither side had won, because if everyone was dead around me then who exactly was there left to win. It was a massacre of fresh bodies recently slain. Bloody, gaping wounds, loss of limbs and severed heads. You name it, and there was a body within my reach that held the mortal blow.

"So much pointless death," I whispered, and as if my voice held power, this was when things started to change. And as I started to really focus on the details, I noticed that each soldier started to change into something else. Startlingly they were changing into something I recognised. It was as if a darkness had swept over every dead body and once the wave had passed, it left behind what they had now become. It left behind a sea of phantoms. An ocean of ghosts all dressed just as the Wraiths we had been fighting back in the office.

Yet they were also slightly different, as before none of their features could be seen, not among the ominous black essence that had floated around them like shadows. Clinging to their bodies one moment like the material of an assassin's attire, and the next as if their darkened souls were trying to keep up with them. But now, instead of the soulless white eyes glowing from beneath their hoods, I could see the face of death. Each of which looked as if they were silently screaming as they were forced to become slaves to the Wraith Master. Each silently begging for mercy. Each one silently begging for a peaceful end.

One the Wraith Master refused to grant them.

"Where am I?" I jerked a little, surprised that my question had been voiced aloud. So shocked in fact to hear my own voice that I reached up and touched my mouth. I didn't know what was shaking more, the quivering of my lips or the vibrations of my fingers as my hand shook uncontrollably. But then, as soon as they too heard my voice, the bodies around me started to change once more.

First they all turned in my direction, doing so together as one. In sight of this, well, I didn't know what was more eerie, the fact I now had thousands of ghosts all staring at me with their dead mouths hanging open still silently screaming, or that they had done so without making a sound.

Then, as if someone had flipped a switch to fast-forward on this *scene, I watched as decaying flesh shrivelled and fell from old bones.* Each of them now starting to wither away quickly as if I was watching months go by before the years started to turn them to dust. And it all started the same as it had done in the office just before I died. A great infection swept across the land like black snakes slithering over the bodies, and everything they touched turned to ash before it started to float upwards towards the sky, taking with it a piece of the history I knew had actually happened.

It was in that moment that I realised I wasn't actually in Hell after all, and I most certainly wasn't in Heaven. No, I was now locked in someone else's nightmare! Someone's memory of events that had been warped into the worst version of itself. As if someone was holding onto it and torturing themselves because of what they had done. It was madness reinvented and a twisted version of their own Hell.

One I was now stuck in.

I finally got to my feet, knowing that I couldn't just sit there amongst the decaying army. So, I started walking through the ash that was now in small piles crumbling around me, as if my movements were vibrating through the ground and disturbing the delicate remains. But then the storm cloud overhead started to swirl angrily just the way it did on Earth before a twister would form.

I wondered in that moment if the next place I would find myself would be in the eye of the storm? Not that it would have surprised me, as nothing could anymore, not after this. Gods, but if it lifted me up right now and I found myself in fucking Oz then I wouldn't have been surprised! But then this thought was quickly followed by another painful one when I thought of my three companions, Vern, Gryph, and most of all, Trice. Gods, but I hated to even think of the pain I had put them through. And Vena, or even Nero… *my friends.*

"No! Stop it, Fae, just stop it right now!" I snapped angrily at myself, knowing I wasn't ready to go there yet. I wasn't ready to face it. Gods, but would I ever be? The tears running down my cheeks told me that I wasn't. Tears that were suddenly stolen by the sharp wind that started up around me. That cutting element that was now whipping against me, and with it taking the piles of ash from the ground. It then became like walking through a sandstorm, and I found myself covering my face just so I wouldn't be breathing in the remains of a person's body. I felt sickened by the thought, like opening up an urn and before realising that someone's remains where in there, you stupidly took a deep breath. The second it touched you, you were left with that feeling that you'd just taken a person's remains into your body and that they would never leave you. Like you had violated their rights or something.

It was haunting.

But this was just another thought I tried to shake off as I made my way through the ash storm. Because I had to cling on to Lucius' vow. *His promise.* His promise that he would come for me. That he would get me out of this place because I wasn't even sure I was actually dead and not just caught in someone else's mind. Caught in someone else's infection. Either way I had to hang on to hope that there was a way to escape. Just some clue or key to unlocking the door to get him back into my own mind. Because I refused to believe that this was my Afterlife. That this was my final resting place.

Lucius was both Angel and Demon just like my father was, hence there wasn't anywhere either of them couldn't go. Which meant bargaining for my soul, because wasn't that how it went? Powerful beings had the right to petition for those they wanted, which was exactly how my father had saved Ragnar. Had saved Takeshi and so many others. But then I was forgetting something. This wasn't Hell and this wasn't Heaven, so the only question left now was what if this was the only place they couldn't go?

What then?

"There has to be a way," I said to myself, after I had stepped through the storm and no longer was at risk of swallowing anyone's flaky testicles. *Yep, that's keeping it real, Fae,* I thought with a shake of my head. Then, as I continued to make my way through the wasteland, having no idea where I was trying to get to or what I was trying to achieve, I tried not to think about what Lucius would be going through. I just knew that I had to keep going as I couldn't sit there and do nothing, so I started walking for what I knew could have been the beginning of an endless journey. It was a dark and twisted place with mountains that grew like giant spiked bones, a land of dirt, black sand and all the harshness a dead world had to offer for there was nothing of life. Not a single blade of grass or flower grew. There wasn't even tumbleweed to suggest that there ever had been. It could have been a completely different planet, one that you had no hope of surviving.

Everything was dead.

It was like wandering aimlessly in the desert, but after what could have been hours or could have simply been minutes, I got was getting closer to something. That was when the sound started. The sound of metal twisting, grating, and breaking away in the distance. The sound of stone crumbling as if it was being chipped away piece by piece. It was as if something was being broken apart, and it was only as I walked around the jagged boulders that littered the wasteland did I see exactly what it was. It wasn't an endless nothingness after all for there, in the distance, was a castle laid to ruin.

And there at its foundations was the ghost of a siege trying to attack it. I paused, not wanting to startle them and make them aware of my presence. The ghostly memories of warriors of a different kind were swinging their war hammers, taking away chunks of stone from crumbling battlements that had fallen. Giant holes the size of cars were spread out over the castle and were most likely from some kind of ancient war machine, like a catapult, a trebuchet, or a ballista. All of which were siege engines used to launch heavy projectiles great distances and doing maximum damage to castle walls. Hence making it now resemble grey swiss cheese. But it also wasn't as if there were any of these war machines around, or even a battering ram trying to get inside. No, if anything, there was just a small group of maybe fifty or so soldiers that looked as if this was a daily thing, not a siege. Maybe some kind of memory on constant replay as it almost seemed mechanical.

They were spread out in groups, all working on a different part, like the group working together to bring down a great metal statue, of who I gathered was once the ruler of these lands and King of this castle. But because I didn't know what would happen should they see me, I started walking backwards slowly in hopes of not being discovered. Then there was that dreaded sound, a deafening crack under my foot, that any other time would have barely been noticed. But not when you were hiding. No, it was then it was always the loudest, and stepping on something meant instantly giving me away as I felt the crunch under my feet. More importantly was what came next as the second I looked up in panic, I knew what I would find.

"Oh, shit," I muttered as fifty plus heads were now all turning slowly to look my way. Then the moment they saw me, they charged, raising their weapons and running straight at me.

Forgetting the King they obviously hated.

Leaving me not to wonder why but more importantly…

Would they turn to ash once more before they reached me, or would I be the next thing they…

Destroyed.

CHAPTER FOUR

TRAPPED IN SHADOWS

I screamed before turning around and running in the opposite direction, yet it wasn't any use as there was nowhere for me to run to. There was no escape and besides, they were far quicker than me.

I knew this the second that I glanced over my shoulder and saw them gaining on me, until they got so close my only other option was to fall to the floor and curl myself into a ball. Doing so now in hopes that they would trip over me or just trample me into another death. But then when nothing happened, I opened my eyes to find them all now running straight through me, disappearing the second they got past me.

I let my head hang down, trying to catch my breath once more before pushing up to my knees, looking around to see that I was thankfully alone. My dress tore as I got up to my feet and once more faced the Castle, only now it was no longer in ruins.

"Wow," I uttered as I pushed my loose hair back from my face, ignoring the rain of dust that floated down off me. Then

I stared up at it in awe, despite living in England for as long as I had, meaning I was no stranger to the sight of a castle, but this one was something else. Of course, Great Britain was full of them and each one was just as beautiful as the last. Some majestic and filled with so much history, that for a geek like me, it filled my mind with endless possibilities of what could have happened there during its time.

Gods, but it was strange to think that my own father had lived in many during his time, but to him, sometimes it must have been like the history of mankind had just gone by in a blur. He had lived in so many places and admittedly there weren't many places left he hadn't seen, so that while growing up when I say he held a world of knowledge, then that was as literal a statement as you could get. His stories had been the best, and as a child I had begged for just one more… always just one more.

Gods, I missed my father.

I missed my mother.

But as for royals and then their castles, well this one that faced me now was different. The black stone towers weren't made up of blocks, but instead just rose up from the ground as if they had been carved from a single boulder. As if some giant had hand sculptured it out of the mountain. Which was of little wonder why it took the soldiers so long to tear it apart.

But now, it was tower after tower, and wall after wall connecting them all. There were arched windows in rows of three down every tower, and six running in lines along every wall. As for the battlements, they were not your standard squared teeth edging the tops of the walls but instead jagged and menacing points. It was as if a mighty beast was opening up its jaws and had frozen that way before turning to black stone. An arched entrance completed the front, with a connecting bridge on top in between two of the tallest towers. A place that called me forward despite the darkness beyond, as it was too deep yet to show me a door. One that I knew would be just as imposing and as frightening as the rest of the place.

Yet, despite this, I was planning to get in there quickly in case the army happened to come back, or time reset and it would be in ruins again. So, I started to run towards it, knowing that the answers to how I would escape would no doubt lie inside the heart of this nightmare, for why else would the castle be there now if it didn't play an important part of the bigger picture? A picture connected to the Wraith Master's mind that I was obviously now connected to.

I made it past where the soldiers had been dead set on destruction, dead pun intended because hey, I might have been dead, but at least I had a sense of humour. But as I passed, I could see for myself the sight of a King now lay on his side, all broken and contorted metal, with its head twisted completely so that it looked towards its back. His handsome face still looked so regal and proud, with features that had a natural arrogance to them. But despite those striking features, I still couldn't ever imagine a face like that even knowing how to smile, let alone producing one. Though surely there must have been someone in his life that he had once smiled for.

I continue to walk past, shaking the image of his face on twisted metal, forever to look behind him and never ahead. It seemed far too symbolic a sight, and one I didn't want to take with me. Finally, I made it to the entrance, where the doors were covered with interlocking spikes from above and below as if a very different beast now had its mouth closed. Yet, the closer I walked, I must have triggered something as the metal spikes started to open up before disappearing into the ground just as they did above. Seconds later, a pair of huge solid metal doors swung open as if welcoming me to the Hell inside, daring me to take that first step into a Wraith Master's domain.

However, the moment I was brave enough to cross over the threshold, I was then transported inside without taking another step. I heard the doors close behind me, but I wasn't quick enough to see when it happened. The large entrance hall was a shell of what it once used to be, with its grand furnishings long left to ruin. All seemed to be broken, shattered, splintered, you name it and it had happened to this place, for nothing worked as it once was... the walls had once been gilded gold, with statues of beautiful Goddesses sat on plinths surrounded by decorative arches that were scalloped like shells.

The whole room was three levels high, framed on both sides by an arched balcony that had elaborate balustrades. Rows of curled corkscrews carved from stone that were once painted gold. Balustrades that were now flaked with old paint, that no doubt used to glow bright under the soft glow of candlelight making them look like solid gold.

Even the floor, that had once been a gleaming black and white marble, was now cracked and covered in a scattering of ash. Yet it wasn't like dust that floated in the air whenever you walked through it before being able to catch its particles in the light. Instead, it was like pieces of tissue paper that didn't break apart like normal ash would as soon as it was touched. No, it stayed the same.

I moved through it, testing the theory, and that's when I realised exactly what it reminded me of. It resembled dead grey leaves long ago fallen from a dying tree. It made me think back to the Tree of Souls and what every leaf represented.

A single soul.

One that belonged to Lucius.

My soul also, yet as a single flower. I wondered if it was now withered with its petals already falling to the temple floor… or would it turn to ash along with the others before it hit the ground? It was a morbid thought, and one that brought tears to my eyes, despite cursing my own weakness for thinking of it in the first place. Gods, but just being here was like sucking all hope from your mind and replacing it with something else.

Doubt… *doubt and fear.*

Thankfully, there were no flowers in sight and nothing to remind me of why my fate had led me here. So, I continued to move throughout the castle, going straight towards the double staircase that lay directly in front of me, sweeping outwards in a mirror image. It was one that reminded me of Afterlife, reminded me of home. But that image only went so far, considering how ruined this place was with most of the steps crumbling at the edge of the treads.

I walked up the steps and again, like the rest of the castle, it seemed that it had been carved from one large piece of stone. I almost wished that it was made from old creaking wood, just to kill the stillness in the room. Hell, at this rate I was ready to start whistling some random tune, but I knew it would just come out shaky for my breathing wasn't exactly steady.

I continued up to the first floor where I found a gallery of sorts, most frames were missing their pictures and the ones that were there had been slashed through as if the memory they held was too painful. But despite this violence, you could still see a beautiful woman and two young boys by her side. Then it was empty, empty again as I walked until finally another picture filled a space. This time it was of the woman on her own and all that could be seen was barely a glimpse of her beautiful features.

But what could be seen of her showed she was young, with flowing curly chestnut hair that almost looked red, and this matched her pale skin that was painted blush over her cheeks. I pushed back the torn canvas to complete the look and saw red lips, a long straight nose, and big brown eyes that looked off to the window she was gazing out of as if in longing. A simple crown that was a band of gold, decorated with golden flowers and a grapevine, sat across her forehead, and along with a single ring... it was the only jewels she wore. A vivid green dress, very similar to the style I wore, made up for most of the colour in the painting as the sky through the window was grey and stormy. Very much as it had been when I first fell into this nightmare world.

I released a sigh, wondering what she was thinking when this was being painted, for I wouldn't exactly say she looked happy. She looked as if she longed for something else in life... for something, *more*. I let the flap of canvas go, thinking that whatever claws had gone through it, they had been strong enough to rip through to the wooden frame too.

These violent reminders of his family most definitely told me what type of King I was dealing with, as the last picture I saw was of the man himself. In fact, it was the only picture left untouched and not even marred by the dust, ash, or anything else. It was as though this was a picture that was to be proud of, a picture to admire and one of strength, for there stood the face of an arrogant King. One who only ever wanted more power. That was his ambition, that was his legacy, you could see it in his dark eyes that seemed to burn even in paint.

It was not like Auberon, the King of Dragons, who wanted nothing more than to ensure his people remained safe and prosperous. His ambitions were only of the noble sort who strived to make his father proud by ruling as he once had. A King who had only ever wanted peace among his land, for the good of his people. Well, not this King, for you could see it in his eyes. That constant search for more power that consumed him. I could almost feel the greed coming from his image.

Hard features that were so serious, it looked as if he spent his days barking orders and nothing more. Had a soft and tender word ever escaped his lips, I wondered? Of course, his deep set eyes as dark as his hair didn't soften the illusion. Nor did the darkness that framed the lower part of his face with the thick beard and moustache. Dark slashes formed inclined brows that looked unimpressed and harsh, creating shadows under his forbidding eyes.

The only part of the painting that held decoration was the crown he wore, gold and gleaming in the beam of light coming from the left of him. It was steepled and typical in its shape, and pushed some of the softer looking curls down slightly at the top of his hairline. But dressed in battle gear it was only those slight curls that gave him any softness at all, for a chest plate of hammered metal lay strapped over a leather tunic. A thick fur pelt lay over his shoulders and long black material fell straight down from beneath it.

But just looking at him now and I didn't realise at first that I was gripping the front of my dress where my heart was, as if it was hurting for me to breathe just by being near that painting. This was what first had me start running as I just needed to get away from that hard, unforgiving gaze of his. If only so I could breathe freely once more.

So, I ran. I ran towards the end of the hall where I found the first door that would take me away and put a barrier between me and that painting. I didn't know why but he utterly terrified me, and I wondered if it was because I now viewed him as my own personal devil?

I pushed the door open and actually welcomed the creaking sound of old wood being forced against a swelled frame. But, the second I made it through, I knew this time I wasn't faced with memories of the Wraith Master, but only of what was happening now.

It was back in real time!

I was back in my old world where I thought I had been locked out of completely. But the further inside the room I went was when I realised that I wasn't really there like I wished. Like I would have prayed for!

No, it was simply like a looking glass into the real world. A giant mirror in a blood-red frame as thick as my hand now stood in the centre of a dark room with nothing else. It was as if this was all that was left of my own mind. This was all the control I had left, and I knew that if this shattered, then that would mean the last sliver of my own void would be left. Because we were connected so that would mean there was at least a piece of me, a piece of my mind that remained.

But then, as the image started to clear, all thoughts in my mind left me and I let out a muted cry as I stepped even closer. I held a hand out towards the man who owned my heart.

"Oh, Lucius," I muttered painfully when I saw him leant over my body, one that was so deathly still and pale it was clear to see that no life remained. Yet Lucius didn't want to give up. He didn't want to let me go as I saw him still whispering things down to me, obviously still trying to get me to respond. It was a painful sight, along with the rest of the figures in the room who all looked devastated by my loss. And in my moment of weakness, I couldn't help looking towards one in particular… *Trice*

He looked as though he had just had his own heart ripped out and I felt fresh tears running down my cheeks seeing all the pain I had caused. But I couldn't hear anything that was being said as if there was only the ability to see what was happening, because suddenly Lucius was up snarling at people and throwing his words around with a face of pure hatred. It was as if something had snapped in his mind and he now set his demonic sights on the Wraith Master, one I could now see being brought into the room by Carn´reau.

I could see now that he was the King in the painting but not as he once had been. He looked more like the dead version of himself, but not quite decayed enough not to recognise him. As though he was half a man and half a ghost, with eyes of milky white, and lips that had disappeared showing only teeth. A nose that looked more skeletal than flesh, and hair that now looked black one moment and white the next. A sickly greenish glow came from beneath the hood as if the ghost part of him was being projected over his flesh.

But he wasn't the only frightening sight, if anything, far from it as Lucius suddenly erupted into his demon form, allowing it to ripple over his body in less than a second. Then he grabbed the Wraith King by the neck and started to strangle him, holding him up and eradicating his ability to breathe. A life for a life and a death for a death, this was Lucius' plan. This was his revenge, and knowing Lucius… only the start of it. But what would happen to me here if the Wraith Master died? Would I be stuck here forever with him or would I simply fade away to nothingness?

This was when panic started to set in and I suddenly slapped my hand to the glass trying to get him to hear me.

"Lucius, no… no please, we don't know what will happen to me! Please, *oh Gods, please… please let him stop."* This last whispered prayer ended with me on my knees, with my hand still held to the glass above me, my head now hung down. Because I didn't know whether I could watch this. I didn't know whether I could lay witness to him being the one who ended the last of me. But then swift movement caught my attention and I looked up.

I could now see the others trying to reason with him, at least that's what I thought it was for they looked panicked. Their lips were all moving too quickly for me to be able to detect what they were saying but one word was clear, and that was '*no*'. I frowned in question, now wiping my tears away so I could see clearly. For some reason they were all trying to convince Lucius not to deliver the Wraith's death, and I doubted I was the only one questioning why as Lucius looked beyond listening. Too far gone in his rage to notice much else other than the revenge he held at the end of his palm.

But then he slammed the Wraith Master down next to my body as if he wanted to take his life close to where he had taken mine. He reached for the blade that had caused my demise and I watched as it shot to his hand.

"NO, LUCIUS!" I shouted in vain as he lifted it up ready to strike it down, no doubt a killing blow. However, it was Trice that came to my rescue as his eyes noticed something, glowing like a dragon when he did. Because he wasn't looking at Lucius, but down at me. Then, in that split second, he made a decision, as if even in death my life was playing out in slow motion. Trice grabbed Lucius by the wrist, preventing him from killing the Wraith, just inches away from death.

Something was said between them and it was enough to make Lucius look to what Trice was trying to tell him. Meaning they both looked towards my chest... no, they were both looking directly at my... *my heart*. I couldn't see for myself what it was that they could see now, only that it was enough for Lucius to drop the blade, falling from his hand as if it had been a snake that had suddenly bit him.

"What are they…?" My question ended there when I saw them start to shift the Wraith Master closer to me.

"No… could it be possible?" I asked, my voice nearly breaking when I saw Lucius now straddling my hips before placing his hands over my chest and starting to push down.

Heart compressions.

"Oh, Gods," I uttered as it became clear what he was trying to do. Then I opened my mouth as a gasp escaped, before a broken sob and then the tears started again, this time coming quicker than before. I didn't know about that heart he was trying to get to beat again, but I knew my own could barely take it. Barely take the sight of the man I loved, the love of my life trying desperately to revive me. His compressions against my chest begging my heart to restart and I put a fist to my mouth just so I had something to bite onto. Just so I wouldn't cry out, despite the tears now overflowing my fingers and running down my hand.

"Oh Gods, Lucius… I'm so sorry, it won't work… I am already gone, and you have to let me go… I'm not coming back, I'm …" Suddenly I heard the only words I ever needed to hear him reply, the first words spoken of this vision, and I didn't care if they were the last. I was just grateful that I got the chance to hear them one last time. Beautiful words whispered so close to my ear,

"I love you."

"I love you too, Lucius."

I said in return knowing he wouldn't hear it, but I didn't care. However, in its place he heard something else in reply and I knew in that moment there was something that he would have chosen over anything else in the world. Even my words of love. Even my last goodbye. And I heard it too. A sound that now made me cry with something more than sorrow…

I was crying with hope.

Then the glass shattered, the image lost.

But it didn't matter because nothing could take away the sound that meant so much more than words. It meant life.

It meant my heart…

It still beat for him.

CHAPTER FIVE

LUCIUS

DEAD ENDS

T*hat heartbeat.*

First one, then a second and then a steady beat of them. It felt like receiving a gift from the Gods once more and a strangled cry of relief tore from my lips. Because that one sound... fuck, but that evidence of life was enough to have me collapsing over her body and thanking the Gods for the sound. I gathered her up in my arms, making sure she wasn't too far away from the fucking cretin that had done this to her.

Fuck, but she felt so fragile in my hold that I knew if I wasn't careful in my emotions, I could have crushed her. I buried my head in her neck and felt for myself the gentle, slow pulse there that represented life.

Her Life

My girl was alive... *she was alive.*

This miracle became my mantra, playing over and over in my mind just so I could keep reminding myself of the fact. I knew I was soaking her with my tears, but I couldn't find myself caring. Let them see this King cry, I couldn't have given a fuck! She was my life's blood, my soul's keeper, and the very reason that my own heart beat! She was my everything, and now to know that there was even a chance that I hadn't lost her, well, then that was all that mattered in that moment. Not pride, not royal arrogance. Nothing but the girl in my arms whose heart beat again!

In fact, I didn't know how long it was that the room allowed me this time before Carn'reau was the first to bring me back to reality. A reality I now wanted to live in once again if it meant Amelia had a chance at living it too.

"My Lord, there is much left to discuss if we are to ensure her life continues." This was the right thing to say and was enough to get me to move my frozen limbs that in that moment almost seemed locked around her. It was as if both my demon and I feared her being snatched from us again, and I knew in that moment there would be no force great enough to tear me from her side. Which was why, without another word needed, I rose to my feet and gathered her in my arms. Then I turned to Auberon, King of this land, and said in a strained voice that sounded as raw as it felt,

"I need somewhere to lay her down." He nodded slowly, and told me with a voice that was thick with emotion,

"But of course."

I looked down at the prisoner and didn't need to say much more, when Trice snarled,

"Leave this shit stain tae me, ah wull carry him next tae ye." I nodded, purposely ignoring the lingering emotion in his eyes. Because I didn't care for his own pain, for rage was not what I needed to fuel my actions right now, not when I knew what that jealousy would do to my demon. No, all I needed to do was focus solely on my girl. So, I followed as the King led us to a place in the castle where most of the guest rooms were situated. This time, the room was one bigger than the last and I painfully remembered all the fun we'd had in destroying it rather than sleeping in it. Gods, but even that thought had me swallowing down what felt like fucking lead caught in my throat, for I wanted that back. I wanted every single moment spent together back, with the chance of reliving each one. But I wanted new ones too, and swore that with this second chance given that I would do all in my power to ensure that future happened.

It just had to.

But with this room being similar to the last in its decoration, it reminded me of only hours ago. I had been so rough with her in my insatiable need to claim her. And now, looking down at her, she looked like some fragile little doll asleep in my arms. Far too pale. That golden blush to her skin long gone, and in its place a porcelain tone. She was so breakable, and I had to be so gentle, more than ever before.

I wouldn't fail her again.

She was mine to protect, mine to cherish and keep safe…

No, *I would not fail her again.*

I pushed the thoughts from my mind and forced myself to concentrate on getting her comfortable. I also realised why the room was bigger, because the bed was double the size of the one that had been in Amelia's first room. Meaning the bed could have fit at least five people in it, which was good considering we had the fucker to place down next to her, something I despised. Yet I lowered her down at the same time as Trice did to him, and I snarled at the Wraith Master when he bared his teeth, something that didn't last long when Trice delivered a punch to his face, hard enough that it knocked him unconscious.

"That's better," he commented gritting his teeth. I nodded in thanks, as it was considerably better having him next to her whilst unconscious and made me feel less murderous.

I sat down on the bed and brushed the hair gently off her face, speaking to the room without taking my eyes from her. I needed to closely monitor her breathing and heart rate.

"Tell me about the Wraiths," I said, keeping my voice steady in case it was possible she could hear me. I didn't want to frighten her with my rage.

"Our uncle must have sent him," Auberon said, at which point I held up a hand and glanced at him.

"At this point, assume nothing. For that is a mistake I have made far too many times in the past. We both have our enemies, Auberon, and either one of them could have been the cause."

"I agree, as I fear that the downside to forming an alliance is the risk of our enemies also forming an alliance," Carn'reau added, making a good point, but at this juncture it was a risk I was willing to take if it meant greater hope at crushing our enemies. Yet I still asked,

"And do you think that likely, for you know of your uncle's nature and his ambitions for power, but what do you know of his means?" This question was directed at both brothers, who looked so vastly different it was like looking at a Fae representation of Yin and Yang, with Carn'reau's darkness to Auberon's light. But this question I had to ask, for I wondered just how powerful this uncle of theirs was? In fact, I needed to know. Because what if it wasn't the uncle that had sent the Wraith Master, but actually the witch? After all, she was the one who orchestrated my girl being here in the first place, even if that was not the outcome she had been hoping for, because she had manipulated the portal and then the King. One who believed himself a promised bargaining chip to use against me in order to get back his brother. And well, as pissed off as I was that it had happened, I was no fool.

He was a King, and that meant making difficult decisions for the good of your people. In fact, without his brother and his army coming back to take his rightful place upon his throne once more, it sounded like an impossible situation to win. Besides, from a selfish point of view, I also knew that I would be even more foolish if I was to let my pride get in the way of forming an alliance and tripling the size of my forces. Because what I hadn't wanted to scare Amelia with was the possibility of a war coming.

Now, priding myself on not being a foolish King, it meant that I'd situated my spies in each of the ruling cities among the many realms of Hell, only to find that a similar account had returned from each of them.

A secret army was amassing.

Now this in itself is not uncommon in Hell, for there was always someone trying to overthrow Lucifer's rule and become the next King of Kings in Hell. But these attempts usually fizzled out before gaining steam. In fact, there was only a handful of close calls for Lucifer during his entire reign, and that was one that began as far back as the dawn of time. I also believed that it was in those near defeats that twisted Lucifer's mind enough to have him dedicate his energy into trying his hand at creation. His ultimate goal was to give birth to a son. A successor to be given the crown and rule by his side. Yet without his mortal Chosen One, this was impossible… at least according to the prophecy. Well, now he had her in his grasp, so why it hadn't yet happened no one knew, but I would bet my own blood that it had something to do with that same prophecy. Something everyone knew existed, but it was also one that if anyone was to discover it, they certainly wouldn't live to tell the tale.

My father's best kept secret.

But this didn't stop him in his quest. In truth, I believed if there was anything he envied about Heaven, it was their ability to create mortal life. Yet I didn't know what lay beneath the root of his obsession when it came to them, just that it was there and growing. A growth in which brought him to trying different methods, hence my existence. It was why he favoured Dariush and I, as we were as close as he ever got to perfecting that dream.

He wanted to create his own race. A perfected version of mortals that lived eternally if they were careful enough. A stronger, faster, and more powerful version of mankind that would beat the Gods at their own creation game. This ideal was where Vampires were first born from. They were the result of some of his first attempts at creating life, but their nature was too wild, too dark, and too unpredictable. But being that they were born from the pits of Hell, then it was of little wonder. No, what he was missing was that tiny slice of humanity that gave a creature an identity.

That gave them a soul.

Then came me… *His success.*

His King of Vampires.

It was genius really, as he discovered that instead of trying to create an army of perfect creatures all he needed to do was create one. One that had the power to recondition all those failed attempts. An entire race of Vampires soon to be injected with the same slice of humanity I possessed, gifting it to all who pledged their loyalty to me. However, what he hadn't been expecting, was that they would all become tied to me and not to him as he had been hoping for. Which meant I might have started off as his intended puppet, but I soon broke away from my strings and became his equal, for his blood running in my veins had made me his son, even without the aid of his Chosen One, doing so in more ways than one. Because where he had used it to create me, I now had the power to do the same by creating my own race of Vampires.

Basically, he might have been successful in obtaining his ultimate goal, but by creating his equal in power it also meant one more thing… *He had fucked up… big time.*

Now, just how many other 'successful attempts' actually remained was now a number I questioned, for I only knew of my brother and myself. But after hearing of the possibility of another who had been in hiding all these years, well I questioned everything when it came to Lucifer. Meaning, if I had to guess who was behind this growing army, then the obvious choice would be someone who had a grudge against Lucifer. But dealing with another son of the Devil with fucking daddy issues, meant that part and parcel of that also meant having an issue with his brother, namely me. The ones who had made the cut. It made sense, for it seemed he had also orchestrated events to make me suspicious enough have my own brother executed by my hand.

It was ruthless and it was tactical, and it was also something I would have done myself in order to eradicate my enemies one by one. Because getting them to turn on each other meant half the work was done and with very little effort on their part. However, fate clearly wasn't on their side as it happened that way.

But as for a war in Hell, well it was something I knew

was on the horizon and one that if I had my way, Amelia would get nowhere near. Something I knew she would have argued against. Which was why my ultimate plan after first saving her life was making her see that for that life to continue, it would be easier if she were back topside and under the protection of her father.

After all, a near death experience wouldn't be without its lingering damage on her mind. For this I could account for, even if there was only one being alive I would ever admit that to.

"In all honesty, I would not put anything past his reach," Auberon said, answering my question of his uncle's power.

"And the Wraith?" I asked on a snarl of barely contained rage as I glanced a dangerous look its way to ensure it was still unconscious.

"Wraiths... well, in truth, not a lot is known of them. Only that it is said they are trapped souls of those that have been wronged or forsaken. Used for greed or some other nefarious reason, either way their souls are at the mercy of the Wraith Master," Auberon said nodding towards the one who obviously currently held that title. But this made me wonder if that was what he was doing now with Amelia's soul. Did he have it still trapped somewhere and that was why she hadn't come back to me?

"Who is he?" I asked, narrowing my eyes once more at the form I didn't exactly relish to see lying next to my Chosen One.

"No one truly knows," Carn'reau answered this time.

"Well, someone must know something, for how else was he summoned?" I snapped losing my patience.

"Well clearly someone knew how tae, as th' proof is richt fucking 'ere!" barked Trice, making the King look to him and mirror the shifter's pissed off stance by folding his own arms, the blood of the fight still there from his injuries that had already healed.

"Yes, and you also don't need to know how to communicate with a snake for it to first bite your hand and release its venom," Auberon said.

"All you have to do is put it where it is not welcome," Carn´reau finished for his brother, making the point that you didn't have to know the origins of the Wraith Master in order to summon him. It also made me wonder if this had been a saying often taught by their father, as it seemed to be one they knew well.

"Dinnae tell me this is fucking useless!" snapped Trice after sweeping his arm out in anger and smashing a lamp on the floor.

"That isnae helpin', brother," Gryph pointed out, trying to calm his brother once more, which these days seemed like a full time job for the big bastard, as it was clear that Trice was quick tempered. As for me, well, I had no fucking time for it as I would show every last fucker what being quick tempered really was!

"Silence, all of you!" I demanded, quickly losing my patience with it all.

"Aye, ah wull be quiet, by getting th' hell oot o' 'ere ," Trice snapped obviously hitting his limit.

"Trice," Gryph said trying to reason with his brother, but it was no use, for he was already walking out of the door, and I had to say I wasn't sorry to see the sight of him leaving.

"Forgive him, he struggles lik' we a' dae, we a' care aboot th' lass," Gryph told me, and I nodded for him to go, and that I understood. Besides, I was glad for it, as the room was getting crowded as it was, and having his negative defeatist attitude at a time like this wasn't exactly something I would class as helpful. No, it just made me want to embed my fist in his face even more than usual.

I dragged a hand down my face and released a frustrated sigh before looking back to the Kings of this realm.

"Someone must know something," I pointed out unable to believe that this was it.

"The Oracle of light," Carn'reau muttered under his breath.

"Who?" I snapped. It was his brother's turn to release a sigh, only his was clearly one of defeat and I soon knew why.

"Unfortunately, the one who would have known how to defeat this poison would have been the Oracle of Light," Auberon answered.

"Great, that's all I need, another fucking Oracle," I ground out through clenched teeth.

"I know what you're thinking, my Lord, but our oracles are not the same as yours," Carn'reau informed me, making me growl,

"Explain!"

"Our Oracle of light gains knowledge not through the Fates, but through casting spells. She is a little like your witch, as she was a woman of great knowledge and held high esteem throughout our people," Auberon told me, describing her indeed as you would a witch.

"And where is she, for if this is true then surely she can help?" I enquired but the moment I saw Auberon's face tighten, I knew there was going to be a story behind why she was not already here.

Not one I would want to hear. I knew this when my first reply was Carn'reau's grim face.

"I'm afraid that is impossible," Auberon said next, and when I let my temper flare and shout,

"Why the fuck not?" This was when I received my next blow.

These setbacks would have only one casualty, that of my Chosen One. A setback that was confirmed when Carn'reau told me exactly why not...

"Because she is dead."

CHAPTER SIX

PAPER CLUES

"*Fuck!*" I hissed as soon as I heard this.

"She was killed long ago by our uncle the moment she spoke of a prophecy that would one day unite our people by birthing four sons, who would each be destined to become rulers of the realms," Auberon told me, a piece of which I already knew.

"So, your uncle murdered her, of this you are sure?" I asked again, needing to be certain. The King nodded, looking solemn before going on to tell me,

"He feared what else she would say, of what she would discover of our uncle and his treachery before our father's death. For like other Oracles, the Oracle of light cannot lie, for the moment that they do, they lose all their power," Auberon said, making his brother add more details to this.

"Which would mean whatever she told our father he would have believed it even over his own kin. Our uncle knew that if she was to discover what he had planned, then it would put an end to his reign of terror among our people before it even began. She was the only one with enough power to stop him and he knew it," Carn'reau said with utter disdain. A disdain born not only to the level of evil which his uncle was willing to go to in his reach for power, but also disdain for being the one accused of his brother's murder.

"So that is it, you're telling me no one else in your realm knows anything of this Wraith Master or the sickness that infects my Chosen One?" I ground out with bitterness, and the dire look on their faces became answer enough. Meaning that had I not been sat next to my girl, the King would most likely have found himself with another room left in ruins, only this time, not one done out of passion and desire but one from chaos and unleashed fury.

Now my mind was racing, trying in vain to come up with a solution where it seemed as if there simply was none. Surely it couldn't be as hopeless as it seemed. Surely something could be done. For I had not fought so hard in bringing her back only to lose her all over again! Because there might not be one powerful enough in this realm to discover a solution but perhaps there was one in my own? Nero perhaps, or even Nesteemia. There must be someone left in this godforsaken world who could help!

There just had to be!

Of course, it was in that moment that fate answered my prayers, and admittedly with the very last person I would have expected. Help that first came with a knock on the door.

"Vena, dear sister, now is not the…" Auberon said, trying to get his sister to leave, obviously believing this no place for the desperate cries of a woman faced with the loss of her friend. But then, as devastating as it was, there was something more I could see behind her eyes…

She knew something.

"No, let her in," I ordered, feeling in that one shy look she gave me that she knew something, or why else would she brave coming in here? Carn'reau gave me a curious look before nodding for his sister to come forward. She was a fearful little thing, that much was easy to see, but there was also a side to her that very few obviously got to witness, and Amelia had been one of them. A kindness and a warmth that made Amelia's time here more bearable. Anyone who had the power to do that, well, I was indebted to them.

"Come forward, little one," I urged knowing there was something she was trying to find the courage to say. It was now that I noticed she held her hands behind her back but not because she was being courteous but because she was hiding something. She lowered her head and I swallowed down my impatience, knowing that any harsh words from me now would only make her regret her decision and leave.

"You have something to say, something to show us perhaps?" I asked in a coaxing gentle tone, one that only Carn'reau had laid witness to before, and no doubt why he believed me to be drawing his sister into some false sense of security. It was most likely why he now looked wary and took a step closer towards her. I gave him a slight shake of my head to tell him that it was fine, silently conveying that his sister would come to no harm by my hand.

As for Vena, she looked positively petrified and it was in that moment that I realised it wasn't because of what I was, but it was because I was a man. I didn't know what dynamics there were between brother and sister, I only knew that in all likelihood she was being protected in some way. She did not hold herself like royalty, and I found this curious seeing as she was a Royal from birth.

In fact, the type of behaviour she displayed was what you would have expected from one who had been thrust into that royalty and not lived with it their entire lives. Very much like Keira in that way, as I thought back to all those times I had seen in her in unsure moments. Like when being put on display in some Royal setting of one form or another. The ball in Venice for example, when Dom had made it his mission to proclaim her as his Queen and announce it to our world.

But unlike Keira, this girl didn't possess any spark of a fire in her belly, not even the hint of fight. No, this little unsure Dove, didn't seem to have a single backbone in her body and the tremble I could see on her bottom lip told me of her fear, which meant only one thing, whatever she had to say was worth finding the courage to do so.

Worth it to save her friend.

Well, I was clearly wrong about that spark then, for despite how small, it was clearly there.

"It's alright, sister, go ahead." This gentle coaxing came from her brother Auberon, the one person she obviously trusted enough, for it was in that moment that she spoke. And as she did, she brought the book she had been hiding behind her back to the front of her and opened it up until a piece of scroll could be seen hidden in its centre.

Then she said the only words in that moment I wanted to hear…

"The Oracle of Light… *she isn't dead.*"

"What, that's impossible!" Auberon said, and Carn'reau quickly followed with scornful words.

"Really, Vena, you cannot waste time like this and give foolish hope!" Her brother's complaints ignored, and not taking my eyes off the girl, I merely held up a hand to silence them both before I motioned her forward.

"Show me." Her eyes widened as if she was surprised that I was the only one in the room that did believe her. But then again, I was the one with the most to lose. She nodded once and stepped closer, showing me a piece of scroll that held some elvish passage. But even I could tell that it had been written in a hurry as half of it had been torn away. There was also a faint print of writing beneath as if someone had grabbed the first book they could and tore off a page, so they had something to write on.

It was evidence.

"Where did you find this?" I asked thinking that if it had been hidden then that was even more proof, and people only hid what they didn't want certain people to find... important information for example.

"I spend a lot of time in the library, it's quiet there, my mother doesn't like the library, she says it's dusty and smells funny," she answered, instantly telling me that her problem here was her mother. I nodded telling her that I understood and for her to continue.

"Some days there's not much else to do other than read."

"Vena, you need..." Auberon started to say but I shook a hand at him telling him to stop, and before she looked around at him and I lost her concentration I quickly commented,

"And you get through a lot of books, I imagine." This I knew would lead the conversation in the direction I wanted it to go, for she clearly needed some help.

"Yes, I do," she replied, more enthusiastically this time.

"Vena, please." Again I held up my hand the moment her brother tried to scold her, for this moment was too important to rush the girl.

"Please, go on, my dear," I prompted.

"I'd been gone for hours one day, getting lost in one story and then in another, so I didn't realise how late it had become. I knew I would be in trouble."

"And did your mother come to look for you on this day?" I asked gently.

"Yes, it forced her to come look for me. Like I said, she

doesn't like the library, well, she doesn't really like me either," she admitted softly, making Auberon snap,

"Vena, that's not…"

"It is true! You're just too busy to see it, brother," she argued back, that little spark of a backbone now shining through. She was a pretty little thing when she allowed it to happen.

"What happened next, Vena?" I asked, ignoring her frustrated outburst.

"I know it was cowardly of me, but I hid. You see there's all sorts of little nooks and crannies in there. Lots of places to hide, yet one of those libraries where there never seems to be enough space for all the books it contains," she said, tucking her hair behind her ear in a nervous gesture.

"Where did you hide?" I asked, and this time it came out as close as possible to a whisper, as I knew my voice was drawing her in.

"I squeezed myself in between two of the shelves and discovered a hidden room." Finally, there it was.

"What, you never told me about this?" Auberon responded as if surprised that his sister could have done anything adventurous in her life without him knowing.

"What did you find there?" I asked, ignoring her brother's shock.

"I think it belonged to the Oracle of Light, or maybe my father. I don't quite know. I was too afraid to go back into the room in case I was caught." I frowned before looking down at the book still held in one hand, the piece of paper still held to the centre page with her thumb.

"But before that happened, you found something didn't you?" I asked nodding to it, and she too looked down making her unusual coloured hair sweep across her freckled face, which made her appear a lot younger than she was.

"I knocked into the shelf and this book fell. At first I was just going to put it back, but then I noticed the piece of paper," she told me, making me ask,

"And what does it say?"

"It is in our old language, one very few now still speak. The Elders, they were the ones who used it. The Elders and *the Oracles.*" She whispered this last part as if it was some holy secret.

"Vena, my dear, we do not know that it is from…" Auberon interrupted, however that spark came back in his sister and she whipped her head back to look at him before arguing,

"But it is, for it is a warning. Look at it, brother, look at it and you will see for yourself that she speaks of our uncle, she says she found a way to survive him… that she… *she found a way to hide,*" Vena said, taking the piece and now handing it to her brother as proof after whispering the part about hiding as if her uncle had the power to hear every word she uttered.

Auberon took it with an exasperated sigh before scanning it as if he already knew it was a hopeless endeavour. However, it was the moment his eyes narrowed that I knew it wasn't hopeless at all.

I had felt it in my core and down to the very depths of my soul.

The piece of paper had held the clue just like Vena had said. And they knew it too when Auberon's eyes shot to his brother's, before telling him,

"What she says is true… this is proof …"

"Of what?" Carn'reau asked, but I was the one to answer him as I looked back at my girl and said,

"That the Oracle of Light is still alive."

CHAPTER SEVEN

ASHES OF THE PAST

I felt my heart pounding in my chest the moment I realised that the only one who could help me save my girl was likely still alive.

"Could this be true, could she have survived your uncle's attack?" I asked, forcing myself to stay calm as I looked between Carn'reau and Auberon. As for the brothers, they first looked to one another before Auberon admitted,

"No one found her body."

"Then how was it she was assumed dead, for surely the word of your uncle wouldn't have been taken as gospel?" I asked, yet I was surprised as it was Vena who answered me.

"The Eternal Light went out," she whispered before looking towards the window and into the night. It was as if she could see something that used to be there.

"The Eternal Light?" I questioned further.

"There is a temple on the top of our highest mountain, it is where the Elders and the Oracles live, a place where they worship," Auberon told me, looking towards the window like his sister.

"There is an Eternal Flame found at the heart of the temple and it is said that it only ever extinguishes when one of its Oracles die," Carn'reau finished for him.

"So, there is more than one Oracle?" Carn'reau shook his head at my question, not allowing time for any hope to bloom.

"There was a time when there were many. But with each coming year no more Oracles were ever born, eventually leaving only one. The Oracle of Light was the last of her kind. Some rumours say it was a curse, but there is no proof to any of it, only that there used to be a constant comforting light that could be seen from all the land coming from the top of that mountain and when it went out, everyone knew the last Oracle had died," Auberon told me, and before I could ask further, Carn'reau knowing this informed me,

"Our father's men went in search to see if this was true, and the Elders confirmed as much, yet no body was ever found."

"And their explanation?" I wanted to know.

"They told my father's men that they had completed the ritual upon her death, and her ashes were scattered to the wind," Auberon told him.

"Then it is possible that the Elders lied, potentially to save her," I assumed out loud.

"That is possible, yes, for I believe they would have gone to any lengths to protect the last Oracle," Carn'reau said, agreeing with me before nodding to the piece of paper and adding,

"She might have known her life was in danger, or my uncle's attack didn't end her life like he thought. It is possible she survived without his knowledge."

Fuck, but I hoped so!

"Vena, you need to show me where you found this in the library as there may be more to discover," Carn'reau said, making her jump a little.

"I… well, I…" her fear was obvious, making me interject on her behalf knowing with just one look why she was unsure.

"Carn'reau, let your brother go for I need you to find the McBain brothers, get them back here." My commander frowned ever so slightly as if questioning why his sister was behaving this way. Yet for me it was obvious, she didn't feel comfortable around him, that much was clear and why would she? How long had it been since she had seen him? Vena nodded quickly and then walked towards the door with her brother Auberon now following.

Then, as soon as they had left, Carn'reau walked towards the door they had just exited, when I stopped him by saying,

"Give it time, old friend." He knew I was referring to his sister, which was why, instead of saying anything, he simply bowed his head once before leaving.

Finally, I was left alone with my girl… *finally.*

I lay down next to her in hopes that she may feel my presence being so close. I rolled to my side so I could hold her, now placing my palm flat against her chest.

"Thank the Gods," I muttered as I felt that slow and steady heartbeat, which was enough to offer me comfort along with the feel of the slight rise and fall of her chest. By all accounts she looked as if she was merely sleeping in a cold place. Which was why I reached over for a woven blanket I saw on the back of a chair closest to the bed. Then I used it to cover her, and at the same time I just hoped that wherever her mind was, that she wasn't frightened.

"Fuck!" I hissed suddenly as a thought hit me and I

suddenly bolted upright. A thought that now made me foolishly want to pound my own fist into my head for my stupidity.

"Of course, you fucking idiot!" I snapped at myself because I suddenly realised, there could be a way for me to communicate with her.

Her Void.

I just needed to access her Void!

I quickly lay back down next to her, mirroring her position, now looking up at the intricate ceiling above before closing my eyes and allowing my mind to delve deep into her own. It was no surprise that at first all I found was darkness as it was very similar to what I would find if I tried to do this when she was awake. But right now, she was at her most vulnerable, so accessing it should have been easy.

Should have.

"Come on, just give me something, my love." I felt my lips moving in actual real time, yet I heard it being spoken in her void. I looked down at my feet and began by trying to concentrate on the most minute detail. It looked like a crumpled burnt piece of paper that was by the toe of my boot and as I moved it an inch to the right I watched as it floated up towards me. Then I snatched out and grabbed hold of it before turning it around in my fingers, half expecting it to crumble into dust, yet it didn't. It felt like a leaf without its skeletal centre.

That's when I saw what it reminded me of, as it looked like a section of a face, one that had been torn from a painting before being set alight. I looked down once again and saw now that the entire floor was covered in them, making it look like the ash was inches thick. It was as if someone had burned an entire library to the ground and scattered the remains, creating a field of ash. One that continued to spread out as though it was growing and growing, until soon it became a seemingly endless wasteland. An inhabitable piece of the earth besieged with jagged rocks of dark grey stone, the sight far beyond what even my eyesight could reach.

"Why here, little one?" I questioned quietly to myself as I took in the expanse of space. This place seemed too dark and too dire for my girl to have created in her mind, so I had to question if I had just stepped into someone else's Hell?

Did this is belonging to the Wraith Master?

I started walking, having no idea in which direction to even start moving towards, but knowing that I couldn't just stand there and wait for it to come to me. Not when it had taken all my effort just to find this landscape in the first place. However, as I continue to walk, I soon found myself turning around to find something that hadn't been there a moment ago.

A ruined castle.

"Impossible," I muttered as I recognised the image. One that was only seen for but a fleeting moment, and long ago. A sight seen through someone else's memories. It was believed in Greek mythology to be half myth and half real. A place only poets wrote about where a legendary people lived in the far northern part of the known world. The oecumene, an ancient Greek term for the known, meant the inhabited. Yet these stories were left over from those who managed to cross over into this realm, one not of man and not of demon but a dangerous cross over of power.

A land and realm known as Hyperborea.

Could it be that whoever this Wraith Master was, that he had been connected to this broken realm in some way? Legend spoke of its demise due to a mad ruler leading his armies into ruin before the entire nation simply faded away like dust. As if its volcanic mountains had all erupted and buried its people under fifteen foot of ash like the eruption in Pompeii had. Was this wasteland a reminder to the Wraith Master of all that remained?

My thoughts went unanswered, so instead I looked down to find footsteps there in the ash. They were small, and not of a man but of a woman. Was this the trail of breadcrumbs that I'd been hoping to find?

I found myself questioning what she would have thought when seeing a castle like this herself? It most definitely wouldn't have been like any she had found in England, as I knew she had often enjoyed exploring the countryside on her days off.

My nerdy little tourist trying to squeeze in as much history into her brain as possible, even when she wasn't working. I found myself remembering looking forward to the chance to talk to her about all the historical events I had been through, to give her first-hand experience from someone who had actually lived there during that time.

She was curious, my Amelia, and it was that same curiosity that led her footsteps towards the entrance of the castle. Because I knew she wouldn't have been able to resist. She was never able to resist anything that fed that eager mind of hers, even when it came to opening the box, one she knew she shouldn't. Every step of the way she had allowed her curiosity to get the better of her and lead her blindly into each dangerous situation.

It reminded me of that old proverb, one not quite as dire as the retelling of it from 20th century Russia. The one people these days would have called the scorpion and the frog. But I knew of its origin, the Persian fable of the scorpion and the turtle. In this telling of it the scorpion and the turtle were friends, and when the scorpion wanted to cross the river the turtle agreed to carry him across, yet the scorpion still stung him despite the hard shell that protected him from harm. The turtle was baffled by his friend's behaviour as he must have known that it would not hurt him. However, the scorpion simply responded that he acted neither out of malice or out of intent to hurt but merely out of nature and the satiable urge to sting.

"Truly have the Sages said that to cherish a base character is to give one's honour to the wind, and to involve one's own self in embarrassment." I recited the end of the fable as it speaks of people who cannot resist their nature. The same could be said of Amelia, for as much as she would be driven to do what she thought was right and to do good, her curious nature often led her to do the opposite. And really, could I even claim it to be a fault? Not when I myself had made so many mistakes due to my arrogant belief that by pushing her to safety would result in saving her.

I shook my head of these thoughts and continued on towards the imposing entrance of the castle, thinking it would simply allow me to enter. Yet this was when things got complicated for the doors would not open for me, no matter what I tried. No matter how much I tried to assert my will over them or use my powers that should have worked in any Void.

So, in my rage, I tried using brute strength, finding the strangest thing happened. I punched the door, and for the first time all I felt was pain. A piercing pain that quickly started to throb and when I looked down, I saw the blood and mangled bone from what now appeared to be a broken hand.

My broken hand.

"What the fuck?!" I questioned furiously, now looking

down at my hand and feeling it pulse with pain like never before. What the Hell was happening?!

However, undeterred, even with my injury, I walked away from the entrance so I could look upon the castle and see if there was another way inside. This was when I noticed that the once ruined castle was now back to being whole again as if my hitting the door had triggered something. Well, at the very least there was plenty of windows, so I released my wings or at least…

I tried to.

"How is this possible?" I asked no one as nothing came from my other side, not even when I tried to call forth my demon. This was when I first felt the silence. The peace and calm I wasn't used to feeling. That unnerving sense that I was alone… truly alone. Something I hadn't been since my rebirth. I could barely believe this was possible for nothing had this power, let alone something that could be connected to Amelia's void.

Unless none of it was Amelia's Void at all? That I had entered her mind only to find someone else had possession of it.

"It's not her mind," I muttered, when suddenly I knew I was no longer alone.

"Ah, now he gets it." I heard the growl of words from behind me and spun around to find the Wraith Master staring back at me.

"What is this?!" I snarled in anger. But the Wraith just smiled and held out his arms, telling me,

"This is my land, this is my world and in it you… you are just a simple mortal."

"That's fucking impossible?!" I argued, wishing my words felt like the truth. But he looked at my broken hand

and grinned once more, a grin without lips as if they had long ago decayed.

"Then be my guest and fly up to your little Princess. Fly up and save her and burn your waxed wings like Icarus, or simply watch them fall for you have no power here and neither does she. Your Princess is mine now!" he said, making me roar at him despite not having my demon to back up the sound. So, I finished it with a hiss of a single word,

"Never!" But even I knew there was no strength behind the word as I begged for just one second to feel that rage burning inside of me enough to ignite my demon. But it never came, and it felt as if I'd lost a piece of my soul. The very essence that made me, I felt...

Utterly powerless

"She's my prisoner now for this is my void, one she will never escape from! I will make sure of that and then when I am ready, I will claim her heart!" I opened my mouth to deny the possibility as her heart belonged to me. But then in that moment I heard her screaming at the top of her lungs. I looked up towards the window to find her shadow running past as if she was being chased by something.

"Amelia! Hold on, I'm coming!" I shouted but once more my wings didn't appear and instead, I felt the burning hand of the Wraith Master grabbing me from behind.

"Time to go and have some fun with your little bitch... but as for you, time to leave, Vampire." I roared out, this time bolting upright back into my own body, taking in a deep breath when finding my demon form there panting as if I had been fighting in a battle for days. I was just glad that my wings hadn't erupted from my back, for I could have hurt my Chosen One lying next to me. It was as if my demon knew we had to be careful of the fact that she was next to us. Yet the moment I made it back it had burst from whatever mental

cage the Wraith Master had put him in to prevent him helping me to reaching her.

"Fuck… FUCK!" I bellowed as I sat up and pushed my hands through my hair and as I did, they were the fingers of a man not of a demon that could tear my scalp clean off. The change rippled down me, so by the time the King returned he did not find a demon sat next to my girl panting like a fucking madman.

"What have you found!" My voice was rough and grated, as if it had nearly been worn down to barely being able to produce the words.

"What my sister said was true, we found the room, one we believe belonged to one of the Elders who assisted my father."

"And?!" I snapped, and his eyes widened in surprise before seeing for himself that something had happened, which was the reason I was on a fucking knife's edge. However, instead of commenting he wisely refrained, and instead told me what I needed to know.

"He left clues, clues my sister believes was prophesied to be found on this very day."

"Please tell me one of those fucking clues tells you how the hell to find this woman!" I snapped, making Auberon smile for the first time since all this had happened.

"We found a clue, one that speaks of a secret passageway. Once a myth that apparently now holds more truth than not."

A passageway?" I asked, and he nodded before telling me more.

"It is said to lead to a protected land, one where my uncle couldn't find her. It is a dangerous journey, but I believe it is worth the chance. I will have my sister look after your…"

"No!" I snapped, cutting him off instantly

"But you must, for the Oracle will not come back and risk

her life for nothing, you must make her see the importance, you must make her understand the…" I growled loud enough to cut him off before telling him,

"I will not leave my Chosen One again… *ever!*" I said as a dangerous vow and, in that moment, the McBain brothers walked through the door hearing the last part of this, and said without hesitation,

"We will go, and we will not fail."

CHAPTER EIGHT

AMELIA

KIDNAPPING OF THE FIRST KIND

My heartbeat.

My. Heart. Was. Beating.

"This can't be possible." I must have said this aloud the moment I realised that the steady beating meant that I was actually…

Still alive.

Lucius had brought me back. I don't know how he had done it, but he didn't let me go, which had me questioning why I was still here? If I wasn't dead, then why was I still locked inside this void? It made no sense!

As soon as the glass in the mirror had shattered, the vision beyond it evaporated leaving behind something else in its place. Just beyond the frame that remained, now looking like a doorway, was a woman's bedchamber. So, I got up off the floor and approached the mirror, feeling like I was in a fucked up version of Alice Through the Looking Glass. I looked down at my feet as they crunched on the glass making me thankful my Fae leather shoes remained, although they were now covered in ash.

I stepped across the crimson frame and found I was right; it was a woman's room. It was also one that from the looks of things, hadn't seen life for a very long time. Yet, after a minute or so, something strange began to happen, as it started to shift into one that I had seen before. A room that had been more from someone else's memory. A piece of the past long before I had even come into this world. Back when Layla was a spy for Lucius and when caught she had been kept in the belly of Afterlife. In my father's prison. And just as it had then, it faded in and out of new and old, richly furnished and totally dilapidated.

"These are from my mind," I said aloud as if calling bullshit on the whole thing. Yet, despite saying this, it did nothing to hide the room I knew she had been kept in, the room Lucius had foolishly broken her free from. It was also when I first found out that the witch had been using Layla as a puppet all these years.

"These memories don't belong here," I said again, only this time more to myself as if this would help. But it was difficult as everything had been the same, just like that night I first found the room. The broken furniture, splinters of wood littered the floor like shrapnel from the rage bomb Layla had detonated. A fourposter bed that sat on broken legs with its useless mattress slashed beyond all use. Those creepy shreds of curtains waving like ghosts.

"This isn't real," I muttered as I took in the torn, shredded wallpaper that barely covered the brick beneath. Royal blue and gold fleur-de-lis, barely more than fragments of opulence. Yet it was those long claw marks slashed through the plaster that made me shiver, because I knew what madness had made them.

"No... no... *not again,*" I stammered as I was too late to tear my eyes from those walls. As just like last time, she appeared, now back to haunt this Void.

"Layla." I hissed her name for the second time, mimicking the past when her image appeared. She was on her knees, facing the wall and still lost to her madness by scratching her bloody fingers into the wall. And like last time there was only one name on her insane mind.

One name written in the blood,

"Lucius." As soon as I said his name she turned and hissed at me like some wild animal protecting her latest kill. Her fingernails were long gone, and blood was all that remained of the tips of her fingers. I flinched back because I was unsure what would happen in the Void. It was obvious the Wraith Master was plucking my past from my mind, no doubt trying to learn my fears. But it was what he intended to do with them that worried me as I knew he had the power to make them so much worse.

So, when Layla rose up without taking me from her sights, I looked around the floor for anything I could use as a weapon and found the leg of a chair. My fingers curled around it just at the same time she suddenly ran at me.

"AAHHH!" I shouted at the same time bracing a foot back and taking my shot when she was within distance, swinging my bat like it had been a mace in my hands. She screamed at me like a banshee as the chair leg travelled straight through her. She started to evaporate into nothing, spreading from the waist outwards where my weapon had struck her. The last thing I saw was her face, turning demonic...

She was horrifying!

It only lasted a second, but it was enough to see the oval shaped skull with its skin pulled tight across the serrated bone underneath. Black hollow eyes were like staring into to two soulless pits of oblivion and the puckered torn skin around them looked as if they had been gouged out. She had no nose, just a frightening mouth that took up most of her face, with metal six-inche pins that spanned from one side of the face to the other with too many to count. In fact, it was as if her razor tipped teeth were locked behind some torture device. The last of the horror was her hair line that was nothing more than a ripped scalp being peeled back from her forehead like demonic fruit. But because I hadn't seen this demonic side of her before, I wondered if this was really what she looked like or was it just something the Wraith Master had created to frighten me?

I dropped the chair leg once she disappeared, and as soon as it hit the floor it too disintegrated. I was looking down, panting and trying to slow my heartrate, one I knew must have been fragile for what it had just been through. But this was when I noticed the room change once more, back into the bedchamber I had first seen through the mirror's frame.

It was your typical bedchamber fit for a Queen. The walls were a work of art in their own right, painted with beautiful white flowers captured inside the gold gilded recess. There was a half-moon shaped little writing table over towards a large arched window framed by thick, blue satin curtains. One that even from where I stood, I could see overlooked the front of the castle where I had entered.

As for the bed, it held a tiara shaped canopy above it with its gold, elaborate design matching the crown mouldings around the top and bottom of the room. Fringed curtains swept down from the canopy in a Royal blue colour, edged with gold tassels. This matched the bedding, which flowed over the high bed like gold edged water. As for the rest of the room, it was filled with expensive furniture that was highly decorated with its feminine touch, each one displaying cute little trinkets that had obviously been collected over the years. A dainty music box, a Fabergé egg in blues and whites to match the room, and a small marble bust of two boys' faces that I recognised from the painting, were only a few of the pieces dotted around the room.

A mosaic floor looked as if designed with the star constellations in mind, parts of which were covered by fringed, thick, blue rugs that tied the room together. Then the last thing my eyes came to focus on was another painting of the woman in the gallery, only this time it hadn't been touched but merely partially covered by a sheet. One I was gently pulling away from the frame as it hung over a side table. The difference with this one as opposed to the other, was that in this picture the Queen looked happy. She also looked younger, more vibrant, but that was most likely down to the small smile that played on her lips. There was almost a sort of naivete to it, as if she had her whole life ahead of her and she was looking forward to every moment of it.

I saw the same ring flash on her finger, but this time it wasn't one that was in the shadows but more as if she was showing it off, making me wonder if this was painted shortly after her engagement? Because the one in the gallery had shown a woman gazing out of the window as if longing to be somewhere else. I also noticed another change, and that was the necklace I saw her around her neck. A stunning blue stone that would have nearly filled my palm it was that big. It looked like a jagged chunk of ice, sparkling as the sun filtered through, something the artist had skilfully managed to capture. It hung from a thick chain and stayed in place by what looked like a crafted silver hand holding on to the stone. A hand that didn't belong to a woman but that of a man.

I had to wonder why this necklace wasn't in the other picture of her, and I questioned if this had been a gift from the King? I also questioned why this painting had survived the rage of the King and had only been covered to hide it from view?

Although, there was another reason why some were slashed through and this one only covered up.

Guilt.

It seemed most likely the cause, making me wonder what had happened to them? What had happened to the Queen and her two boys and where were they now? Had they managed to flee from the King, from her husband and the boys' father?

I wished that I knew, maybe then I might have stood a chance of understanding this creature and his mad mind, one that I seem locked to. A mind that was frighteningly merging with my very own. Because this room might have been a memory from the Wraith Master's past life, but Layla's prison had been stolen from my own. Which meant that we were obviously connected, and I knew that maybe the only way I had a chance to break that connexion, was to first understand him. To know what he wanted was in return.

Besides, what else did I have to do?

Okay so granted this was a bit like playing a life-sized game of Cluedo, one that I would no doubt find ended something a little like Mr King killed his wife in the dining room with a candle stick. But then again, at least it beat playing battleships with his Phantom army outside.

So, I left this room knowing there was nothing left for me here and went back out the door into the gallery. But before checking out the other parts of the castle I decided to make sure I wasn't missing anything important, so I tried the door opposite. It was unlocked and I stepped through only to find myself sucking in another startled breath.

"What the Hell?" was my reaction the moment I found myself standing outside Jared's club...

The Devil's Ring.

Well, to be more precise, I was standing outside a pub called Ye Olde Cheshire Cheese, found in the heart of London, just off Fleet Street. I hadn't been there in years, in fact the last time... well, it hadn't ended so well for me. Meaning this memory was a strange one to be reliving, that was for damn sure.

But just like before, it was the early hours of the morning and yet still dark enough to be creepy to anyone who hadn't just stepped out of a demonic Fight Club... because come on, the real horrors were buried two hundred feet underground in Jared's demonic playground and if that didn't scare the shit out of someone, then a dark street wouldn't. And back then I had been a sixteen-year-old girl who had never known a single day of danger.

Not until that night.

I'd just discovered Theo was my brother, a fact that had been purposely kept from me and the reason my over emotional mind had made me go running out of there. A place I never should have ventured into. But the very reason I snuck inside to begin with was because I had been searching out the one who ruled Hell's fairground on earth. Jared Cerberus was like an uncle to me, so in my defence I didn't think I had much to fear. He was the King of the Hellbeasts after all and had owned this underground demonic Fight Club for centuries.

But the reason I was searching him out was I believed he was the only one I would get any information from. Because I had been dreaming of Lucius since I was seven years old, but it was not long after my sixteenth birthday that my dreams of Lucius had started to change. And this was all before I had really even met him. Of course, I had seen brief, fleeting sights of him, although he hadn't seemed to notice me on these rare occasions... *nothing like in my dreams.*

Yet these dreams when I was younger were barely even more than just a sighting or the feeling that I was being watched. I remembered one dream where I'd been playing the piano, and I swore that I saw someone watching me in the reflection of the beautiful instrument my uncle Zagan had bought me on my birthday. He had been stood by the doorway, with just the barest hint of him in view. I had no idea who it was at first, I had just continued to play as if they weren't even there, hoping they liked it. But then the moment I heard that creak by the door I spun round quickly, missing the chords as I did. Yet it was in vain as no one had been there. But I never forgot that reflection, and as soon as I had my first real dream of him after meeting who I now knew had been his witch Nesta, I knew it had been him in those past childhood dreams also.

It had been Lucius watching me.

After my sixteenth birthday, my dreams of him started getting stronger and stronger as time went on and by the age of eighteen they were definitely more of a sexual nature. I had always wondered if he'd ever had a hand in them, like our minds were connected and in my sleep he could control what I dreamt of. After all, I knew he could access my mind when I was at my most vulnerable, as he had proven that when he had tried to find me the very first night I had run from him.

But after I turned sixteen it was as if someone was pulling me in his direction and of course, growing up around my parents meant that I knew all about the Fates. But more importantly I also knew all about Chosen Ones, which meant to me that fated fairy tale endings of finding your one true love was all too real. I had believed it down to my core. So, after that first dream, it sparked the beginning of my obsession.

My obsession with Lucius.

Because I also knew that it was usually fated that the woman was the one who found the man, who found the other half of their soul and well, this silly notion in my mind wouldn't leave me, to the point that for the first time ever I went against my parents' wishes. I even had my parents' signatures forged and I left on a school trip without their knowledge. Although, this rebellious act had been heavily influenced at the time, and unbeknown to me or even Lucius, it had been done by his witch Nesteemia. Someone who had intervened on the Fates' behalf.

Of course, this was my parents we were talking about, so it didn't take them long to hunt me down as a quick phone call to my school was pretty much all it took. However, they did surprise me, as I wasn't marched back to an airport and onto a private jet to be whisked back home within the hour after they found me. I believe this was mostly down to my mother, she so desperately wanted me to have the human experience that I felt more part of. But what they didn't know was that I had an ulterior motive, *one named Lucius.*

I knew of my uncle's Fight Club, and I also knew of the tournament that was being held there. This was a place all the teens that were being groomed into the supernatural fold were going to fight. And well, seeing as I knew that Lucius was in charge of his own school during this time, it made sense this would be my one and only opportunity to see him.

But I had been wrong. Because I had believed the tournament was on that night I snuck out of the hotel, after first getting my cousin Ella to cover for me. Someone who, thankfully, went to the same school as me and who I had dragged along on this trip convincing her it would be fun... oh, it was fun alright, but definitely not in the way a mortal who didn't know anything about the supernatural world would consider as fun. Because I never expected her to get suspicious and secretly follow me. That was pretty much the start of my plan going to shit, as soon she was also being followed. Theo had been playing the hero since the very first time I ever saw him, and that night had been no different. Hell, but he had even been the one to catch me as I was climbing out of a window and leaving Afterlife for the first time unprotected. Even then he had asked me if I needed his help, as if something compelled him to help those in need.

Just like he had done that night when believing he was following us to keep us protected. My brother is the most noble person I've ever known... that, and the ultimate bad ass, as I discovered that night!

No wonder he made a good Thor.

However, what happened that night was not the way I had planned for it to go. This was because the moment Jared had realised a human had infiltrated his club, well, let's just say he wasn't exactly thrilled about it. As for my cousin Ella, she had been found dancing on the stage, after being coerced as a way of dishing out a humiliating punishment once discovered by Jared's guards. However, little did they know that my cousin used to dance professionally, *until her illness that was.*

As for Jared, well, he had found her on the stage and after spending a night of horrors discovering this secret supernatural life that she had no idea about, well let's just say what happened next didn't help. Because suddenly finding herself being faced with an angry Hellbeast King who threatened to take a bite out of her, was not exactly what she needed to top the night off.

However, little did I know that Ella finding the Devil's Ring that night was actually fated… or should I say, finding a Hellbeast King was fated. Because thinking back to that night and remembering what happened when he found her, well, I don't think I'd ever seen anyone as gentle when delivering such a stern warning. Making it clear there was something about Ella that the King was drawn to. Especially when Jared was known for his dislike of humans. However, the way he had pinned her against the wall and snarled at anyone who approached, it had been more like he had been guarding his most prized possession.

That was when I knew they were destined to be together. They were fated. Now if they could just realise that too, then things would move along a lot smoother for them. Although, that was easier said than done considering she was utterly terrified of him. Because she had fled from that place as if the Devil himself had threatened her never to come back. Yet, to contradict this threat, Jared still ensured she got back to the hotel safely by having his own men take her. And well, when I eventually managed to get back myself, let's just say that it wasn't the easiest of conversations to have with her. But no more difficult than what came after she left as I watched Theo fighting on stage. I remember finding myself confused as I had been so worried about him, as though there was some strange connexion between the two of us, a connection I understood the moment he released the full extent of his power.

When he had looked exactly like my father.

Our Father.

That was when I knew. In that very moment I knew who Theo was to me. Which meant I also knew that my parents had lied to me all those years. Naturally, I had done exactly what my cousin had done when faced with the impossible. I had fled from Jared's world, soon finding myself exactly where I was now. Staring not at an empty street that I had hoped for, that I had been expecting. This was because men were waiting for me.

Just as they were now.

Only this time they were faceless phantoms dressed the same way as in my memories. But instead of the Devil masks they had worn that day, now it was the featureless Wraiths in hooded cloaks, like some demonic cult all waiting for their sacrifice to arrive.

"Ohh hell no, this is not happening again!" I turned around ready to run as if my instincts were playing out one more time, just as it had done that day. I was grabbed from behind and the motions played out as if my mind was reliving the moment all over again. And just as it did in the museum that day, my father's training came back to me in a rush of movements.

I uppercut the guy next to me, only instead of making his nose explode as it did that day, my fist went straight through. Then, as if I was caught in this replay, I dropped to a knee and elbowed him in the leg, my arm going through just as my fist had done.

A punch to the gut and sweeping my leg around didn't make him land like it had done the first time. So, there was no body collapsed on the floor groaning and bleeding. And that was when I realised that just like that day it didn't matter how hard I fought, I hadn't been strong enough. I hadn't been the supernatural I had needed to be.

Not like Theo. Not like my brother.

My father had been right and now as not a single Wraith fell, I knew he still was. I was living that shame, that defeat all over again. And just like that night, it was that doubt that had made me fall. It had been that first punch to the face that I hadn't managed to block that took me down to my knees. Blood had poured out of my nose, just like it had done that day when training with my father. I hadn't been quick enough with the staff and my father's had accidently connected instead of being blocked like he taught me.

But then I saw his hand.

My father's hand helping me up and teaching me the most important lesson that day. After that moment it had then been a mantra I lived by. Which was why I growled angrily, before I swiped a sleeve across my face. Then I did something they didn't expect as I looked up at them and growled. I had pushed myself to my feet and charged. But the first time it had happened I had taken them by surprise. The men who had been sent to kidnap me. They had expected fear, not the rage they found in me as I charged at the one who had punched me. He hadn't expected me to rugby tackle in him into the brick wall behind. He most certainly hadn't expected me to kick the shit out of him, letting loose my anger until he was bloody and screaming for someone to drag me off him.

But it wasn't like that this time, as the moment I ran at him, I just travelled straight through him, landing at the wall. But their motions were the same as one yanked me back before spinning my body and throwing me to the floor. I knew then what was next as I was kicked in the ribs, making me cry out in pain.

But that's when mentally I saw my father's hand. It was what I always saw when I got knocked down.

Because… *Dravens don't stay down.*

And besides, if this was anything like the past, then I knew just like the first time…

Lucius would come for me.

CHAPTER NINE

WHEN LOVE FIRST MEETS

"Dravens never stay down, Amelia." My father's voice rang out in my mind. His words coming back to me after the first hard fall and every time after I was knocked to the mats. And that fight in the street had been no different. I had blocked a hit, and then another, before cracking my fist into a man's jaw. A few more hits were all I managed to get in but the moment I felt the pinch in my neck, I knew that it was all over. However, despite going through the motions of what happened that night all over again, not a single hit had connected. Because I wasn't fighting men this time, I was fighting the ghosts of them.

So, even as I got up and started staggering towards the main part of the street and away from the black van that I knew awaited me just like the first time, I still didn't give up. Because this had been the point where they had used drugs to knock me out.

I even tensed knowing what came next as I felt myself being grabbed from behind one more time. I struggled for as long as possible trying to reach that main street where I knew even at this late hour the city never slept. Someone would help me, someone would notice a girl being abducted. But just like that night, I was dragged backwards and lost consciousness before I was dumped inside the van.

Whilst back then, all I could wish for in that moment was the sheer strength of the supernatural world beneath me. The ones that could have torn these people apart, and because I decided to run from my problems instead of facing them, no one knew what was happening above them.

That a Princess, daughter of the King of Kings, was being kidnapped by humans. But now, well I was no longer that same princess, and these beings were no humans. Which meant I had no idea what would meet me when I opened my eyes next. Hence, when I did and found myself tied up in a dilapidated office, I released a sigh of relief. Because I knew what would soon be walking through those doors like a wave of terror. Like a one-man army set not just on war, but on an eradication...

My saviour.

A Vampire King.

I blinked my eyes a few times, thinking it strange that even the same groggy effect of the drugs lingered in my senses. It was as if the memory the Wraith Master had playing out was also connected to what my mind had remembered feeling in that moment. Because it was clear he had chosen this one as he believed it a traumatic moment in my life. He was searching for my fears and believed this to be one of them. In truth, it might have been had it not been for who would soon appear and save me.

The first time destined lovers would find each other.

So, as I tried to shake off the lingering effects of the drug, I also held on to that moment I knew was coming. Yet, like the first time, I didn't know how long I had been unconscious, but my guess had been not long. I was back in what I had guessed had been a factory of some kind. One that hadn't been used in a very long time, from what little I could see through the few clean patches of glass. As for the small room, there wasn't much left in it, with only a broken filing cabinet and desk left to indicate it had obviously been used as an office at one time. However, the lights flickered above me that told me the place still had power at least, as I could also see it outside the wall of windows lighting up the dirt on the glass.

I had been tied with my arms over my head by a chain hanging from a metal girder above from the exposed ceiling. Also, I must have been here for a while if the ache in my shoulders was anything to go by. It was not long after this that I remembered hearing the first of them... the first of their screams.

I hadn't known how he had found me that day, but the moment I heard the first cries of terror from outside the office was when I first understood what it meant to be really afraid. Because back then it could have been the Devil himself come to get me, as that was exactly what it had sounded like. Those furious demonic growls and roars of anger were the stuff of nightmares bred from only one place... *Hell.*

A Vampire King's place of creation.

But the glass box I was being kept in hid nothing of the horror and bloodshed despite the dirt on the windows. Windows now being marred by much more than dust and decay, and I remembered jumping when I saw the first blood spray hit the glass. It looked almost clean compared to where it landed. That bright crimson line now slowly dripping down, it had reminded me of a ladder on its side, and I stared at it, hoping it would turn into one. But it never did. No, it was only the first. It was only the beginning. Because as each bloody line appeared, I jerked, making the chains I hung from cut into my wrists.

Thankfully, I wasn't just dangling in the air and my feet were actually touching the floor, but the sudden movements still weren't pleasant. Yet the pain was nothing compared to the sight of what was coming now, as I saw bodies flying past. This was followed by the sound of glass breaking, and through the gaps of dirt and blood I could just make out bodies being thrown out of the windows.

Another body was thrown down the hallway just beyond the office and I could see their blurred form hurtling down through the air until landing with a deafening thud. A roar of anger and another snarled growl, and I remembered it had me wondering if it had been Jared himself that had turned up in his Hellbeast form. Of course, now I knew the truth of what beast would actually be walking through that door.

But at the time, I had just known that whatever was beyond that office was the most frightening thing I was ever to encounter. And I had been right, but I had also been wrong, because the moment he kicked the door open I gasped at the sight of him.

The Vampire from my dreams.

Then suddenly, everything stopped. My heart, my breath, not even a single muscle moved. Because in that moment I knew that nothing would ever be the same again. So, when my heart got over the shock and continued to beat, now pounding in my chest, as it only ever did so for him. A heart that became his the very second I saw him, not in my dreams and not as a man, but as the deadly predator before me now. The one with blood covering his bottom lip and dripping down his chin to his neck. The one with hands painted crimson, even the strange black glove he wore on one hand, their death was dripping from him.

It was like looking at the deadliest creature, one whose beauty wasn't diminished by that danger but instead seemed enhanced by it. A stunning monster who had walked in there, intent on creating a massacre. A right hand of the Devil who knew no such a thing as mercy but only revenge. Which had made me question at the time...

Why had he come for me?

This demon from Hell, this King of Vampires looked as if he was close to breaking out of his human skin, he was that tense at the sight of me. His crimson eyes glowed as he scanned the length of me, taking in every injury. He narrowed his eyes for a brief second as if torn between helping me down or going back out there to find the ones who had done this to me. To find them and make extra certain they had suffered. Even the light over me flickered again, as if feeding from his thunderous energy.

But then he took that first step and I gasped, before I felt his gaze now scan the length of me for another reason. And the heat of that gaze transferred to the heat in my cheeks, for that look was nothing short of primal need. I realised in that moment that it was silent as he had eradicated every last threat before coming for me. I swallowed hard and must have made a whimpering sound the moment he made that second step towards me.

I tried to tell myself this was Lucius, the man I loved and knew, but then my mind kept shifting back to that night and it was like I was seeing him for the first time all over again. I even felt myself start to shake as his footsteps brought him closer to me. He took in my reaction to him, gritted his teeth a moment before he then held up his hands as if he was surrendering.

Then he spoke for the first time.

"Easy now, I will not hurt you, Princess," he said softly,

as if worried that he would frighten me even further. I nodded slowly, telling him silently that I understood and that it was safe for him to continue without me screaming in his face. But as he moved closer, he continued to do so slowly and cautiously, making sure to keep his hands up. But I wasn't an idiot, as even I knew that this wouldn't matter. If he had wanted to hurt me, he would have done it in seconds. He didn't need a blade or a gun, as his hands were the only weapons he needed, and he must have thought me a fool if he believed that I thought otherwise. But then I suppose what else could he do, as it was after all the universal signal for 'I come in peace'.

So, I watched wide eyed as he approached, unable to take my gaze from him as he was the same with me. Then, when all space between us had been eliminated, he looked down at me with his greater height and told me,

"I'm going to release you now… just be brave for me a little longer." His soothing voice that I remembered so clearly from my dreams was what made me close my eyes. It was like being put under hypnosis, and made me wonder what else I would have done for him if he had only asked it of me. Which was why I forgot completely the situation I was in. I forgot all about the bloody scene that I knew was just beyond the office. I forgot about it all and focused solely on that voice. A soft and tender voice that took me back to my dreams and away from this Hellish nightmare called reality.

My breathing had stopped and must have been running out as I felt his lips come to my ear and whispering tenderly this time,

"*Breathe for me, my Amelia.*" I did as he commanded, as I knew in that moment I would have done anything for him. Especially when I had just heard him making the claim that I was his. So, I took a deep breath for him and I felt his smile against my skin before he praised me,

"My good girl."

I let those words linger in my mind and held on to them, getting lost in how good they made me feel, until eventually the crunching sound of metal above me made me jump as he had snapped the chain. I felt my weight fall to my feet and knew the moment they would fail as my knees buckled. Something that would have had me crumbling to the floor had he not wrapped an arm around my waist and tugged me forwards suddenly. The strength in that arm I felt at my back as he held me to him, made me suck in a shuddered breath for a very different reason. There was not an inch of space between us, and I wondered if he could hear the pounding of my heart and scent for himself the evidence of what being so close to him was doing to my body. His intense gaze told me that he could.

He knew I wanted him.

The shame of this had me lowering my head, trying to hide it and in doing so, it just made the difference in our size even more prominent. He was so tall, so full of muscle, and being held tight to his frame... well, I didn't think I'd ever felt safer in all my life. Not even with who my father was. I had never felt a more powerful being in all my years, and by the Gods I wanted him to want me. I wanted him to keep me here like this with him forever.

Forever in his arms.

"Look at me," he ordered, this time with a slight bite of authority that had my body responding to his every command. Meaning my head snapped up and the slight blood-soaked grin appeared as if my easy submission had both amused and pleased him. But then I homed in on those blood-stained lips and my breath left me on a small gasp. Because I realised in that moment that…

I wanted that blood to belong to me.

However, he must have mistaken this reaction for some other reason as he told me,

"Easy now, I've got you," before suddenly I was swept up into his arms like some demonic fairy tale. All I was missing was some dark woodland setting around us, a long, virginal white flowing dress and being surrounded by the beasts he had just killed for me, thus saving my life. But then the reality of our situation came back to me very quickly as before he stepped out into the office, he paused. He knew what was out there, he knew of the beasts he had slain and what they looked like. He knew of the destruction he had caused and the evidence of it was no doubt flowing crimson just as the blood dripping down the window was. That's when I knew why he had paused because it was obvious…

This was a side of him he didn't want me to see.

Which was why he said something strange to me. In fact, until this moment and now reliving it, it was something that I hadn't remembered the first time. As I had always remembered passing out in his arms and only waking again when he was laying me down in a bed back at the hotel. But now that wasn't happening, and I was soon to discover why.

He started by lowering me to my feet and positioning my back against the wall. I sucked in a startled breath wondering what he was going to do when he spoke in his demanding tone once again.

"Give me your eyes, sweetheart… fuck me, they are even more beautiful close up," he said, saying this last part as if more to himself, making me swallow hard. He had told me my eyes were beautiful, even back then.

"Even more so when they have tears in them like now…

Gods, my Khuba, you are a gift," he said, and I sucked in a startled breath, now realising why he wouldn't have wanted me to remember any of this. Which was when I knew he had hidden those memories from me, yet somehow the Wraith Master had found them.

"Lucius." I whispered his name for the first time, and he closed his eyes as if hearing it meant something profound to him. Which was when he did the same by saying my name on a whispered breath, and coming from him it sounded like a prayer.

"Amelia."

After this I must have felt braver as the next thing out of my mouth came a question, one I wished with everything in me that I would have remembered the answer to.

"Are you…"

"Ask it of me, my Semsa." His voice rumbled as if thick with the emotion of our first moment together.

"Are you my Chosen One?" I asked, feeling my hands shaking in fear that he would say no. But instantly he answered me,

"Yes, I am." It was such a statement, such an absolute that there would have been no questioning it ever again. Not like I had done for years and years after. With the way he answered I would have believed it until my last breath. But then I asked one more thing and it just showed how naive I was, and my blush belonged both to the memory and to me reliving it as I heard myself say,

"Will you kiss me?" His knowing grin was warm, yet I knew him well enough to know it also amused him. This was when he shook his head a little and said,

"No, I will not kiss you."

"Why not?" I whispered before I could stop myself, even if I could no longer look into his eyes and lowered my gaze to

my feet. But then I felt him hook a finger under my chin and lift my face up to grant him my eyes once more. Then he told me,

"For two reasons, the first being I will not have our first kiss stained by another mortal's blood, for I will not allow anything to come between us."

"And the second?" I asked in a shy voice that slightly trembled. At this he got closer and whispered his answer directly in my ear, telling me,

"Our first kiss will be one you will remember for the eternity we are together." At this my reaction was to reach out for him, grasping hold of his shoulders so I wouldn't fall like I feared I would. But he pulled back slightly, yet not enough that it would break our connection as he wanted me holding onto him.

"Now you must do something for me," he asked, and I nodded before admitting,

"Anything." Again he smiled, that same knowing grin that liked hearing the word, liked hearing the proof that I belonged to him and would do anything he asked of me.

"I want you to think of a door," he said, making me blink up at him in surprise.

"A door?" I questioned.

"Close your eyes and think of a door, perhaps the one to your bedroom at home." At this I made a nervous little sound and his grin turned into a smirk. Then I must have sighed at the thought, and the last thing I saw before closing my eyes was a full grin as he knew what it was he was doing to me. He knew the power he held over me.

"Can you see it?" he asked the moment I did as I was told and closed my eyes. And of course, with his gentle smouldering voice playing out the picture for me, there was little I could do but see my bedroom door. But then he told me,

"I'm going to knock on it. You will hear this and stand from the bed you are sitting on. Then I want you to walk to the door and open it... open it for me," he said, playing out the scene in that seductive voice of his and I did exactly as I was told. The moment I opened the door he didn't just step into my room but actually stepped into my Void.

I sucked in a deep breath, seeing him now as if my room was real and he was right there in front of me. The office was long gone, and my geeky room was all that remained in sight. I opened my mouth ready to ask, ready to speak when he just shook his head down at me. So instead of explaining, he took me by the hand and walked me over to my bed, one that I was embarrassed by as it looked like a Landspeeder from Star Wars. I couldn't breathe wondering whether this was it, even in my mind I was confused believing this was real. That he was actually leading me to my bed before telling me,

"Lie down, Amelia." I did as I was told, letting him continue to lead this hidden memory. Then he followed me down, stretching out next to me before I felt his soft fingers gently stroking the apple of my cheek. That's when I received my last command.

"Close your eyes and sleep for me," he whispered, and I would have liked to have argued against it, telling him I didn't want to sleep. However, the moment he said the words it was as if he had that power over not just my mind but my body as well, as both obeyed. I had closed my eyes in my mind and fallen asleep in his arms.

I remembered very little after that, but I must have been in a car with him at one point as I remembered him whispering to me, telling me he was proud of me for fighting back. It was like being semi lucid but not being allowed to be fully wake. Yet it was still enough that I remembered elements of it. Like when I felt him checking my body for injuries, this was along with him lifting up my top so that he could expose my stomach and no doubt to see for himself the damage to my ribs. But I must have sucked in a sharp breath when I felt him there, as his hand stilled.

I knew what I would have found the next day when looking in the mirror. A bruised face, scraped knees, cut knuckles, and bruised tender flesh all down my side. Along with two cracked ribs, that hurt whenever I moved or took in a deep breath. Yet, despite these injuries, I had refused to let anyone heal me. I knew to many it might have seemed foolish and it was even to me looking back on it, but I had my reasons, and they were all named Lucius. It was a sickness really, but hearing the way Lucius had said that he had been proud of the way I fought them, well, it had made me want to keep hold of the proof of my fighting for as long as possible and wear it like a badge of honour.

The last of this memory continued to play out as I remembered it, coming awake the moment he lay me down back in my bed in the hotel room. I knew that was my one and only chance to tell him the truth in hopes that he would know who I was to him. Because I hadn't remembered our conversation in the office. The one where Lucius had confirmed who I was to him. Because he had taken it from me when he had access to my mind. Well, now I knew, and even in this nightmare world the Wraith Master controlled, the lost memory had felt like a gift, one he never intended on giving me.

In this memory, I opened my eyes and said,

"I must be dreaming because you are always in them when I sleep." It was the first time I'd heard the tiniest hint of emotion, for he sucked in a breath and whispered back,

"You are always in my dreams too, Princess."

I would never forget those words for as long as I lived, for they had given me so much hope after that point, that I played them back to myself like a daily mantra. But then I was left thinking because of those words he would come back for me. All I had to do was wait and one day he would come back for me, declaring to my family who he was, that I was his Chosen One.

Sometimes I would play the fantasy out like some damn Cinderella story. However, instead of being the girl that arrived late at the ball, it was Lucius who arrived late. Then he would part the dance floor, stride through a sea of people either side of him and come straight towards me. Then when he reached me, he wouldn't ask me if I wanted to dance as that wasn't his way. No, instead he simply claimed me, taking me in his arms and gliding our bodies around the dance floor, refusing to ever let me go.

It had been a great dream but that was all it ever had been...

A dream.

A wish that had never come true.

Just some silly childish dream that I wasted my time romanticising about. Because days turned into weeks, then weeks turned into months and months eventually turned into years. Then I would convince myself he was waiting until I grew up and turned more into a woman. But then I went from seventeen to eighteen, and then finally the last of my hope died that it would happen at the age of twenty.

This had been when I'd had enough of waiting and I took it upon myself to make the first move. When I made the foolish mistake of going to Transfusion... the belly of the beast. But then that was what happened after years of hoping. Years of dreaming of him as being my one true love. I had naively thought he had been waiting for me to come to him. That all he would need to do was take one look at me and be reminded of the connection we shared.

But that's the thing with dreams. The problem with fairy tales. The dangerous truth about hope. Sometimes every single one of them only leads you to one place. A place Lucius had taken me to that night. The night he had ripped my heart out and killed all my dreams, killed my fairy tale and killed my years of hope. Killed by the very same man who had been so tender and gentle with me all that time ago.

Yet our future had only really begun, because yes, he had been the man who had broken my heart, but he had also been the man who put it back together again. Because eventually I got my fantasy, my Cinderella fairy tale, as gothic and as dark as it was. I got to experience that moment of being swept off my feet. That moment on the dance floor by my not so Prince Charming, but by the deadly Vampire King.

I remember thanking him that night. Thanking him for the gift of him, but what I had never said was what it had really meant to me. Thanking him for all he had given me, as it was so much more than he thought. Because I might have had to wait over a decade for my moment, for my dreams to come true, but on that single night he had given me back my hope.

A hope for the future.

A future that I now knew I had to fight for.

Even if it killed me…

Again.

CHAPTER TEN

A TREE OF MEMORIES

The next time I opened my eyes, it was to the sound of a fist banging violently on a door making it rattle on its hinges. At first thought, I wondered briefly if it had been my father angry at what had happened. But then I remembered that it hadn't happened like that. Yes, he had been furious with me for sneaking into Jared's club, something I had overheard when he was arguing with my mum, but his main concern had been my kidnapping and my wellbeing after it. I remember him coming to my bedside not long after it had happened and I had lowered my head with guilt, forgetting all about Theo. But then he lifted it gently and after seeing that angry tick in his jaw on seeing my injuries, he ran the back of his fingers over the bruise at my cheek and said,

"Oh, my dear daughter, I hope you made them bleed." At this I grinned and said,

"And broken." At this he winked at me and then leaned in to kiss my forehead, saying,

"That's my good girl. Get some more rest and we will

speak of this day no more." I remember being shocked that I wasn't in for an ear lashing, however the next day it had come from my mother. But I think this was because my father had felt some guilt on his part. He obviously believed that by keeping me sheltered from their world for so long that I had let my curious nature win over my good sense. Of course, I had allowed this peace between us until my mother's anger had bubbled over, making me throw back at her,

"And when were you going to tell me I had a brother!" At which point her argument stopped and her mouth dropped. Then, as I ran from the room with tears streaming down my face, the last I heard was her whisper,

"*Oh, Fae.*"

They knew then, after this point, that they had been in the wrong also and arguing with me on my actions became nothing more than making them both hypocrites. Because I had only run into danger after discovering Theo was my brother and needed to get away from the painful situation. The lies they had weaved around me.

I pushed the memory from my mind, knowing the reason it hadn't played out that way was because it wasn't one the Wraith Master had been interested in. Because having my father's comforting words by my bedside didn't instil fear. Which was why the pounding on my door continued and the room started to morph in between the hotel room and a Queen's bedchamber.

The bed I was lying in was modern and covered in muted yellows and greys one moment, then to the same bed of royal blue with its fringed gold canopy that I had seen before. However, as soon as the scene settled on the Queen's room, the banging grew louder and now had angry shouts being added from a furious male. This was when I heard the whimpering off to one side of the room in the corner. It was the sound of a woman crying and begging to be left alone.

I quickly scooted off the bed and saw the shadow of the woman crouched behind a privacy screen, which she obviously used to get undressed behind. It was then that I realised the room looked more lived in than before. There were various garments tossed over the top of the screen, with a full dressing table off to one side that had little pots of makeup and creams with their lids off.

The panels of the screen were sheer white, meaning that I could see her silhouette easily through it, making me wonder what the point of it was. It looked to be made of paper-thin material as if I could put my fingers straight through it and was as easy to tear as tissue paper. Perhaps it had been created to provide a teasing moment to a husband or lover as they got ready for the night ahead. Either way I looked back towards the door that still rattled on its hinges and doubted it had been used for that reason in a while. Especially as a furious man I assumed was the King was demanding that she open the door. This made me so angry, as it made the queen cry louder, her body shuddering with every loud bang against the door.

"Okay, I am so sick of this shit now!" I snapped, grabbing the first heavy thing to hand before storming my way over to the door, ready to deal with this angry fucker myself! I was sick of his twisted Horror House of Fun. Sick of him playing on my fears and using his own violent past to intimidate me. So, I turned the key and grabbed hold of the doorknob, raising above my head what I turned to see was a fucking candlestick.

"Well, wouldn't' you know, time to kill Professor Plum after all!" I said yanking on the door ready to batter him. However, as soon as the door swung open, there was no one there, making me frown in question before I felt a hand on my shoulder. I screamed and stupidly dropped the candlestick then I turned to find the same woman standing opposite me who had been in the portrait. The queen that I could see as plain as day on the wall over the side table. She was even dressed the same, as if she had crawled out of there herself, the only difference was that she was missing her necklace.

"You can't stop him, no one can," she said in a composed way as if she hadn't just been terrified and crying her eyes out.

"Okay lady, gotcha... husband's crazy... brilliant," I muttered, knowing that she wasn't real and was just another one of his memories. I knew this because she reeled off the next line as if I hadn't even spoken, as if she was having this conversation with someone else.

"Greed will always be his first love, *I know that now,*" she said sadly, so I shrugged my shoulders.

"Men, eh? Can't live with them, can't bash their brains in with a candlestick 'cause they're not really there," I muttered, and again it meant nothing to her.

"He's already made the deal, the Gods are angry and the Devil in his heart is hungry," she said, and this time it ended with her floating away into a cloud of ash, very much like the one that had covered the land outside the castle.

"Well, I wouldn't go as far as putting it on a T-shirt, but I think I get the point," I said to myself, finding comfort in making jokes and hearing them. Because I was done being afraid and I was done running. I needed to get to the bottom of this, and if discovering the root of his obsession and exactly what this deal had been, then maybe that was the key to unlocking this mental prison I seem to be stuck in. If only I could go back and allow Lucius access to my Void, then I wouldn't be faced with this alone.

I thought back to how he had got me to sleep that night. He hadn't wanted me to witness what he was capable of. He didn't want me to be afraid of him or view him as a monster. As some bloodthirsty demon. So, he had told me to imagine a door to a safe comforting place like my bedroom. He had then wanted me to let him in. To open that safe door and let him walk inside because that's all it was, just a symbolic gesture my mind needed in order to allow him access.

If only I could do that again. Because I was sure that Lucius would know what to do. Perhaps that was it, the key to getting out of here was to find a way to reach out to Lucius.

I continued to think this way as I once more stepped out onto the gallery wondering what I would find this time.

"And what's behind door number three, Monty?" I said, wondering now if like that show, I could just make a deal. But then the door opened, and I gasped before forgetting about any deal and just outright begging for it to be anything else.

"Oh, Gods no! No, please, anything but this… anything!" I muttered in horror the moment I saw that this time it was a memory of my own making. Why I couldn't just shut off my brain completely was beyond me, but it was as if the Wraith Master was drawing on every fear… feeding on the fucking things! Something that was hard to find for a girl who grew up with demons. Well, now he was digging deep and finding things that had the power to bring me to my knees!

Because he took me back to that winter garden, which had started by feeling sand beneath my feet. As soon as I felt it, I knew what it represented. The worst memory of all. The one I was forced to see by first the witch, and now this Wraith! Because nothing was worse than being forced to watch the death of the person you loved the most.

Judas.

What had been done to him had been truly horrific and unjust, yet the history of the world had made him into the ultimate villain. For centuries there had been painting after painting and book after book, passage after passage of the evils and wrongdoings that Judas had done against God and his Son. His crime was painted and portrayed as the worst of man's treachery and deceit... the ultimate betrayal.

But it was all a lie, for it spoke nothing of his sacrifice, the one he made for that same God and his Son. Yet it was one he was punished for even further and far beyond death. Which is why having that reminder of his past life nearly crippled me. All the research that I had done during my time away from Lucius, every single thing I had read, every picture I had looked at, had brought tears to my eyes. He was the most misunderstood figurehead of betrayal in history. And as Jesus had been made into a martyr that day, saving a religion and solidifying its future, it had been achieved not only off the back of the life of Jesus sacrificing himself, but also the sacrifice Judas had made.

Yet what had his reward been, an eternity of hatred, that's what. Well, it was unsurprising that he hated the name so much. He was never ready to talk about it and really, I didn't blame him, as who would want to remember such a day... *no one.*

But this all meant that what I saw now was even harder to witness. For right in front of me was the very tree that had started this Hellish nightmare. The very same tree he had been hung from, just as he was now. That haunting sight that had tears running down my face as his form hung lifeless with his back to me. The blood pooled on the ground, his feet torn beyond recognition from being forced to walk to his death. The suffering he must have endured, once again it brought even more tears to my eyes.

"No, please, anything but this... anything but this," I begged, tearing my gaze from the sight only helped slightly. Because I knew it was still there. Yet I shamefully knew that this was the price the Wraith Master wanted me to pay for mocking his own pain. The Wraith Master's own suffering. But when I heard a crow crying out, I opened my eyes and the second I did, the rope suddenly snapped, and Judas' body fell to the ground. Then, just as quickly, I felt myself being pushed from the front by something I couldn't see. The force of it made me fall backwards and I noticed that we both landed at the same time, only I slipped straight through the floor and the world tipped upside down until it was back right again. I then found myself standing inside the temple of the Tree of Souls.

Only this time it was different.

The walls of the temple started to fade away, revealing in its place a vision I had seen before. Back when I was in Hell and staring down the length of an alleyway where I saw a girl who had pretended to need my help. Then it flashed to the crimson umbrella floating on a river of blood. Blood I had created. It was coming back to me. That monster that had come from its depths had been the stuff of nightmares, lying in wait as if an ocean lay beneath the surface like a different level of Hell was waiting to drag me under and drown me.

Was this why the Wraith Master had plucked out another memory because he thought it might be one I feared? But then something started to change, and before the creature could take hold of me like it once had, it shifted quickly to another memory. As if someone was manipulating it. Because the Tree of Souls came back suddenly and became that of a tree growing tall on top of a small hill. However, the startling difference now was the small, cloaked form of child who stood with her back to the tree, a gaze I couldn't see, dead set and frozen on the sight in front of her.

I knew instantly what I was looking at now.

The witch's void. It had been one of her memories.

I slowly approached, questioning what connected the witch's memories to that of the Wraith's? Because the memory I had seen had only been from a distance and this… *this felt like so much more.* Something important and more than just an elaboration on a distant memory. So, who was in control of this now, the Wraith or the witch, I wondered? Had he extracted more of what I had seen in the witch's void. Was such a thing possible? To be able to drag a small slither of her past life from when she had been trying to drag me into her darkness by the monster she had conjured from Hell.

As always, I had no answers.

But there was only one way to find out. So, I continued to step closer until I was stood next to her, seeing that most of her was covered in a crimson cloak that reached her ankles. She reminded me very much like the girl I had encountered that night in the winter forest. Other than her height of course.

I didn't know what I expected but I found myself surprised when the girl raised her hand and pointed ahead of her. So, I turned to see what she was watching, and found the woman burning at the stake once more. And like the first time I had seen it, she was screaming about her revenge. Screaming about how she would return, only next time she would be the most powerful witch the world had ever seen and when she did, she would kill them all.

I found myself questioning how she even formed words with the agony of being burned alive. However, revenge was a strong motivation if ever there was one. So, I looked to all of those she had cursed with her threat to see the village people all stood around watching her demise. But this time it was strange, as it wasn't like when I had seen it the first time, just like so many things that were different.

No, before all the villagers had appeared as vampires, each with glowing red eyes, extended fangs glinting in the firelight and clawed fingers curled into the torches they held. But now they were just people. Mortal people that, despite being the cause of what was happening now, all looked horrified by the sight of the woman burning. Each one standing behind a man of the cloth who was reading from the Bible, no doubt asking God to spare her soul and grant her forgiveness for her sins.

Why was this vision different to the one I had seen in her own void? Well, I was soon to find out as another figure approached. It was one that had remained out of sight when I had received a glimpse of it in Hell. I could tell from the size that it was a man, even if he too remained hidden beneath a layer of material, cloaking his features. However, his voice I recognised…

Lucius' unknown brother.

"Now, do you see, child? Do you see what you must do, what she must become?" his brother said, but the child did nothing, her shoulders lightly shaking as if she was silently weeping.

"They are the cause of all of this. A disease against the Earth that must be eradicated, a vile virus against God." At this the girl looked back up at him and said,

"Then what does that make my mother if she is being burned by one of God's hands?" I was amazed at how steady her voice sounded.

"It is by the hand of vampires, for look closely and you will see the truth." The girl looked back again, and I knew it was in this moment that what she was seeing was what he was making her see. He had manipulated the images of the villagers to look like the enemy.

"It must be done, it is the Gods' will, for they have chosen you, my child," the man said, clearly trying to coerce her into something she didn't want to do.

"I am not your child and my mother is dead," she said sternly, and I looked to see that she was right, her mother's screams had stopped and an eerie crackle of flames in the distance was all that remained. Lucius' brother said nothing to this, and it was almost as if he feared to. But then the girl looked back towards her burning mother, a sight I couldn't imagine anyone laying witness to, let alone a child.

"What will happen to him?" she asked softly, and I found the question strange.

"He will burn, just like the Tree of Souls," he replied, and I knew then that they were talking about Lucius. Then, as soon as his words finished, she reached out behind her, placing a hand on the tree. It instantly caught alight, and I stumbled back to get away from it, knowing what it meant.

However, this was when something new happened, as the vision wasn't finished despite the memory of it being over. Lucius' brother disappeared, floating away as if now ash as well. The girl turned to me, and with a hood covering most of her face, she told me,

"You should have given me the box when you had the chance, but now it is too late... the River of blood is your own fault... just as the burning of the Tree of Souls will be mine... blood is the only key in defeating a heart of darkness... remember that... Vampire born," she said and then she, along with the rest of the image, simply floated away, with the last to go being the burning tree of raining ash.

Then as I closed my eyes, I heard the first of his voice.
Lucius.

"How is this possible?" I frowned, wondering who he was talking to. So, I opened my eyes and found myself in another part of the castle. I was sat in a long hallway I hadn't seen before, one full of high, arched windows. That's when I stood up and walked to one of them to look out, doing so now to find the front of the castle where the entrance was. I looked down and sucked in a startled breath as I saw a shadowed figure standing there looking down at his hand. I narrowed my eyes to try and make out who it was, hoping and fucking praying that it could be him! But then when I heard his voice once more, I knew it was. I knew he had found a way!

"Lucius!" I shouted. However, this time his voice sounded as though it was in the room with me, making me look around the space frantically searching for him.

"It's not her mind," he said, and I frowned, looking out of the window again. Another figure was there, standing opposite him and though they were too far away to make out any details, even I could tell who it was... the King. They were talking and I wondered if the King was taunting Lucius and if so, why hadn't he yet released his wings and flown up here?

Where was his demon?

But this was when I heard something else and just before I could bang on the window to get his attention, a deep growling and snarling sound made my hand drop. I swallowed down the hard lump that had suddenly formed and I looked towards the door. There I saw the glowing of red eyes in the darkness.

Another memory.

Another fear.

"The Wraith Master will never let him in," a voice next to me said and I jumped, screeching in shock before turning to see the witch was stood next to me once more, still as a child.

She was standing by the window, staring out towards the two shadows. I heard more snarling coming closer and my head snapped back in time to see as one Hellish paw emerged...

Hellhounds.

"Only memories have power here, that and blood... now run, save yourself from them and run!" she said shouting this last part, and in that moment the Hellhounds charged, and I ran from them screaming, now hoping I could reach another door, praying that just another madness was not lay behind it.

And as I ran from yet another feat, I did so hearing Lucius desperately shouting my name, along with his promise,

"Amelia! Hold on, I'm coming!"

Then, as I fell through the door, I no longer questioned if Lucius would come for me, knowing deep in my heart that he would find a way.

No, instead all I questioned was...

Why had the witch helped me?

CHAPTER ELEVEN

A DATE TO REMEMBER

As soon as I fell through this door, I found myself back at the castle's entrance hall as if I had just stepped into this nightmare for the first time. I was just thankful that, for the moment, there didn't seem to be any new memories or fears facing me. I bent over trying to catch my breath, and most definitely needing the reprieve from such an ordeal. Because it had been one thing after another, and I had wondered if this nightmare was ever going to let up?

But with everything that had just happened, I now knew that I needed to help get Lucius in here. Because whether the witch had been on our side or not, what she had said was true, the Wraith Master would never have allowed him inside his mind. Which meant there was only one hope left…

Me letting him inside mine.

I was the key, or should I say, my memories were. Because my mind kept lingering on the past we shared. That first time we had met and the first time he had entered my void. Then I thought back on the words being spoken about blood being the key to the heart of darkness. I knew there had to be something more in that. After all, the King had made some sort of blood oath to someone, or how else would he have gained his powers in the first place. The Queen had spoken of his greed, maybe it was the greed of supremacy, of ultimate control over all men? Something he exchanged to become the Wraith Master and therefore using his Wraith army to eradicate his enemies.

Maybe blood was all that mattered here?

But then it came to me, what that message could be and how I would get it to him.

"Of course!" I shouted as I started running! I ran up the stairs, and knowing exactly what I was looking for I found the gallery once more. Because I knew what room was at the end of it, and just what window to use to get my message to him. So, I ran to the end, praying like never before that when I opened this door, it wouldn't just hold another one of my nightmares, but instead the room I was counting on.

"Please, just give me this one thing," I pleaded when placing my hand upon the cool doorknob getting ready to turn.

"Oh, thank the Gods," I whispered on a breathy sigh of relief as I was faced with the Queen's chambers once more. I also found myself thankful that I was doing this alone and without the shuddering figure of the terrified Queen hiding in the corner. I quickly scanned the room looking for something sharp enough to use and found a letter opener on the old-fashioned half-moon shaped writing desk. I grabbed it and then ran over to the window, one I knew faced the front of the castle, where Lucius had been closest to and despite its height, he would see it… *he just had to see it!*

"And now I'm back to this shit," I muttered in annoyance as I held the blade to my palm, remembering the last time I had been about to do this, when I had got it in my head to open that damn box!

It briefly made me wonder where I would be now if that moment had never happened. If I had not allowed the witch to manipulate my thoughts enough to get me to do it. If I had never found that map and discovered where it led to. Would I still have seen what I had between Lucius and my mother? Would I have still got the wrong idea and left Afterlife anyway? Or would Lucius have left me in the protection of my parents as he went off on his quest to eliminate all threats against me and his people?

But then I could have questioned everything that had ever happened between us, as after all, that was what prophecies were all about. Everything was meant to happen for a reason. An end goal the Fates were counting on, and each and every one of us were playing our part in an outcome we could only hope meant good won over evil. But then this made me think back to what the witch had said, about me giving her the box, I don't know why but the way she had said it made me question everything about her.

She had said it in a way that seemed as though she had been trying to prevent this very thing from happening. Because that was the only part of this that didn't make any sense. Why would she have tried to take the box back if she needed me to get into Hell in the first place. If she needed me to get the eye?

"Fuck, but why have I never questioned this before!?" I scorned myself aloud before answering my own question.

"Because her creepy child image of a witch that usually wants you bleeding hadn't ever spoken to you before now, Fae, that's why," I said to myself with a shake of my head, knowing that I needed to concentrate on one thing at a time. So, I sliced my palm, hissing at the pain and letting it drip down my hand so it coated my fingers. Because that was one thing the witch had said, *my blood was the key.* Of course, this seemed to be a running theme with her but still, it was all I had left to go on. Because I assumed it meant that finding some good old-fashioned ink and paper wasn't going to cut it and make it through the Wraith Master's void. Because after all, wasn't sacrificing blood the thing that held the most power around here?

"This has to work... it just has to," I said as I started to write the only clue that I could think of to get Lucius to understand what he had to do to break into my void. Just as he had done that day. How he had accessed my mind and told me to show him a door. A door I knew he would recognise as belonging to me, and one I would hold onto in my mind in hopes that he would come looking for it.

So, I wrote the only date that mattered and one I knew he would never forget. After all, it was the combination to his safe in the wall. I then stood back once it was done and read the four numbers written in my blood,

13.06

The date we first met and the day he saved my life.

I closed my eyes and let my hand drop the moment it was done, wishing that when I looked out that window, I could still see him there trying to get to me. But there was nothing, not even the battle that could sometimes be seen raging on in the distance. It was as if parts of this world were on some Hellish loop, all playing our parts and having our strings pulled by the Wraith Master.

And speaking of Hellish loops, the moment I heard crying behind me, I knew she was back, the ghost of the Queen and just another of us who had been wronged by the King. I knew I couldn't put it off any longer, as I needed to look. It was almost as if this was what she had been waiting for. Someone to understand her pain. Someone to finally lay witness to the horrors that had been done to her. I knew that when the blood first appeared. It started flowing from beneath the screen and consuming the stars that were inlayed on the floor. It continued to overflow, as if there was an endless supply.

I braced myself for this new nightmare I would find, having no choice but to get my shoes tainted by something other than ash. Yet I soon discovered that there was no amount of preparing myself for the sight that met my eyes. And if I had ever naively believed that I had seen it all, then I could now eat my words because this... well, this was something else entirely. It was giving birth to a new nightmare the Wraith could use against me.

For there was the Queen, now slumped to the floor in a hopeless position. Only the difference now was that she was no longer hugging herself in fear and shaking at the thought of what her husband would do to her. There was no point to that now. Not when she had her hands held out in front of her, and not when in those hands she was holding her own heart, one that had been cut out of her chest. A heart that was still beating and pumping the last of her blood onto the floor... something that wasn't an endless supply as I had first thought. It was the most sickening sight I had ever seen, especially when she looked up at me and said,

"I can't get it to stop, I can't stop the blood from flowing... will you help me?" In that moment I would have pointed out to her that the only thing to stop the blood pumping out of her was death. But she was obviously a ghost, so that was a moot point, one I decided best not to point out in that moment.

"What happened to you?" I asked her softly, hoping to understand how this had happened to her. Why, by the Gods, would the King do something like this, let alone to his own wife!

"He wanted my heart, a payment, I told him he had my heart, it wasn't enough, he needed them all." This was when she opened her mouth and screamed, a sound that seemed to pierce my skull as she threw her head back, bellowing at the ceiling. A sound I knew would haunt me forever. I squeezed my hand tight, letting the pain anchor me to what I knew was real and what was not before the vision burst into ash just like all the others.

"Gods." It came out of my mouth like a prayer at what I had just witnessed. I started walking backwards and looked towards the window, checking that the numbers were still there. Thankful they were, so I could leave the room. I had to get out of there! I had to get away! So, I grabbed a length of material that was hung over the screen, and started wrapping it around my hand as I ran towards the door.

However, just like so many times before, I opened the door believing it would lead me back onto the gallery only again, it didn't. Because nothing made sense here, and now finding myself in some sort of banqueting hall shouldn't have come as a surprise. Hell, but at this point, finding myself in a cage dressed as a gorilla and scratching a pair of hairy balls right now wouldn't have fucking surprised me!

As for the banqueting hall, the floors shone to a high gleam from the polished black and red stone floor that created a diamond pattern. The walls of this grand room were panelled in a dark wood that reached the halfway point before a pale grey stone reached the high vaulted ceilings. The upper parts held a collection of swords displayed in a fan shape, and at its centre were the remains of some of hunted trophy. They had been displayed like some hunting lodge would display them, antlers and the stuffed heads of the game they had shot down.

But this was different as they looked more like the skeletal remains of a demon's wings, or perhaps belonging to some creature that I had never seen before, one that used to roam the land of whatever realm the King had once ruled.

Large recesses in the panelled walls held red up-lighting, giving an eerie glow to the room. His phantoms added to this creepiness as they lined the walls, now all dressed as servants in their double-breasted jackets with hoods that hid any features that would distinguish them between what they were now and what they used to be. I narrowed my eyes in a wary way as I stepped further inside, after hearing the grotesque sound of someone eating. They were tearing through something and slurping it as if there was a wild animal at the table devouring a meal.

It didn't exactly go with the setting that was laid out in front of me. A long table, that could have sat at least forty people, dominated the space and was now covered in what first appeared to be a blood red tablecloth, no doubt to match the Hellish setting. Two larger seats, that resembled thrones were the only seats occupied, and these were naturally situated at each end of the table. In the one facing me I could just about see that it looked like the Queen, slumped over as if asleep on the table.

As for the other seat, which obviously held the King, his back was to me and he seemed to be the only one eating. The sound of tearing into meat was a sickening sound that echoed around the high ceilings. I didn't know whether to turn around and just run straight out of the door and save myself what I knew was no doubt a new nightmare. But then I also knew that I was here to discover the truth and if that meant putting myself in this horrifying situation, then I knew it was a sacrifice I had to make.

So, I slowly continued forward, trying to make as little sound as possible as I wanted to keep the King occupied on his meal and not on me. Because I didn't know what it was he was going to do when he found me. However, the closer I got, the more this unsettling feeling in the pit of my stomach doubled and this terrifying situation revealed itself to be something so horrific, it was beyond my comprehension! A sight so horrendous, it had me making excuses in my mind, for surely those organs along the table set out on silver platters had to be the insides of some recently hunted beast. No, the blood overflowing the once silver platters and spilling onto the floor belonged to the same unfortunate animal.

It couldn't possibly belong to anything else!

"Oh Gods, no," I whispered the moment I came to stand in front of him and saw exactly what the Queen had said was true. Because now sat in front of the King was a large platter with three hearts on it, two of which were smaller than the other. My mouth dropped and I instantly looked towards the slumped form of the Queen to see that she wasn't asleep at all. Her dress was stained crimson and had, at one time, been a pale lilac, barely now seen in patches on her arms. Blood had poured out from having her chest cut open and her heart removed. The very heart the King was now consuming, with black tears running down his face as he wept.

A blood-stained dagger sat next to the platter and I had wanted to reach out and stab him with it, but I couldn't control my body. It wouldn't stop fucking shaking!

"Monster… you fucking monster!" I shouted suddenly as I started backing away, because I knew what those two smaller hearts meant, and I was just thankful that the two small boys were not at this table. The only thing I had left to pray for was that the mother hadn't lived through knowing what he had done. That she hadn't had to witness it!

So, this is what the King had done to become the Wraith Master, to win his precious wars! It was beyond sickening!

"You're sick! A fucking sick bastard!" I shouted again, and this time he turned slowly to look at me, with the eyes of a cruel dying King for he was losing the last of his soul with every bite. I could see it. I could see it in his eyes that were slowly turning black, being consumed by darkness.

"All is gained and lost, in love and war," he said reminding me of Lucius. Reminding me back to that day in his training room, the day I had claimed him for myself after biting him. Yet that was not the saying. It was 'all's fair in love and war', and spoke nothing of gain and loss, yet in his warped mind that was all that mattered… what he had gained and what he had to lose in order to get it!

As soon as he finished this, the phantoms that played as his servants all started whispering the same thing.

"Fearful Hearts feed the Wraith of Fire… Fearful Hearts feed the Wraith of Fire…" I backed further and further away before suddenly the King looked back to me and, after making a show of licking his bloody finger, he said,

"I wonder what I would get for eating your fearful heart."

This is when I wisely turned and started running, now doing so for my life, as it was clear exactly why I was trapped here.

The Wraith Master wanted another heart, and he wanted it full and bursting with not just blood, but one…

Filled with fear.

CHAPTER TWELVE

LUCIUS

BLOOD IS KEY

I didn't know whether I made the right decision or not by allowing the McBain brothers to take on the important task of finding this Oracle of Light. I only knew that I couldn't leave her.

I just couldn't.

Because I could feel her pain, I could feel her fear, and I could feel her desperate need for me to come rescue her. Now all I needed was for a way in, but she was locked in the prison of her own mind and it was one that was now combined with that of the Wraith Master. I knew I had to try again, I wouldn't give up. I would never give up. Not when it was my girl's life on the line, so I would keep trying until I managed to break my way in. Which meant I had gone with my instincts and what was in my gut, knowing it was the right thing to do by staying by her side. In truth, I was close to praying that the brothers managed to come back with this Oracle.

For nothing else mattered!

This also meant that time had started to merge to the point I could barely tell what day it was. In fact, the only reason I knew it hadn't gone past three days was that it was still dark outside. So, I continued to take care of my girl, trying a few more times for her to take my blood in hopes of at least keeping her strength up. The only thing she had managed to consume and keep down was a bit of water but even then, I had to go slowly.

I had checked with the King to see how long it would take, but considering no one had been to this place, they didn't know. I found myself worrying about Amelia starving to death and started to have broth made in hopes this would help.

It had not.

In truth, I had never felt so useless in all my years, including the time when I had been searching for her, both across Hell and in the mortal realm. Yet the frustrations that presented themselves back then were nothing compared to how I felt now. *I felt fucking useless!*

Of course, I had done the best I could in caring for her. I had stripped her of her bloody torn dress, washed her down and placed her in fresh clothes. All the while trying my best to ignore the Wraith Master. A being that was blindfolded, gagged and wrapped in Elvish steel chains that were strong enough to keep even Adam from breaking them. But being forced to keep him close to her was like having spiders crawling under my skin. I was constantly having to remind myself of the necessity of keeping their connection constant, all so my Chosen One's heart continued to beat. As for the infection, it hadn't moved any closer to her heart, yet it had moved further down her arm, telling me that over time it would only get worse. But for now, it remained on that side of her body, closest to the Wraith Master, as if it was his essence trying to get back to him.

I wished there was some way to stop it, but I had spoken to Auberon's doctors, men of both magic and medicine. One had even mentioned bloodletting by leeches, which took me back I don't know how many years to the practise. Of course, my version of bloodletting would have been as easy as taking a meal, and admittedly not one I often practiced as it wasn't something I craved, contrary to popular belief.

But as for the most common medical practice, one that lasted over 2,000 years and continued up to the late 19th century, the withdrawal of blood from a patient was thought to prevent disease or cure an illness. When, in actual fact, in the majority of cases, the historical use of bloodletting was harmful to patients. However, as for bloodletting by leeches, this was a practice used for poisons or harmful toxins that managed to get into a Fae's bloodstream. A particular type of leech that latched on and only took what wasn't meant to be there in a host. This was because their main source of food came from a poisonous plant known as the mother's eye. It was similar to deadly nightshade, yet when the flower bloomed it looked like an eye.

The Fae used these types of leeches for not only medical emergencies but also to keep their livestock free of disease. Of course, I had been willing to try anything, yet when even the leeches wouldn't take hold, I knew without them saying anything that it wasn't a poison, it was the essence of evil, and no fucker wanted to feed on that unless you were... well, an evil fucker!

So, after snarling for them to leave, I had gathered her up close and continued to talk to her, hoping that somewhere in that mind of hers she could hear me and would find it a comfort. I would stroke back her hair knowing how much she loved the feel of it and found it soothing. I hoped that she could feel it too, but with not a single movement or breathy sigh, then I doubted that she could. So instead, I continued to spend my time talking to her, telling her all we had missed out in the months we had been apart. Telling her of all the times that I nearly found her and that she had only barely managed to slip past my clutches. I told her how difficult it was for me to keep my promise and stay out of her void just so I knew that she would sleep and was safe in doing so. This had been one of the hardest things during that time. I had wanted to infiltrate her dreams so many times, just so I could get a glimpse or clue as to where she may be hiding. But I also admitted to her that discovering clues of her whereabouts wasn't all I had wanted from her dreams, as I had missed her terribly. I had been like an addict needing another fix and being only an arm's length away from the drugs I craved.

Yet, I knew the damage it could cause, and just the thought of her driving when too tired and falling asleep at the wheel was what kept me from doing it ever again. Since meeting Amelia, I could honestly say that I had never worried so much in all my life, for it was one thing after another. There were so many on the fucking list, with her being taken from my club, waking up and finding her missing from my bed and having her be the one to run from me, and those were just the ones to happen before she had decided to step into Hell. No, after that she had been thrown into a prison and attacked, then taken once more, this time from a place that was a fucking fortress and by a fucking Harpy Queen, one who even when dying had managed to release her Hellhounds to hunt Amelia down!

But, like I said, it had been one thing after another, yet

nothing… fucking nothing in this world could compare to watching her die on the floor! Doing so after she had thrown a blade thinking she was saving my life. Nothing in all my years had ever come close to haunting me as much as that sight had, and I knew it was one nightmare that I would carry with me forever more.

A nightmare I was still living!

Yet, in sleep, I told her all of this. Every single word, every single time I worried, just hoping for one moment there would be a squeeze of my hand, or a short intake of breath. Fucking anything to let me know that she had heard me. But there was always nothing.

That was until the moment I was just recalling the day she had claimed me down in my training room. A scar from her blunt teeth I still wore like a fucking badge of honour or more like a wedding band on my finger. It was the claim she had made and one that only a short time later she had fled from.

I had just paused my story when Vena had entered, as she did most days. A sweet girl who had made it her mission to try and get me everything that I needed in caring for her friend, for my Amelia. She had just been setting down some more broth in hopes we had better luck this day at getting her to keep it down. I had been instructing her to put it next to me when it had happened. The moment that I felt Amelia's hand in mine jerk before it became wet. Then there was a horrified gasp that belonged to Vena the moment I lifted up my hand and saw it was now covered in blood.

"Oh no, did you cut yourself… wait is that…Amelia's blood?" she stammered out in confusion, and my astonished gaze went to Amelia's hand before I turned over her palm to see that it was right there, a fresh slice in her palm. It was exactly the same as it had been that day when she had opened the box. Gods, but I had been so angry at her, not just for being foolish enough to open the box, but also to do such damage to herself. Because the truth of the matter was, I may have been a bloodthirsty vampire, but the sight of seeing blood on my girl made a pit in my stomach grow like a sickness. For unless I was the cause of that blood when it was coating my lips, then it only represented one thing…

That my Chosen One was hurt.

But that cut, the way it had been made, made me question if she had once again done this to herself and if so, then why? Knowing Amelia and the way her mind worked, then there would be a reason… There always was with her.

"Quick, get me some bandages," I demanded, and Vena didn't need to go far as the room had been equipped with medical supplies in case of an infection or something happened to the wound in her shoulder, one I made sure to clean often. Vena handed them to me, and it was as I started to wrap up her hand that I notice her index finger started jerking. I frowned in question.

"What are you doing now, my love?" I asked softly before it started to come to me exactly what it looked like she was doing… *she was writing something.* Could it be that she was using her blood or some way to communicate with me in her void? I had seen her briefly the one time running past the window, but that had been the only time and I had tried many times since then to get inside the castle. But with no powers and no access to my demon side or that of my angel, then it had been hopeless. What made it worse was that I had come back out of the void with the same injuries that I had made breaking my hand on the door, yet within moments, it had healed back in the reality of my own world. This made me realise instantly that whatever injuries she would receive in their joint void, it would carry through to her mortal body that lay next to me now. This worried me more than anything else, and my mind had been in turmoil ever since thinking of the harm that could possibly befall her.

Of course, I say mortal but after being in Hell for as long as we had, then it was obvious that a lot more was going on with Amelia and being in Hell had obviously started to draw something out of her. However, between the McBain brothers foolishly taking her from me, and the moment I had barged my way into King Auberon's castle to reclaim my Queen, we hadn't yet had chance to speak of it... Nor anything else for that matter.

Alright, to say that we hadn't had time may be a bit of a false claim considering we did have the time, we'd just spent it more wisely in my opinion. By reconnecting our bodies and our souls in a desperate need to be with one another, was there any greater time spent...? No, not in my mind, because in that moment that had been the only thing important to either of us, and yet I still couldn't find myself regretting that decision, for if she was to be taken from me now, then that was how I would have wanted our last hours spent together. Not the serious conversation of all that had happened since that moment she had been taken by the Harpy Queen.

But looking down at that hand now and I knew time was definitely of the essence, because whatever horrors were in that castle locked away by the Wraith Master, I knew now without a shadow of a doubt that they had the power to hurt her. Something I could not allow to happen. I had to get in there and save her, even if she was still locked in that void, then by the Gods, I wanted to be locked in there with her!

"I need to be alone with her, Vena," I told Auberon's sister, and she stood instantly. She then bowed her head once and excused herself after giving me a gentle look of understanding. I could easily see why Amelia was so drawn to her, for she had a gentle soul, that was to be sure. It made me think back to that look I had misinterpreted when we had first entered her brother's office. Amelia's attention had been on Vena as she met with the McBain brothers outside the door and Vena, in her shyness, had clumsily knocked into a vase. I had growled Amelia's name to get her attention back, believing foolishly at the time she had been engrossed with the sight of Trice, who had been standing there with his brothers. However, after the single look I had seen Vena give Trice before their departure, I knew what that look had been about. My girl had matchmaking on the mind. Good, Trice could get his own damn girl. However, whether he deserved someone as sweet as Vena, well that remained to be seen.

The moment Vena closed the door, I lay next to my girl after carefully attending to her wound. Then I forgot about the soup, deeming this far too important to wait. I closed my eyes and found myself back outside the castle as I had done so many times before. However, this time I had been right...

Amelia had left me a message.

"Thank the Gods," I muttered, looking up at the stormy sky for a moment before taking in the four numbers I knew better than my own damn birthday! They were written in blood on the window I could clearly see and the second I did, it was like a fucking light bulb had just gone off inside my mind!

"Oh, my clever girl!" I said aloud, thinking back to that very day that we first met and knowing it was the first time I had ever attempted to access her mind. The day I had saved her after being kidnapped from outside of the Hellbeast's club, the Devil's Ring. I remembered that day like it was yesterday. Of course, I had known the possibility of who Amelia could be to me since she was a baby, one admittedly I had denied up until that moment I first saw her.

It was the very reason that when Theo had mentioned his

sister's name in panic after his fight had been won, that I had run after her. In all honesty, I had simply believed all I was to find would be a stubborn teenager walking home by herself in the dark. What I didn't expect to find was evidence that she had been taken. It was the first time I let my connection with her grow instead of pushing it away like I always had done.

Then, with Dante's help, I had soon discovered where they had taken her and only thankful that not too much time in between her being taken and me getting there had elapsed. And on a rare occasion I had let my rage get the better of me. As a result, it was the first time that I had been ashamed enough of my own nature to not want to show Amelia my true self. I hadn't wanted to frighten who I knew deep down in my heart was my Chosen One. But the moment I had walked inside that office to find her hanging there by a chain, I found myself forcing down my demonic nature that wanted to erupt at the very sight. For the demon in me knew instantly what I had been pushing away.

Our Electus.

I had taken her in my arms and in that first moment of doing so, it was as if every single shred of my soul belonging to the man I used to be and the demon I had become were as one. A calmness swept over me like nothing I had ever felt before. I had struggled with myself, for I wanted nothing more than to sweep her off her feet and keep her in my arms forever, taking her somewhere where no one else would ever find her. The primal instinct to do just that was one I had no other choice but to fight against, and one I had to keep fighting every day since. For that moment in time, I knew she was but a girl. A girl too young and too fragile for my dangerous world, and one far different than what she had grown up in; the world that belonged to her father as his sheltered little Princess. But by the Gods, I had never seen a cuter sight than her. In fact, I never thought that cute would ever be my thing, but for years after that night, I would only have to recall the sight of those big blue eyes staring up at me over her glasses and it was one that would get me hard in seconds. Something I would often replay in my mind whenever I had to fist my cock to relieve the pressure.

My girl was an enigma. My nerdy little geek who could fight with the heart of a warrior. I knew this after seeing for myself what she had done and how she had fought, even being just the tender age of sixteen. But despite this, I still hadn't wanted her to see what horrors I was capable of. Meaning, I first had to access her mind so she wouldn't see the massacre beyond that door and have that as the everlasting memory of me.

However, the moment that I came up against her barriers, I knew she was definitely her mother's daughter. Yet there were still ways to manipulate a mind, even one as strong as hers, for all she had to do was let me in without even realising it. To create a doorway to somewhere safe and I knew for a teenage girl, then surely nothing was safer than her own bedroom. I remember thinking how compliant she had been and how so very sweetly she had offered me her submission. Admittedly, this was another thing that could easily get me hard in seconds just thinking back to that moment. Then again, this wasn't surprising considering my dominant nature and how I would need my Chosen One and Queen to yield to me often… *and mainly in the bedroom.*

Yet yield to me she did, and it was fucking perfect! I could barely keep the knowing grin from my face when she had opened the door to her room and invited me into her sacred space. I could have left it at that after commanding her to lie down and go to sleep, but something in me snapped and instead I had taken her hand and led her there myself. Her heartbeat had been through the roof, as if this was a fantasy she had played out in her mind so many times before. However, the moment she obeyed my command by falling asleep, I'd had full access to her mind, seeing for myself the dreams of me that had already started to take root and play out as a nightly treat.

Dreams, I ensured, after turning seventeen had taken on a more sexual nature, granting her what I knew was her first orgasm. Yet despite having no intention to take her untried body at this young age, I was still determined to claim her first sexual release as my own. One, which admittedly played out like soft porn coming from a girl who had no idea what she was doing and allowed me to take the lead in her mind. I had laughed many times at the thought of what she had seen of me, as I knew it had most likely been like watching a Prince Charming version of myself being gentle and tender with her. Oh, if she had only known the things that I had wanted to do to her. Well, then the massacre outside the office wasn't the only thing that would have made her run for the hills.

I remember carrying her unconscious body through that factory, relishing in how right the feel of her in my arms became. This was to the point that I snarled like a wild beast when the suggestion for me to let her go came from Dante, as someone to take her back. Fuck, but I wouldn't even let go of her when positioned in the car on the way back to the hotel. I kept her in my arms the whole time, praising her on what a good girl she was for me, even though I knew she couldn't hear me, I still wanted it to be said. And as I finally laid her down in the bedroom of her hotel, doing so before fetching her father, she told me that she had been dreaming of me. This being said in her sleepy way, and I admitted to the first soul in the world that I had been dreaming of her too.

Because I had done the moment she turned sixteen. However, what she didn't know was that the dreams of her were vastly different to her dreams of me. They were nightmares really, nightmares of how I was constantly losing her. How some dark hooded enemy was always there waiting to snatch her from me, or he was pulling the strings like some puppet master orchestrating every kidnapping. It was why I'd had a stone-cold fear and a pit of dread in my heart the moment I reached the street level and realised that those nightmares were actually coming true. Those dreams were one of the main reasons why I fought against announcing to the world that Amelia was my Chosen One sooner than I did. I was convinced that she would only be safe without me in her life, and I hated to admit it, like fucking acid and bile combined rising up my throat, but since the moment I had brought her into my life it had been one Hellish thing after another.

Even to myself I didn't want to admit ever regretting the decisions that I had made that day when finally claiming her as mine. For every day since, the simple fact remained that I couldn't go back to how it was before, so why should I torture myself? Because there was no giving up on Amelia. I couldn't be without her, not now, not ever. I would do anything and everything in my power to keep her safe, but I would not lie about how I felt about her. I would not betray her trust in my feelings or hurt her by trying to get her to leave me... to get her to leave so she may be safe.

I didn't have enough strength to do that.

And speaking about strength, I knew now that was what she was referring to, the day I took control of her void. So, believing that I had that capable connexion, I called out to her in this joint void, telling her to create a door. Create the same door as she did that day, and I would come and rescue her again.

I made my way around the castle, getting more frustrated with every step I took when I didn't see one. I continued to try and reach out to her, telling her what I needed her to do. The castle was enormous, yet I didn't give up and nor would I until I found that door! I didn't know how long it would take me, so I started to run, a strange feeling doing so in what felt like a mortal body again, as my muscles started to burn and ache with exertion. But my body would have collapsed to the floor before I stopped, and despite my heavy breathing and my heart pounding, I continued on.

In fact, had my mind not been as occupied on its task, then I would have thought more about how strange it felt to be a mortal once more.

But what I was doing now was far more important than the oddity of exhaustion or fatigue.

No, nothing was more important than this, and just as I thought that I may finally reach the beginning of where I started, nearly giving up hope, that was when I saw it.

That was when I saw the beauty that was…

Her bedroom door.

CHAPTER THIRTEEN

AMELIA

LOCKED DOORS

Once again, I found myself running through the castle, only this time things had changed. As now I was also running from a mad King, one covered in blood after just consuming his wife's heart. Now I believed myself resilient to most things and I'd had my fair share of fights since Lucius had come into my life... but this was something else! Because long past was that girl who used to sit in her flat at weekends, making Lego ships and watching Star Trek reruns. Where excitement came in the form of the Enterprise battling its way through space, or knowing me and my clumsy side, the pain usually found by stubbing my toe or catching my skin in between two pieces of Lego.

But as for being afraid, then there was nothing I really feared, well, other than the usual phobias like my fear of spiders. Yet I had to say that I most definitely had more reason to fear them now after encountering the Spider Queen.

As I think it was safe to say that this was a slight step up from the common house spider scuttling across your floor and making you scream. In fact, the most traumatic thing that ever happened to me was the day that I had been kidnapped and admittedly, it had ended within the hour thanks to Lucius.

Besides, it would never be an experience I regretted as it meant meeting my Chosen One for the first time. But like I said, since Lucius had stepped back into my life, then I had found myself fighting far too many demons, mercenaries and every other Tom, Dick and bad guy.. Yet despite the odds set against me, I had managed to survive each time, and this I could mainly put down to my ability to keep calm and focus on my training. However, no amount of training or life's experiences could ever have prepared me for this horror world. Gods, but Hell was starting to look like an all-inclusive holiday on a tropical island compared to this nightmare.

I had never been one for running. I had always been the type who stayed behind and fought until I was knocked down, only to get up again. Because not only did Dravens never stay down, we also didn't run. We fought. We faced our enemies head on, but now my only weapon against this King and his castle of 'not fucking fun!' was to run, because this wasn't just impossible odds I faced, this was fucking insanity on steroids, one that I had no chance of ever defeating!

Because it had been like the time we had fought the wraiths back in the King's office, no matter how many times we hit or what weapons were used against them, nothing worked. Meaning that they could hurt me, but I had no chance of hurting them. So, I continued to run, not really allowing myself the time to feel ashamed or cowardly as survival mode had kicked in and kept me running from danger.

I'd hoped that after spending as much time trapped here that I had, then I would know my way around this fucked up castle. But this wasn't the case as every door I went through led me somewhere completely different. If anything, it felt as if I was playing the doorway lottery in hopes of trying to find anything that I recognised. For example, one door I opened took me back to an old schoolroom as if this place had randomly just been plucked out of my childhood memories. Of course, I had wet myself at the time, and was sat in the corner crying about it, too ashamed to tell the teacher.

But then when the phantoms had started to appear, each one sat at a desk and one playing teacher at the front, my response was instant,

"Oh, Hell no!" I shouted and turned around to walk straight out the door, quickly finding myself in a different section of the castle. This time it was the armoury, and finally a smile came over my face, but then when I reached out to grab one of the many swords that hung in racks on the wall, my hand just went straight through it.

"Ah!" I shouted as I heard the thundering of feet behind me, making me jump out of the way and hide behind a barrel. An army of wraiths came marching in, now grabbing weapons as if readying themselves for war. I heard whispers around the room as if the very walls held memories.

"We will never win this fight!"

"The King is lost to madness!"

"We have no choice, for if we do not die in battle, we will die by the King's hand."

"The Queen is missing."

"I heard the young princes are too."

It continued on and became a haunting account of the army's final days. By the time the last of the ghosts had left, it became obvious that his own army believed the battle they were being forced to fight in, was a hopeless victory. They spoke of their King's madness that had been growing like a disease. They also spoke about the missing Queen and Princes who hadn't been seen in days. That the kingdom feared for their lives. It made me wonder about the Wraith Master, who had obviously started life as their King. It made me wonder who he had made this deal with and sold his soul to, for the longer I was here the picture became clearer of what had happened in this kingdom's last days. The price of his victory against his enemies was consuming the heart of his wife and children before seeking the souls of his army.

I left this room and unfortunately was met by the angry King, now storming towards me, fully clothed in armour ready for the battlefield.

"YOU!" he roared at me the moment he saw me, now shouting,

"INTRUDER!" The clanking of his armour sounded like a war drum thundering behind me as he started to run after me, pulling his sword free and getting ready to strike me down. I grabbed what I could nearby, throwing it at him, but everything evaporated mid-air making him untouchable. I understood why because, like everything else in this void, he had more control over it than I did.

My own visions were warped memories and hints of my past life he controlled. I was a prisoner here, that much was clear from the very beginning. So, once again I continued to run from him, this Master of nightmares, and soon I saw a window open and thought this might have been my opportunity to escape. However, I ran towards it ready to jump and thankfully stopped myself just in time before plummeting to what could be my death as I was too high up. The glass was missing, and in the distance, another battle had begun its constant time loop once more.

I watched, unable to tear my eyes away as so many lives were being slain. The other side, believing they had victory, despite the great casualties to their own army, all raised up their weapons after the last of the King's men fell. As for the winning side, I could see their King sat upon his noble steed, now splashed with blood from his victims. But then he said something strange, as he pointed his sword at the castle and ordered his men,

"Bring me the Queen and her sons, for it is time to claim and crown my beauty!"

"Claim his beauty?" I whispered to myself, now wondering what else of this tragic love story I was missing. My thoughts, however, were cut off abruptly when the King's order didn't get chance to be obeyed, as it wasn't quite the victory he had in mind.

As for me, I sucked in a startled breath the moment I felt the King approaching from behind and as soon as I saw the gauntleted hand come and rest against the window frame by my head, I knew I was caught. I waited for him to push me through, or to feel the stab of his blade as it pierced through my torso... yet it never came.

"This is my favourite part," he told me, his deep voice so close to me making me tremble. Then I saw another armoured hand reach over my shoulder and point towards the battlefield. He wanted me to watch what happened next. He wanted me to witness the moment when his dead army started to rise and the very instant their souls became forever trapped to this place. Trapped to his void and eternally at the mercy of this mad King. One who had not only sold his own soul to some Wraith devil, but also that of his entire army.

One by one they rose up as the phantoms I had seen in the office, the Wraiths that moved like there were three of them. They each took up their weapons and fought as they had done that day. Tripling the King's army as one become three to fight against. Each of them now moving with a trail of death following the first swipes of their blades. They became untouchable, for the opposing army had no hope and not a single chance of beating them. Especially when no one's swords could inflict even a single blow.

The King at my back, whispered down at me,

"Time for me to play with my army." I refused to look back at him, admittedly too afraid to. But just like that night, I knew he commanded them as he clenched his fist in front of me, still positioned over my shoulder. This was before he spread out his fingers in a quick motion, which mimicked the actions of his wraiths on the battlefield. They all charged as one, descending on the now fleeing army like a swarm of death, hitting into them and flowing over their bodies like a murky black wave.

It didn't take long before they decimated the opposing side and once they were all dead, the wraith army all looked up at the sky and screamed as one. It was the most horrifying and painful sound of death before each of them started to turn to ash and float away until the next time they were summoned to fight for the King's amusement. What he classed as his greatest victory, and one he wanted recreated over and over again… the thought sickened me.

Enough for me to hiss,

"You're a sick bastard." I heard his chuckle behind me before he whispered back in my ear,

"A sickness that will soon consume you too." After this I was suddenly pushed hard from behind and felt myself falling through the window.

"AAAAHHH!" I screamed and it was one that echoed all the way down, believing this was it for me, as the moment I landed I would die in my reality. My only thought went to

Lucius and the utter pain and heartbreak that my death would cause him.

"Lucius." I let his name be the last from my lips as the ground came closer and closer, and then...

I landed.

However, it was obvious then that King was far from done with me and falling to my death was too easy an end. Because the moment I landed, it was as if I had only fallen to my knees. I lifted my head in confusion and found myself in a new place...

No, that wasn't strictly true.

I had seen this place once before back when I was in the land of the living and fighting his wraiths. It was when I had kicked my body back up from the floor and the momentum had taken me straight through one of the wraiths. I had then caught but a glimpse of the sight that now faced me.

"Gods," I whispered, before my hands flew to my mouth as I took in what looked like thousands of prisoners before me. Rows and rows and rows of them, all in a room that looked endless. Each one a soldier locked away, behind glass cells and chained up like animals. Each one ready for when their master wanted to call them to the real world and use their souls, their very essence, to create an army of wraiths on demand.

I could barely believe this was real, as I had never seen anything so horrifying on this scale! I also couldn't help but wonder if this was soon to be my fate as well. To find myself locked away with the rest of them, just another being at the ready for him to use whenever he wanted?

He was nothing more than a jailor of souls.

It looked like a library of cells, I could count at least fifty of them in each row as I now stood in the centre of one of the aisles. But then the sound of a door banging behind me echoed like thunder around the large open space, making me jump. I snapped my head around to see who it was and found the King was back, hunting me. But unlike before, the image of the King was no more and in its place was something despicably more terrifying than before.

It was as if the moment he stepped into this place he became something else, a demonic general ready to control his army of death. His armour had turned black, with demonic golden symbols now glowing at his chest and the edges of his long dark cloak. One that moved around his body like a separate living entity, the bottom of which look like black souls reaching out along the floor as if they were contained inside very depths of him and were desperate to get away and free themselves. A pair of overly large shoulder pieces were covered in ten-inch spikes that matched the foreboding dark helmet covering most of his face. He had also grown in size, for now he was huge, and three times that of what he used to be. None of his features could be seen clearly, other than his eyes now glowing amber in the darkness and a creepy smile that also burned bright, showing me just how much he enjoyed the sight of my fear.

He raised an armoured hand and pointed to one of the cells. I looked behind me and saw the wraith that had been inside now disappear, slipping free of his chains when he turned to ash. I jumped like some skittish creature in the woods when its heavy restraints clattered to the floor. Then, when the glass cell door swung open, I knew what he planned for my fate. I was to become another one of his prisoners, chained down here for the rest of my eternity, because as soon as my body died in the real world, then he would own what was left of my soul. One that was connected now and forever to him.

"No! I will never let you take me!" I shouted, breathing

hatred into every word. Then, at the first sound of his footsteps coming towards me, I did what I had no other choice but to do…

I ran.

I ran like I had never run before, knowing I couldn't let him catch me. I couldn't let him put me in that cell, as that was the moment it would be all over for me… because I had been wrong. I had thought the moment I discovered the truth of what happened to this mad King that I would discover a way out. But in fact, it was the other way around, he had wanted me to discover the truth. He had kept this little game going for as long as possible and why, because it had amused him. The game of cat and mouse was one that he had continued to let play out as part of his entertainment. But now that game was at an end.

An end that had only one destination.

My eternal cell.

But I refused to let him win. So, I continued to run, barely having time to look as I passed each poor soul that had been here for, I don't know how long. Then, when I thought all hope was lost,

I heard his voice.

A voice from the past.

"I want you to think of a door."

"Lucius?" I uttered his name like a prayer.

"Close your eyes and think of a door…" he said again, just like he had done in that stolen memory. But then the footsteps following me grew louder and leaving the past behind, Lucius now shouted in panic,

"Do it now!" That voice echoed around me and I heard the roar of anger behind me, knowing that it came from the demonic King that was hearing it too. So, I did what I was told, I closed my eyes and let my mind focus on nothing else but the sight of my bedroom door. I could see it so clearly that when I opened my eyes again it was no longer just in my mind's eye. but right there in front me at the end of the room! So, I ran with every ounce of strength I had left as it was right there, all I had to do was reach out and open it. Suddenly the whole prison started to seep into my bedroom at the edges. I could even smell the room, the scent of my sheets, my candles and the plastic of my Lego. Then I started to see the posters on the wall and feel the rug beneath my feet. I could see it all so clearly that when I reached out to grab the handle and open the door, I believed with everything in me that he would be there.

I wrenched open the door and before I had chance to take anything in, I threw myself through the opening. But the second I was through the door, I was grabbed from behind and I screamed before a hand was quickly held over my mouth to silence me. Then I was pulled quickly against a hard body just as I heard the roar of anger get louder as the Wraith Master was getting closer towards the open door.

However, before he reached me, the door slammed shut and just as it started to shake, I watched wide-eyed as molten lava started to seep up from the ground. It continued up the door, consuming it entirely before it cooled into hardened black rock, now preventing anyone from getting through.

I started struggling in the arms that held me tight, but then stilled the moment his voice penetrated through my panic as he whispered tenderly in my ear,

"I told you I would come for you, my Princess."

CHAPTER FOURTEEN

LILY OF THE FIELD

"*You're safe now… you're safe now, my Amelia.*"

"Lucius, is that really you?" I asked on a whisper, the disbelief in my voice clear to detect, fearing that it was all a trick. That this was just another part of his game. Just another level of cruelty with the Wraith Master being able to access my emotions, twisting them and luring me to a false sense of security.

"It's me, Amelia, I have you now," he told me, pulling me to him, and cradling my head against his chest as I didn't realise until that moment that I was crying, unable to stop the flow of my tears.

Tears of utter relief.

"I can't… believe it, you… you made it through," I said, pulling back and looking up at him, needing to see him to make sure that he was really here. That he wasn't just a ghost of my memories. But then as his gaze softened, he took my hand in his and lifted it up before running his finger gently over the strip of material I had used to bind my hand. Then he told me,

"I got your message."

Then he took my face in his hands and tipped my head back, and the look he gave me was one that had the strength to burn itself to my soul forever. It was bursting with love and the same utter relief my tears had shed. Then he told me fervently,

"I thought… Gods, Amelia, *I thought I had lost you!"* Then he pulled me the last few inches and kissed me as if we had been torn apart for years. In fact, I didn't actually know how long it had been, only how it had felt like a lifetime. Which is why I practically fell into his kiss, clinging onto him as if I never wanted to let go. As if I would never have the strength to. I closed my eyes to imagine this was happening elsewhere, not in this world of horrors. For the beauty of this kiss didn't deserve to be tainted by the truth of our current situation.

It was perfection in my heart, and I wanted nothing to stain it. And Lucius knew. He knew exactly how I felt as he pulled back slightly.

"It's alright, Amelia, you can open your eyes now," Lucius whispered over my lips once the kiss had finished, and I found myself stood in a beautiful field.

"Where are we?" I asked in astonishment, shocked I was now seeing something completely serene and peaceful.

"Come, sit with me," Lucius said instead of answering me as he held out his hand for me to take.

"Are we… are we safe here?" I asked as I placed my hand and trust in his so he could lead me over to the peak of a hill. The moment we came to the peak, I gasped at its beauty.

"Gods!" I muttered in awe, making him grin back at me.

"You like it?" he asked before pulling me down and situating me in between his legs so he could wrap his arms around me from behind, encouraging me to lean back against his chest.

"Like it, Lucius, it is one of the most beautiful places I've ever seen." And it was, because what lay in front of us now was a blanket of red flowers going as far as the eye could see. They looked like poppies, with their crimson petals that looked as fragile as silk and their black centres creating a startling contrast.

"What is this place?" I asked, making him lean closer to me so he could whisper,

"This is one of my mortal memories." I sucked in a startled breath by this admission, now knowing we were somewhere in Israel.

"Anemone coronaria, Lily of the Field," he said, making me smile.

"Is that what it means?" I asked, leaning my head back, slightly resting it on his shoulder. I just caught the hint of a grin before he tightened his arms around me and gave me one of my favourite things, *a history lesson.*

"Anemone, anemos, is the Greek name and in mythology, Anemone was the name of the daughter of the winds. Now, in Latin it is known as Coronaria, Corona, meaning crown." I released a deep sigh, loving the sound of his voice and easily getting lost in it.

"But do you want to know my favourite?" he asked leaning closer again.

"I do," I said in delight, making him smile against my neck before commenting in a knowing and amused tone,

"Of course, you do." Then he told me,

"In Hebrew, the name of the flower is called Kalanit, this is related to the Hebrew word for a bride, Kala, referring to its beauty, just like a bride on her wedding day." His voice sounded as if he was dreaming of such a day and I had to say, his words were pulling me under and encasing me in that same dream. But despite how beautiful this setting was and how I could have easily remained getting lost in the feel of his strong, safe arms holding me close, I knew I had to break the spell by asking,

"How are you doing any of this?" I was surprised when he laughed before telling me,

"You are the most curious person I have ever known." The look I gave him over my shoulder said it all.

"Err, no offence, handsome, but do you blame me?" He laughed again and I turned around so I could face him. Handsome was not a strong enough word for him, as he was beautiful, and even more so with this field of dreams he had created.

"I never would, sweetheart, I am just happy to hear that curiosity voiced once again and with you in my arms," he told me, making me smile, but then when I thought of what I had just been through, that grin fell away. Then I framed my hands either side of his head and lay my forehead to his.

"I don't know why this keeps happening," I admitted holding him close and I felt his hand come to the back of my neck, holding me to him before whispering back,

"Neither do I, sweetheart, I just know that I can't lose you again, I would not survive another time." At his own admission I swallowed hard before pulling back a little so I could look at him.

"Oh, Lucius," I uttered softly at the pained look he gave me.

"I lost you... Gods, Amelia, the pain... the fucking agony... it was unlike anything I've ever experienced... I..." I cupped a hand to his cheek and said his name again, telling him that I was here.

"Lucius."

He reached up and wrapped a hand around my wrist, as he needed to keep me in his grasp before he took a deep breath and allowed all his emotions to come spilling out.

"You died, Amelia…" I sucked in a deep breath and closed my eyes, feeling the tears build at how pained those three words sounded.

"I know," I whispered, knowing that now my words felt thick and almost too hard to say.

"You died…" he said again, and this time I was powerless to respond as the tears fell.

"Right there, in my arms… you died right in front of me… died, and I was fucking helpless to stop it! I couldn't…" The emotion broke within him as his agonised words trailed off and like my own, every word had been thick and heavy and weighted by the pain of his memories. The memory of my death that I knew would stay with him forever. Which was when I decided to remind him of another.

"But, Lucius, you saved me, you brought me back… my Chosen One, you saved me, *saved my heart,"* I told him softly before pulling him to me and burying my face in his neck so he could feel my tears wetting his skin.

"How do you know that?" he asked, his quiet voice amazed by the knowledge. So, I pulled back slightly, making him grip my waist as if unwilling to allow too much space between us.

"This place… this crazy void I'm trapped in… it shows me so many things, most of which I can't even make sense of. But when I saw you, saw the way you tried to save me, I knew."

"Gods," he hissed before running his gloved hand through my hair, pushing it back from my face.

"Please tell me… Gods Amelia, please tell me that you didn't see the moment you died?" he said as if this realisation was too much to bear. So, instead of giving him my answer by way of a pained broken voice, I nodded. It was in that moment he crushed my body to his and wrapped both arms around me as if he never wanted to let me go. Then he continued to whisper how sorry he was, even though none of this was his fault. Yet, despite that, he was just sorry that I had seen it… seen what he had seen, knowing now that it would forever haunt us both. So, I continued to remind him,

"I saw the moment you brought me back, Lucius. You saved me…"

"Sweetheart…" His voice said he was about to stop me when I placed my hand to the back of his neck before squeezing him there and told him more forcefully this time,

"You made my heart beat again, Lucius… don't you understand that… you saved me, *you saved me,*" I told him fervently before finishing it on his lips, kissing him with all the passion I had inside me. I pushed him back so I could lie down on top of him and show him everything I felt. Make him feel every breath, taste every word, and feel every beat of a heart he had brought back to life.

I wanted him to feel it all.

He wound his arms around me, one coming up to the back of my hair where he buried his fingers, keeping me anchored to him. God's but I wanted to remain there forever! It was like being reunited with an obsession, an addiction that only ever helped you live the best life you could. Like taking your first breath of fresh air after spending years suffocating in a cloud of dust.

I knew that there was so much we had to say to each other. So much we needed to talk about, so many important things left to discuss. But right in that moment, I felt as though all I wanted to do was celebrate the fact that we were together once more. And it felt like a gift. A gift from the Gods. One I wasn't about to throw away.

I'd spent so long running, so long being frightened of what I may find around every corner, behind every door, and now I was here in this beautiful field with all the beauty that was Lucius, holding me close. Finally, once again, I felt safe. Safe in his arms.

I needed this. We both needed this. We needed this connection, this single moment that was like reuniting two souls meant to be together. Simply put...

My heart needed him.

After this kiss, one that felt powerful enough to erase the past and reignite hope for the future, I asked him,

"So, you've been trying to get through?"

"Of course, I never stopped trying, sweetheart, but I was powerless," he said. We were currently lying down with me tucked to his side and I was drawing circles over his pecs as I listened to him talk. He was wearing pretty much the same thing he had been before all this had happened, which I assumed was classed as comfy wear in Hell. A pair of loose fitted black trousers, made from a material I didn't recognise. As for his solid, muscular torso, it was covered in a tight fitted jacket that, like before, wrapped around him and tied at the sides, this meant that it left his impressive shoulders and large biceps bare.

"What do you mean?" I asked, finding the statement strange coming from Lucius, seeing as it was hard to imagine him being powerless at anything.

"It was as if I had been stripped of the supernatural part of my soul, in truth... I was nothing more than a mortal man," he told me, and I sucked in a surprised breath. I had just assumed he had been locked out and nothing more.

"But I saw what you did, you made the door disappear

with the lava, you brought us here... how did you do any of those things if...?"

"It wasn't me, Amelia, it was you. You were the one who gained power over the void, and that in turn gave me power enough to break through," he told me, surprising me enough that I stopped making circles on his chest and instead found myself gripping onto him.

"Is that even possible?" I asked, making him nod to our surroundings, telling me without words that it clearly was.

"So that means you have power over it too?" I asked, obviously getting excited about the idea.

"I do, which means there's no more running for you, sweetheart, I'm here now and I will keep you safe," he replied, making me sigh and relax more of my weight into him, which made him tighten his hold. However, this was when I realised the truth of our situation.

"You can't get me home, can you?" He cupped the back of my head and pulled my hair enough for me to grant him my eyes before he told me the truth.

"I am not going to lie, Amelia, it is complicated at best." I nodded, silently telling him to continue.

"It's as though you're in a coma. The knife used against you was infected with his blood, with his essence and that has connected you to him. The infection travelled to your heart which is what made it stop beating for a short time. However, when we discovered that his essence was drawn to him, it was enough to save your heart. The truth is that right now the Wraith Master has to stay next to you so he will continue to draw back his essence and prevent it from happening again." Once he had finished, I let out a whoosh of air and said,

"Oh great, I bet that looks good, three in a bed and the little one said, 'please don't roll over or I will die'." At this Lucius frowned, but I was on a roll and said,

"Not exactly the threesome I had in mind." At this, that frown turned into a growl and I threw up my hand, as the other was tucked down his side.

"Joking... jeez, you do remember I was a virgin before you, right...? I would think jumping to threesomes at this point would be quite a sexual leap," I joked again.

"As funny as I find you most of the time, I believe any jokes that include another man in our bed is not exactly one that you will find me laughing at," he informed me, making me smirk.

"Noted, and while we are drawing comedy lines here, I will also say, likewise, buster." Now at this he smiled. Then after a moment of silence I said,

"So that's it then, we now have to carry him around with us wherever we go... umm, I wonder if Louis Vuitton does a pet carrier?" He gave me a pointed look at that joke, and this was when I reminded him,

"Come on, if I don't make jokes, Lucius, I'm gonna cry." Thankfully, this was enough as his gaze softened.

"I have not given up yet and neither should you," he told me, making me release yet another sigh.

"Yes, but what can be done?" I asked, now sitting up and bringing my knees up so that I could rest my arms on them. This made Lucius release his own sigh before doing the same, so now we both sat next to each other staring across the sea of red flowers.

"There is something, but I don't want to give you false hope, Amelia," Lucius told me, making me do just that... *get my hopes up.*

"What, what is it?"

"Your friend, Vena, found a clue." This was when Lucius told me about the Oracle of Light and how she may still be alive. That if anyone knew anything about the Wraith and breaking this connection, then it would be her. He then told me how he had sent the McBain brothers on a mission to find her and I instantly realised something.

"You didn't leave me." He gave me a pointed look before telling me,

"You really think I would after I just nearly lost you? Gods, Amelia, after all we've been through, I want to fucking tie you to my body with an unbreakable bond!" he replied in earnest.

"Well, I would say it's called a wedding band, but hey, the divorce rate isn't exactly in our favour with that one," I joked, making him pick up my hand and start rubbing his thumb on my wedding finger as if this was something he was imagining right there. But when he didn't say anything, I decided to cut through the tension the only way I knew how... *with humour.*

"It's far less subtle than a collar and lead, that's for sure." I elbowed him in the stomach playfully, making him grunt as his only reply.

"What are we going to do if they don't find her?" I asked, my voice sounding small and seemingly far away.

"Don't think like that, Pet... besides, the McBain brothers are proving themselves quite useful, time and time again... have faith," he said, making me reply,

"Well, that is my name after all." At this he gave me a small grin that managed to lighten my fears and worries somewhat.

"Now, are you going to tell me what this place is?" I asked, because my curiosity had got too much. Beside me, Lucius released a deep sigh that almost sounded pained. It made me look over to him to see an expression I hadn't seen there before. Actually no, I had seen it once before, before we had come to Hell. Back to a time I had called him a boy scout and believed we were on a camping trip.

It had been when Lucius had been speaking of his father.

I remember being fascinated hearing him recalling his days as a boy, yet nothing prepared me for what he said next...

"This, this place, it's the last memory I have of..." he paused, before finishing off what was clearly a painful memory,

"Of my mother."

CHAPTER FIFTEEN

MATTRESSES AND FLOWERS

The moment Lucius mentioned his mother, I tensed, holding myself still, not wanting to distract him from telling me about his past.

"She used to call me her little Kalanit, her favourite flower," he said, looking out to the field and letting his fingertips graze the flowers closest to us, as if this was done subconsciously and something he used to do as a boy.

"It's all I remember really… that, and this field," he said, making me have to clear the emotions from my throat before I asked,

"When did she die?"

"When I was a boy, I rarely remember it now, only that this flower reminds me of her. She would bring me here and I'd run through the flowers," he said, looking off into the distance as if he was seeing it play out and when I turned and looked in the same direction, I sucked in a startled breath. As I could just see the shadow of Lucius as a boy, of course it didn't look like him, as Judas and the vessel Lucius had been reborn into were not the same man. No, only his soul remained the same.

But there was no denying his beauty, as he was a cute little boy, and the sight made my heart ache. Even more so when the hint of his mother appeared in the distance, even if it was barely even a whisper of an image and obviously all he remembered. But it didn't matter, for it was such a profound moment all the same.

I continued to watch as the mother chased the little boy, before grabbing him under the arms and swinging him around, dropping a basket of red flowers tied in bunches to the floor. She looked so carefree, so happy, and so did that little boy. The echoes of laughter from them both made me well up and before I knew it, a single tear fell for them both. For his memory. I couldn't imagine how hard it must have been for him losing his mother at such a young age, and someone he obviously adored and idolised. And to know he was sharing this with me now, well, it felt like another gift. Which was why although I might not have known the right words to say in comfort, I did know the right thing to do. It would mean the most to Lucius, and let him know in return how much sharing this piece of his past with me meant to my heart.

So, I shifted behind him until I was on my knees and at the right height to wrap my arms around from behind. Then I told him the only words that mattered in that moment.

"I love you, Lucius."

He reached up and put a hand to my arm, holding me to him as he released a contented sigh. Then when he wanted more, he twisted his body and at the same time he reached behind him, taking hold of my arms so he could pull me over his shoulder and position me across his lap. Once there he told me tenderly,

"I love you more."

After this he kissed me, letting the memory of his childhood fade away as if carried away with the wind and back to the recesses of his mind. But as for me, being here with him and getting lost in his kiss, it was as if this nightmare world I had been running from quickly turned into the heaven I never wanted to leave. Lucius simply unravelled me, making my heart soar and my soul come alight, burning for him. I knew that this was my everything. Right here in this field of his dreams with his most precious memory still floating away on the wind, and one I would now never forget.

A gift given like no other.

But Lucius wasn't done, as there was another gift he wanted to give me, and this one would make both our souls come alight. Something that started with him taking hold of my waist and lifting me, so I was straddling his lap. Then he started to kiss his way up my neck, making my head fall back and my hair cascade down my spine. I let out a soft moan at the feel of what his lips were doing to me. My body burned for him, ached to have him inside me as he created a pathway of pleasure along my skin. I closed my eyes for long moments, then reminding myself to open them again just so I could see the sky above us. So, I could believe that this fantasy was real, that it wasn't just our minds that were connected, but our bodies as well.

I didn't want to think of the reality. Of the two of us just lying in a bed next to each other, still and unmoving, as if frozen in time. I wanted to imagine that this was our reality. Despite knowing that where we were now was as real as it ever could be, I wanted to believe the dream, and I knew if I closed my eyes all I would see is where our bodies were actually lying, wasting our precious time together.

"One day, Amelia, one day and I will bring you back

here, I will find this exact spot and I will make love to you and in that moment, it won't just be a dream," Lucius told me as if he was reading my thoughts. I let out a breathy one worded sigh,

"Yes." I felt him lowering me backwards, so I was now lay on a bed of flowers that represented a beautiful bride on her wedding day. Yet that same beauty reminded a mother of her son.

It was perfect.

"But for now, let's lose ourselves in the fantasy," he added, now looking down at me, the sun shining behind his sand-coloured hair, making it glow. I became transfixed by the sight, because in that moment, he had never looked more like an angel. However, his actions soon contradicted this as he fisted a hand in my hair at the top of my head before lowering down for a dominating kiss.

Then moments after, in a crimson field of beauty, he made love to me and as he did, he never once lost the connection. With his lips on mine, with hands entwined with my own, not once... not for a single second did I not feel...

Loved, owned and cherished.

"Well, at least we didn't destroy any rooms this time," Lucius pointed out not long after we had finished making love. I was also now wearing a pretty white summer dress after Lucius had naturally torn my other one. Because we might have just made sweet, tender love, but this was still Lucius we were talking about, *he had to rip something.*

As for him, he was only wearing his loose fitted trousers, as I guess that was the handy thing when you controlled every aspect of a dream world, you could conjure up anything you liked... including comfy pants.

"No, but we crushed the hell out of some flowers," I replied with a smirk and a wink, making him growl and playfully nip at my cheek.

"That does nothing for my manhood, sweetheart," he replied, making me giggle before my wit returned.

"Well, I don't know, I think at this rate we could totally turn into a pair of hippies. What do you say, stud, want to take another go at the 70s?" His face was a mask of horror before shouting,

"Fuck no!" I burst out laughing before asking,

"What's the matter, bell bottoms and large collars not your thing?"

"Laugh it up, Princess, but just remember who has the power to change this void here," he threatened, making me enjoy this game.

"Well, I think I've had enough of castles, so how about some hotel spa somewhere... I could do with a massage." At this he laughed. We were still lying in the field together, where I was absentmindedly playing with one the flowers in front of me as I lay on my belly. As for Lucius, he was lay on his back with arms behind his head looking towards me with a bit of a squint as the sun was in his eyes.

"You know you could just magic up a pair of sunglasses or even make the imaginary sun go behind the imaginary clouds." To this my reply came in the form of a handsome grin that lit up his face. Then he shifted so he could run the backs of his fingers down my cheek.

"My funny girl," he muttered in what seemed like more of a statement made to himself than to me.

"I wish we could stay like this forever, but

unfortunately…" Lucius started, and I released a sigh and said,

"Yeah, yeah, I know… we have serious shit to talk about."

"I hate this as much as you do, sweetheart, but I have to know everything that's happened, as this is far too important for us to miss something," Lucius said, making my eyes widen in surprise before I felt like this conversation had become a little one-sided. So, I sat up and quickly made my point.

"Yeah, I agree, let's do that, let's tell each other everything… oh wait, you first considering you're the one who has been keeping stuff from me." I folded my arms across my chest when I had finished, making him sigh as he had no doubt hoped I would have forgotten this particular, 'let's tell each other everything' pact.

"I should have told you about Dariush," he admitted right away, however I didn't let my surprise stop me from scolding him.

"Damn straight you should have told me. Seriously, Lucius, what were you thinking?" This was met by him running a frustrated hand through his hair before he looked away.

"No one has ever known of my brother, other than our father."

"No one?" I said in a questioning tone because I had a feeling that wasn't strictly true, and his look said it all.

"But of course," I muttered, now looking away from him. However, after hearing my tone he looked back at me and obviously wanted me to do the same. I felt him take hold of my chin in his thumb and finger before bringing my face back around to look at him.

"I think we're past that, sweetheart," he commented,

making me jerk my head free and roll my eyes before pointing out,

"No, what I thought we were past was all of the lying and the keeping shit from each other, and when I say we, I really mean you keeping shit from me," I said, motioning with my hand between us.

"I agree, I should have told you about my brother, but as for your mother knowing, then that isn't my story to tell and besides, it would be difficult for me to do so."

"What do you mean?" I asked in confusion. He rubbed a hand to the back of his neck before telling me,

"This may be hard to understand, but I wasn't there." I jerked back a little in surprise and repeated,

"You weren't there… when you told her…"

"I didn't tell her, and by all accounts it is something your mother discovered after seeing my brother and I together," Lucius told me, and I didn't know what to say, other than,

"Oh."

"Please understand, Amelia, that I did not keep knowledge of my brother from you intentionally, for if you remember, the last thing I expected was to be taking a trip to Hell together." Okay, so I had to admit even to myself that this was a good point, one he unfortunately continued to make.

"Something I will remind you wasn't my idea and when we first got here, I spent the whole of my time trying to find you. If I'd have known that you were going to be as reckless as you were, then I would have thought to mention it." His tone of voice said it all and after everything that had happened since, then I couldn't really say that I blamed him. However, I still said,

"You still could have told me." And damn him but after I said it, he continued to make good points.

"When, sweetheart? No seriously, when? Think back, Amelia, to all that has happened between us. It has been one thing after fucking another and not exactly a vast amount of time spent with each other to talk about life or our future or anything else that I don't know that couples talk about in bed together."

"Okay, okay, you can stop making good points now, Lucius, I get it." At this he got closer to me and said,

"Oh no, one more I think."

"Lucius." I said his name in warning, but it was one he simply chose to ignore.

"Just before we came here, Amelia, I'd spent months searching for you, scouring the Earth looking for my Chosen One who decided it would be a good idea to up and run before listening to reason." This unfortunately was true, and I hated to admit that he was right.

"Alright, Lucius, that's…" At this he placed a finger over my lips and told me,

"I am not finished." At this point I rolled my eyes, and he raised a brow at me, telling me what would happen if I did that again. Hell, it most likely would have happened then had he not been in the flow of telling me off!

"Now, had I known what was facing us in our future, of course I would have told you, but Amelia you have to understand there are things in my life that do not come easy for me to speak about… *with anyone*…" He paused to emphasise this, making a silent point about my mother before carrying on,

"And as hard as it is to believe that in over 2000 years, you are my first girlfriend, despite how juvenile I believe that to sound, it doesn't negate the fact that this is my first relationship and well, in all honesty, I haven't exactly read a book on it. I've been kind of focused on the keeping you alive part," he said, surprising me with that honesty.

"We have kind of had a Hell of a time, haven't we… no pun intended?"

"Ha, with you, pet, it is always pun intended, but yes… case in point, sweetheart," he said, holding out a hand to gesture to the field we were currently still sat in, knowing that if he hadn't manipulated the scene around us, we'd have most likely been sat in some creepy castle with a madman chasing us. Or even a wasteland of ash with the sounds of a reoccurring battle raging on, as our not so romantic music of no choice.

I felt Lucius' fingertips skim down my back where the hex had once been.

"I wish I could have been there for you, to hold you through the pain, it must have been agonising for you," he said as if pained by the very thought of it.

"I'll be honest, it wasn't exactly a party. However, the quirky, perverted goblin who removed it though, was… well, now he was a character," I said, telling him about the goblin's antics in both the pub and after he had removed the hex after taking it upon his own body and displaying it proudly in front of the mirror. Lucius laughed when I told him what Vern and Gryph's faces were like when they found him dancing in front of the mirror, swinging his grotesque little body around as if he thought he was the sexiest thing in the room. Lucius threw his head back and laughed so hard I swear I saw tears form. Then he shook his head before pulling me to him and whispering,

"Just what am I going to do with you, pet?" It was sweet the way he was looking at me, but recalling this time made me realise what else had happened not long after this point.

"I'm sorry I failed you," I said looking down at my lap.

"Failed? Come now, how could you ever fail me, Amelia?" Lucius asked as if this was impossible, so I told him,

"The witch, she got the eye, Lucius." At this he made a scoffing sound as if it didn't matter to him.

"You failed me in nothing, sweetness," he said softly, pulling me in for a gentle kiss.

"Besides, I doubt she can do much with it or this mysterious brother I'm supposed to have, whoever he may be. No, I am not worried, as it is clear that he too cannot use the eye, despite him obviously believing himself worthy," Lucius added, and it was clear that he wasn't too concerned about the outcome.

"So, where does that leave us with that particular evil, I mean not including the obvious one we are currently dealing with... man, we need a holiday, one without people," I muttered, making him smirk.

"Let's take it one thing at a time, yeah?" was his answer.

"Speaking of time, how long do you think it will be before they find this Oracle of Light, *if they find her at all?*" I muttered this last part, making Lucius turn my face to his again so I may see the sincerity in his eyes when he told me,

"They will find her, Amelia, have faith."

"Again, you do realise that's my name, right?" I joked making him smirk before replying,

"Yes, sweetheart, the irony is not lost on me." I couldn't help but giggle at this before asking in a playful way,

"So, what do we do now?"

"Well, for once at least we find ourselves alone and together," Lucius replied, making me add,

"If not in body then in mind at least."

"Indeed, perhaps we should make the most of it," he teased with a wink and then stood, now holding out a hand for me to take. He pulled me to my feet as I made my next point.

"I think we just did that by having mind-blowing, make love sex. Oh, God, I hope no one was in the room with us when we were orgasming." At this, Lucius burst out laughing and I smacked him on the side of the arm playfully and shouted,

"Oi, this is serious!" He simply laughed harder.

"Don't worry, sweetheart, I think your modesty is safe. Besides, the entire Kingdom heard me fucking you into oblivion and you seemed fine with that." Man, but just his sexual words had me getting wet again.

"Yes, but we didn't exactly have an audience that was in the room with us as I think I would have noticed," I pointed out.

"Sweetheart, with my cock inside you, you wouldn't have noticed a brass band going through the room playing your favourite tune." I rolled in my lips to try and stop myself from laughing so I could say something witty in return, which turned out to be,

"Did anyone ever tell you that you are a cocky bastard?"

"Once or twice." He smirked before giving me a wink and making me roll my eyes, but then the moment he clocked it, I held up my hand and said,

"Don't you even think about it. I think after everything that's happened between us, I am definitely due a few more eye rolls before I get a spanking, thank you very much."

"My rules, sweetheart, but yes, I will allow you this one time." I barked out a short laugh and said,

"Oh gee, thanks."

"However, I have been known to change my mind quite rapidly, and more inclined to do so when my Chosen One is being a sexual brat that needs taking under hand." At this he reached down and pinched my ass hard, making me yelp.

"Oww," I moaned making him rub it gently and say in a tender but mocking tone,

"Aww, poor baby."

"So, this quality time you were talking about, what did you have in mind exactly? You want to take me on a date or something, cause the first time that happened it didn't end so well?" I asked, making him fake surprise and say,

"What are you talking about, you mean you don't usually deal with mercenary attacks or seeing your new boyfriend massacre some humans on all your dates?"

"Hey, that might be normal for you, vampy, but for us humans, we usually just go with dinner and a movie and the only blood and gore is usually what's being played on the screen." He rolled his eyes this time, and kept up the charade when commenting in a dry tone,

"Well, that sounds boring to me." His teasing made me giggle.

"So, what did you have in mind, gun range or axe throwing?" At this he grinned and said,

"With you, sweetheart, I am thinking you could get into trouble mattress shopping." I laughed again and asked incredulously,

"Really, you can imagine anything right now and you want to choose mattress shopping?" He grinned again and looked close to biting his damn lip.

"Answer me this, have you ever even been to a shop to buy a mattress or did you just have one of your minions do it, because I really doubt you would even know what one looked like... whoa!" This ended with a cry of shock the second I felt myself being tossed in the air and landing on a soft mattress, soon finding myself in a store. However, it was one that only had a single bed for sale and some counter with an old-fashioned cash register that could have been one of the first ever invented.

"If this is supposed to convince me that you bought your own bed, then you're going to have to pick a card machine to go with that antique on the counter," I teased, making his lips twitch again.

"Or I could just fuck you so hard on this bed you won't even remember what the fuck a card machine is." At this I gulped and said in a high-pitched voice,

"Er, yeah, let's do that."

His bad boy grin said it all…

Mattress shopping was going to be fun.

CHAPTER SIXTEEN

LUCIUS

SHOPPING AND SEX

Fuck me, my girl was funny!

Gods, but how much I had missed her!

The moment I had seen that door, all I had been waiting for was for her to open it. I just needed her to know that I was there waiting for her. Of course, then I had felt her panic, I had felt her terror when I had called out to her, but then the door opened, and she ran straight into my arms and I was so fucking proud of her. Then I had seen the Wraith Master in his true form running after her and I swear I had never been so torn, for I wanted nothing more than to set her aside as I let my demon erupt, showing him the true meaning of fear! I wanted to walk in there and rip him to pieces myself, to tear his fucking heart out for making my girl scared!

However, two things stopped me, the first being the most

obvious, for he could not die, as that would only mean Amelia would also die right alongside of him... literally. The other reason I didn't give in to this mad impulse was that I knew Amelia took precedence over everything else, and in that moment, she was fucking terrified! So, I had slammed the door and made it so that he could no longer reach her.

I swear feeling her there in my arms for that first moment since losing her, well, I thought my heart would pound right out of my fucking chest! It was as if the cracks surrounding my soul had healed and everything in me centred as peace had swept over me.

I was whole again.

Therefore, in that moment, I had wanted to share something with her, something that I had never shared with anyone. A piece of history I thought long ago buried, and one I dug back out just for her. Her reaction had been better than I'd ever hoped for, as I could feel the love pouring from her and how grateful she was that I'd shared it. In the end, having her there experiencing it with me for the first time, had been what felt like the true gift, the one she had given to me, not the other way around.

A moment in time I would never forget, and one only the two of us shared in our minds. It was the reason I had vowed to her that one day I would make it real, and I added to this vow a promise I made myself. That I would turn this moment into a reality once I had finally made her my wife. After I had made her the Queen she already was in my heart.

Now, if anyone had told me I would have come from that romantic moment after making love to her in a field of flowers, to being in a mattress shop... then yeah, considering Amelia was involved, I probably would have believed them.

Of course, I had no fucking clue what a mattress shop

looked like. And little did she know but I didn't have my 'minions' go shopping for me to buy one. No, I usually just had shit custom made, like most other things I wanted. But I didn't say this to her, as this game we were playing was too much fun to spoil it now. No, instead it was time to make it even more interesting, starting with me getting to rip another fucking dress from her.

Gods in Heaven, but she looked like some virginal sacrifice spread out on the bed like that, all dressed in white. A dress I had chosen for two reasons, one, it was tight, and two, it was indecently see-through and as close to keeping her naked as I could get.

But I had just adored the way she teased me, her funny quips about the cash register being an antique made me want to punish her in the most delicious ways possible. But I also knew I had to take care with her because whatever injures she sustained in the void would carry over to her body in reality, and I wouldn't risk any harm coming to her, not when she was so weak. But this being said, I could also tell by the way my girl was restlessly fidgeting on the bed, that this time she didn't want it soft, slow, and sensual as I had given it to her earlier. When I had made love to her in the field of crimson flowers. No, this time she wanted to come screaming my name and not breathlessly speaking it over my lips as she had before.

My girl wanted to scream.

And by the Gods, I would make it happen.

I stood by the edge of the bed looking down at her, getting a sick satisfaction when I knew that my dominating look could make her squirm. Then I reached out and grabbed hold of her ankle before pulling her to the edge of the bed, doing so until her legs hung over the edge. The action made her dress ride up to her waist, and considering I hadn't awarded her the luxury of underwear it meant that she was bare to me. I could see her arousal glistening on her skin along her inner thighs, making my mouth water.

It may have all been in our minds, but it didn't mean that it wasn't also affecting her body right now, as I knew if I had been there, I could have spread her legs and run my fingers up between the folds of her sex and come away to find my fingers soaked. Because arousal was all about your mind and how it interpreted every touch. Every dirty, raw sexual word whispered in her ear would make her wet and that was without any touching at all.

Which was why I knew that when I finally came back to my body, I would unashamedly find my trousers soaked with my own release. So, opening her legs I found what I had allowed to remain from before, left by my mind from when I had pumped my seed into her beautiful pussy. Relishing in the feel of her tight, wet channel fisting my cock and its unyielding hold on me had drawn out my orgasm for longer.

However, this time around I wanted the start to be all about her. So, I lowered to my knees and ran my fingers gently along the inside of her thighs, grinning when I saw her flesh quivering at my touch. Then, when I had finished teasing her with all my gentle caresses, I gathered up my dripping seed with my fingertips before I raised myself up so as that I could reach her mouth.

"Suck!" My commanding tone didn't go unnoticed as her mouth opened instantly. Ah, my good little submissive, she knew who her master was. I put my fingers inside her mouth, letting her taste me, and when she moaned around them, then it was nearly my undoing. I loved how greedy she was. Greedy for any part of me she could get, and I relished in the fact that no other man would ever get to see this part of my girl. This sexual fire I could spark with just my touch. No one would ever get to experience the heaven that I did every time I bedded her.

She had always been mine to claim, I knew that. Even from the very first moment I saw her when she was untried and at the tender age of sixteen. No other man would ever have her and after I'd claimed her virginity once both of us were ready, I knew that would be it for her. She would never know of another's touch, another's cock, never taste another's seed. She would only ever know me, and I didn't give two fucks on how primitive that sounded... how possessive it was, for I would not pretend that I was apologetic to the fact that she was mine and belonged to me. Nor would I claim to think otherwise just to appease anyone else's opinion of me.

"Deeper!" I commanded putting my fingers in and relishing the sight of her gagging around them before fucking her mouth with two thick fingers coated in my cum. She was stunning! Everything about her was utter perfection, and seeing how well she took my sexual deviancy was nothing short of spectacular.

I pulled my fingers from between her lips, grinning when she made a small sound of disappointment. But before she could speak, I went back to her sex for more, this time putting my fingers deeper inside her and making her arch her back at the same time crying out with pleasure. I hooked my fingers a little knowing that I was rubbing against her G-spot and then pulled from her slowly, gathering up as much of my cum as I could so that I could feed her more. Once again, she moaned knowing that it was coming.

"Open!" I ordered, knowing this time there was enough there that as soon as I tipped my fingers up my seed would drip down the digits and into her mouth. I wanted to watch her take it this time. She didn't disappoint as her tongue came out ready for it, like a sweet little pet of mine ready to lap it up. Once it dripped onto her tongue and rolled down her throat, I then coated her lips with it telling her,

"Lick it off, slowly." She did as I commanded, and the sight was so fucking erotic that I could have come there and then without even having my dick wet.

"Beautiful," I praised, making her blush before putting my fingers in deeper so she could get the last of my seed, gagging once more. Then I pulled my fingers out one last time and lowered down again in between her legs.

"Arms above your head. If they move, I stop, do you understand?" I asked in a stern tone and she nodded before raising her arms up and gripping on to the plain black covers I had conjured up in my mind to cover the bed. One that was still situated in this make-believe shop that held little else other than one large bed for sale and a counter she had mocked.

I lowered my face to her sex and just to tease her further, I blew along the centre of her glistening lips, first spreading them with my fingers like an erotic flower, one I was near desperate to fuck! Her quick intake of air made me grin before I lowered down and kissed her opening, before running my tongue up the length and then sucking in her clit, hard enough to have her arching from the bed once more.

"Gods!" she said, making me grin as she finished it by letting out a long, greedy moan. But there was no one greedier than I, for that first taste of her sex burst across my tongue and I was nearly lost to madness, for I wanted to devour her! She was fucking exquisite!

I sucked in that little bundle of nerves, knowing that I

wanted it swollen and engorged before I bit into it. I wanted as much blood to rise to the surface as possible before I was ready for my feast. Knowing that the blood I would take from her there would make her orgasm all that more stronger, igniting it like a fucking rocket! And she wanted it, she craved it in fact, as she was writhing on the bed, begging me to let her come. Because I had been teasing her, drawing it out as I knew every time she was about to orgasm, I would leave her clit and kiss my way along her soaked inner thighs.

I was a cruel bastard, but I was one that was enjoying myself, so naturally I continued. Besides, I knew how powerful an orgasm could be when you prolonged it, something quite difficult to do by yourself, especially for one as greedy as Amelia was. But it also meant that it was time for me to indulge her in her release, despite the few times she had moved her arms. However, she had soon got the message when I would stop and growl my commands over her bare mound. One that had just the slightest amount of hair starting to come through. I usually liked my women bare and soft for me but strangely enough when it came to Amelia, I often wondered what her hair would be like if she allowed it to grow. Would it be soft curls I could grip onto and yank to cause that delicious bite of pain I knew she liked?

That would be fun indeed.

"Please, Lucius, please, can't hold it… please, I'm desperate." This had been one of many out of breath pleas that had come from her, begging me so sweetly during my time devouring her sex. And only because I didn't want to push her body too much, I decided to let her come. Allowing it by biting down hard over her clit and releasing the blood I craved, I sucked it back hard and fast making her go wild as her whole body tensed.

She came so hard she nearly flew off the bed, and I quickly put a hand on her stomach to pin her down. Her screams were the sweetest song, and I closed my eyes as I relished both the sound and the taste of her. Then, before she could come down from her sexual high, I stood up and raised the bed to the right height so I could slam my cock inside her, giving her no time to adjust to it before I was hammering my length in her still quivering channel.

It was fucking spectacular!

In fact, I could barely wait for my own orgasm to erupt, being too turned on after licking her out. Gods, what this girl did to me, she had no idea how much she unravelled me! The control she had over me. I often wondered if I should be the one calling her 'mistress', as she most certainly fucking owned me!

However, the collar and leash idea was definitely going to come into play at some point during our sex life, and I knew I wasn't going to be the one fucking wearing it. Just the thought made me collar her throat with my palm, only applying enough pressure I knew she could take and one she would enjoy. The feel of her screams beneath my palm made my balls tighten up as if ready to explode. I kept trying to hold myself back for fear of hurting her, but it was difficult when her screams of pleasure spurred me on all the more.

I fucking adored how rough and hard she could take it, how rough and hard she enjoyed it. And as much as I enjoyed making love to her, I knew that deep down my nature could not have delivered the softer side of sex every time. Besides, the times that I had made love to her meant that the intimacy we shared would not have been as profound had we done it that way daily.

Besides, I was a fucking Vampire King, so one could barely expect anything else from me other than my dominant need to control and rule over my Chosen One when being fucked in my bed. These thoughts and the sight of her at my sexual mercy, and I could feel myself close to the edge as I continued my brutal, punishing pace inside her. Yet despite this, she still wrapped her legs around my hips and clung on, digging her heels into my backside as if anchoring herself to me. As if fearing any minute she may lose my cock.

Not. Fucking. Likely.

I wanted to live, sleep and breath with the thing constantly buried inside her!

"I'm going to come!" she shouted for the fourth time, as her screams and orgasms were starting to merge into one. Yet I knew that this would be her last, for I could not hold out any longer. But I wanted us to find our release together, and after ripping down her dress and releasing one of her perfect breasts, I gripped the nipple and squeezed hard, knowing that the bite of pain would tip her over the edge and the sound of her screams would do the same to me.

"AAAHHH!" *Fucking beautiful song!*

I threw my head back and roared out my release like a wild beast was breaking through. Then I felt the pulsating pleasure tear through me and into her, as once again she milked my cock of everything it had. She was screaming my name, and it sounded hoarse and rough, evidence that she had been beautifully used.

I landed over her, making sure to take my weight on my arms, so I wouldn't crush her but needing to take her lips all the same. And as I did, I whispered over them,

"I fucking love you, my perfect girl," and then I kissed her, and when her kiss wasn't given back in return I smiled, knowing that I had worn my girl out. Like many times before she had passed out on me. And like many times before, I grinned to myself.

I laughed before pulling back and gathering her in my arms. Then I created another scene that I wanted her to wake up to.

After that I chuckled to myself and said aloud,

"Now that is what I call mattress shopping."

CHAPTER SEVENTEEN

AMELIA

A BELL RINGS

When I opened my eyes, I knew that I hadn't really been asleep, because wasn't that kind of what I was already doing in this void to begin with. Unless my mind had just switched off for a time? Seriously, this was as confusing as time travel stories and all the loophole questions you found yourself asking. It would be at this point now that Pip would have been reciting about the time space continuum from the movie 'Back to the Future', which was one of her favourites. I remember her once watching it when my mum walked in, she had taken one look at it and strangely said, 'oh Hell, no!' and then walked straight back out again with no explanation. My Aunty Pip had admitted to weeing a little, she laughed that hard.

Well, whether it had been the illusion of falling asleep or not, opening my eyes now and finding myself encased in Lucius' arms was a dream in itself. Or should I say, a dream within a dream within a dream... or was that too many dreams? Can anyone say melty brain much or time paradox... wow, Doc Brown would have had a field day with this one!

Lucius was holding me tightly when I open my eyes, and when I saw that we were back in Lucius' bed in Blood Rock, I couldn't help but smile. I also couldn't help but wish that everything since the moment we left Lucius' castle hadn't happened the way it had. As, in reality, it had just been one long, endless nightmare... one that was far from over.

"Good morning, sweetheart," I heard next to me, finding him watching me and I knew now that he was creating this illusion after what I had said to him. That I had wished for just one normal day in what our life could be like, for what our future could possibly hold. This had been not long after we had made love in that field where I was free to dream of the day this was all over, and we could be free to live our lives however we wanted.

Well, now it looked as though he was trying to give me a taste of it, and I couldn't help but smile at the idea.

"I see you take my wishes quite literally," I said as a way of my own good morning and if Lucius had any say about it, then it would be better than good. Lucius just shrugged his shoulders before bolting out of bed, and I watched him get dressed, not exactly expecting this was how the 'normal day' was going to begin. I almost pouted at not getting more sex.

"Err, what are you doing?" I questioned, and after he pulled the dark red t-shirt down to join the dark grey denim jeans, he came back to the bed. He lent his weight on his hands after putting them to the mattress so he could lean in closer to me. Then he kissed my nose and told me the last thing I expected him to say.

"Time to go to work, sweetheart." He then winked at me and smirked when he saw my mouth drop in shock. I frowned in confusion before laughing nervously. But as he walked out of the door, I quickly called after him,

"Work for you or work for me?" I really didn't expect his reply to be,

"Both, as you work for me now!" he shouted back, something that finished on a chuckle.

"You cannot be serious," I muttered, and it was one he heard as I could still hear him laughing outside the room. So, I got up and walked into the closet, seeing as I was naked once more, and stopped dead at what I found. All the shelves were stripped bare, with only one outfit now hanging up ready for me, and there was no denying that Lucius both had a sense of humour and was clearly the horniest vampire in existence.

"I can't wear this!" I shrieked knowing he would hear me, and I heard his reply in my ear like a whisper,

"Then wear nothing... your new boss won't mind." I jumped and turned around only to find myself still alone and that's when I realised, Lucius intended to have some fun in this void, starting with that sexy outfit. I released a sigh and grabbed the damn thing, muttering about what human resources would say about this one.

"Oh, come on!" I complained when I quickly realised 'my new boss' hadn't given me any underwear, just a push up black bra that would make anyone look indecent in the workplace. As for the rest of the outfit, well that was just as indecent, if not even more so! I now wore the tightest black pencil skirt in existence, that had a long revealing slit up the back that would have shown my bare ass if I bent over. To this I had sheer black stockings with a seam up the back, and black stiletto shoes with that trademark red sole that screamed Louboutin.

As for the top, if you could call it that, it was a white shirt that only buttoned up to partly cover my breasts, meaning that thanks to the bra I was practically popping out of the shirt, one that I tucked into the high waistband of the skirt. A thick black belt was to be worn under my breasts and when I saw the black L in the centre, I looked up at the ceiling and muttered,

"Why not just make it a dog collar with a tag and a little bell so you can hear me coming." I looked down again and knew then that he had heard me as on top of the dresser was exactly that, a leather collar with an admittedly cute leather bow and a little silver bell dangling down from the middle. I picked it up and read the tag beneath the bell, it said,

'Naughty Kitten
Property of Lucius'

I burst out laughing and turned it over to read the other side.

'If lost please return immediately,
Her owner is worried.'

At this I couldn't help but smirk as it was sweet, cute and funny. I also knew he would never expect me to wear it in a million years, so I decided to surprise him and wear the damn thing. I gathered my hair up into a bun, adding to the fantasy he was creating, and walked back into the room expecting it to be the bedroom. However, I was wrong as the room had now changed again, this time into his office. There was also a very distinct difference as to what I remembered about the last time I had been in it, and that was a new desk that had been placed next to his, creating an L shape. He was also sat behind his, already with paperwork in front of him. He looked up from his desk when I entered and his gaze, holy shit, but I swear my girly parts fluttered at the sight. Talk about heated, it felt as if it had the power to burn me it was that hot. It was like someone had ignited two crimson pieces of coal.

He raked his burning gaze up the length of me, and I wouldn't have been surprised in that moment that by the time he got to the top, I would have been naked. He took his time as well, looking over every inch of me before he homed in on the collar. The grin he now wore could be classed in only one way… utterly sinful.

"Come here, *Pet,*" he said, emphasising the word 'Pet' for that very reason. I swallowed down my nerves as best I could because, despite all our times together, he still managed to intimidate me, especially with the way he was now undressing me with his dominant gaze.

As I approached, he stood up, and after moving back a little he nodded in front of him where he wanted me to be. So, I continued crossing the room, and only stopped when I was positioned in front of him. Then, being brave and showing some sass, I looked up at him, in what I hoped was a cute and innocent way, and said,

"Yes, boss?" His reaction was worth it as he groaned before biting his lip for a second, then he hissed,

"Fuck me, but I could come at just the sight of you." At this I grinned, and he reached up and tapped on my bell, saying,

"This was a nice touch I think, and good of you to recommend it, *My Pet.*" I smirked at that and replied,

"I think you will find it was less of a recommendation and more of a sarcastic comment." He grinned in return before shrugging his shoulders, feigning a tone of indifference when he said,

"That's up for interpterion, besides... *I like hearing you come.*" He added this last part on a sexual whisper and obviously one that had a double meaning. Then he growled,

"In fact, let's see what it sounds like again, should we?" Then before I could respond, he spun me around and pushed me down over his desk, now holding me there by a dominant hand to the back of my neck. My shocked cry soon turned into a moan as he started to trail his fingertips up the backs of my legs, continuing all the way to my ass thanks to the large slit up the back of the skirt. Then he leaned over my back and pulled my hair free, so it was now loose and spilling into his hand as he gathered it up in his fist. With me clearly at his mercy, he tugged my head back and told me,

"Oh yes, I am going to enjoy being the boss..." he paused so he could bite my ear before whispering on a growl of words,

"...my fuckable little kitten"

Then after that, it was precisely what he did... he fucked his new office 'kitten' on her first day of work, to the sounds of my screams and...

A little bell ringing.

CHAPTER EIGHTEEN

PARTNERSHIPS

"Your work awaits you, my dear," he said after our quickie over his desk. One that ended with him needing to gift me a new outfit as the last one didn't last long and was ripped off me in seconds, starting with utilising the rip in the back of the skirt… one that soon became a lot longer and ended at the waistband. Then he had peeled the edges back as if he was opening a pair of curtains to reveal my prized backside beneath. As least this was the way he made it feel, especially after paying special attention to it after kissing it, grabbing it and biting it, telling me how fuckable it looked.

I had frozen when he also added how one day soon, he was looking forward to taking yet another virginity from me, one of a different kind that had me squirming at the thought. Then he had leaned down and whispered,

"Don't worry, Pet, I will have you well trained and ready for it before then." Needless to say, I squirmed even more and silently questioned exactly what he meant by 'well trained'.

After I don't know how many orgasms and being held in his lap in his chair as I shuddered through the aftermath of them, he held me close and peppered the side of my face with gentle kisses. No doubt making up for my now sore ass cheeks that had met his palm during the act, that had admittedly made my orgasms as mind-blowing as ever.

A short time after this and I was grateful to find myself in a soft pair of jeans and loose-fitting navy top with white flowers, just like one I already owned and had obviously been plucked from his memories. It was then that I found an array of artefacts on my new desk, which included a gold belt buckle excavated in Pyongyang, North Korea during the Proto-Three Kingdoms period. There was also a Mycenaean stirrup jar from Ras Shamra, Syria, in 1400–1300 BC, and a 2nd century AD Sarmatian-Parthian gold necklace and amulet from the Black Sea region. All three got me excited, however I still asked,

"What is this?"

"Your new job," Lucius replied, nodding down to it all after leading me around to my side of the desk.

"Erm, not that I am complaining here but I thought we were just role playing?" I asked, making him say,

"Well, I'm certainly happy to make what we just did a morning routine when coming into the office," he said, making me give him a wry look as he retook his own seat, now making a point of moving a desk lamp out of the way so there was nothing obstructing his view of me.

"I don't remember you hiring me?" I said, making his lips twitch as he fought a smile.

"No? That's strange because I remember the interview process going quite well for you," he said with those perfect lips showing a knowing grin, one that was all bad boy, and spoke of exactly what he would have done to me during this interview of ours. In fact, I think I had just experienced a taste of it moments ago, and even I had to admit that I would have got the job... *bell or no bell.*

"So, this *is* one of those boss and employee fantasies of yours?" I said, making him comment,

"I think I just lived out that one, sweetheart, but it's one that I'm definitely happy and more than willing to live out every single day..."

"Oh, I bet," I muttered, making him smirk before he carried on.

"Yet despite how sexy it sounds and how sexy it clearly was only moments ago, this is actually what I had in mind for your future." At this, my mouth nearly dropped in shock as my voice turned high pitched.

"You want me to work for you, as in... for real?!" His lips twitched again as if he was greatly amused by the idea, before telling me,

"Sweetheart, I have no problem if you want to call me your boss, however, I had more of a partnership in mind."

"Okay, so you're gonna have to help me out with this one, honey, as I'm totally confused." His gaze softened when hearing me calling him 'honey', before he replied with a strange statement,

"I have a lot of money."

"Yeah, babe, you live in a castle and you collect Lamborghinis like normal people would collect holiday souvenirs. I kind of got the memo." He chuckled once before explaining what he'd meant.

"I wasn't bragging, sweetheart, I was merely trying to explain that with that wealth comes the ability to indulge in certain passions, one of those is acquiring artefacts... but then you will already know this after you broke into my vault," Lucius said reminding me of that night, and if there was ever a moment where I would claim a relationship do-over, it would have been deciding against breaking and entering into a vault owned by the man I also hoped one day to date.

But getting back to his 'indulgences'.

"You want me to be your antiques dealer?" I said, laughing as it suddenly came to me.

"Why not? You're more than qualified for the job, after all," was his serious response.

"Lucius, be serious," I said, making him look surprised.

"I think you will find, love, I am being serious."

"This is the job you want me to do?" I asked again as if this would help clear it up for me.

"I fail to see why this is such a hard idea to grasp. You love your work, that much is clear, but I can't give you that job as I don't live in London and due to my commitments here, I never will live there," he said, coming right out and saying what he refused to say back when he was trying to convince me to move in with him. Although, I think it was obvious we had come on far more in our relationship since those unsure days when I was still half expecting him to break up with me.

"I know this," I said in a quiet voice. So he reached across and took my hand in his before telling me,

"I would give you anything in my power to give you, you know this," he told me sincerely, and my gaze softened as I said again, this time in a tender tone,

"I know."

"So, this was the only thing that I could think of as a possible way of making you happy, with me, in Germany," Lucius admitted, and I had to say, that it warmed my heart to know that he cared so much about making me happy and understood what my job meant to me. He was so thoughtful, by trying to keep my dream job alive by giving me the same thing, yet still being with him when doing it. I found myself biting my fingers and grinning around them until eventually he couldn't take any more.

"Amelia, you either say something from that cute, adorable, and very *fuckable* mouth of yours, or it's going to find something else in it rather than your fingertips." I swallowed hard, and despite how appealing that idea was, I let my fingertip go so I could tell him,

"What if I was to get a job in Munich, and we were to live half the time in Transfusion, as I'm sure a museum would be hiring?" I asked as the idea came to me. However, he looked a little taken back, and I hated to say it, hurt by the idea.

"You don't want to work with me?"

"Lucius, it's not that, working in the same office as you, I mean come on... I really don't think we'd get much work done, do you?" At this he relaxed enough to grin.

"Besides, knowing me and seeing your sexy ass all day, I think I would probably break more of the artefacts than I would have the ability to restore them." At this, his grin grew bigger and definitely more cocky at being called sexy. But then he shrugged his shoulders and told me,

"How about I give you your own office, your own space to work in where we both do a normal working day and like most couples, see each other in the evenings and who knows, we might even get the occasional weekend off... you know, to take you Lamborghini shopping." I laughed at this and said,

"You're serious right now?" It was at this that he got up and walked over to me, before leaning down to tell me,

"I am *deadly serious.*" This ended with a kiss after tilting my head up and the moment he collared my throat with his large hand, I felt myself getting wet causing a breathy moan to escape in his mouth and in turn making him growl in arousal. Then when the kiss ended, he said,

"That felt like a yes to me, sweetheart." His cocky tone spoke of his victory and if I hadn't remembered what happened the last time I was in his office, then I would have been tempted to roll my eyes at him. But I thought about what he'd said and his offer. Sure, it wasn't exactly what I had in mind for my future career but then again, I knew being realistic about it, he was right. I couldn't exactly carry on with the job I had at the museum. Sure, it had been my dream to work there ever since I was sixteen but being with Lucius was more important than anything else in my life. And he was right, he had responsibilities in Germany, and it would have been selfish of me to expect him to move his entire life just for me. Because it wasn't just Lucius who would have been affected, but an entire kingdom he ruled.

Which meant that I would soon be a part of that kingdom also, and therefore I had to do what was right. Besides, this way he was still giving me a slice of what I love to do. I could research until my heart's content on the pieces that we could potentially purchase together. The idea was suddenly one that got me so excited and gave me hope for the future ahead, assuming we managed to get out of this current, Hellish mess first, of course. But right now, I pushed all thoughts of 'what ifs' to the back of my mind and allowed myself to get excited, to the point that I even found myself asking,

"And would we potentially, maybe, I really hope so, go on trips together to acquire these certain artefacts?" At this he grinned and ran a fingertip tenderly down my cheek as he said,

"Sweetheart, as long as you're not expecting me to sleep

in a tent and dig in the sand, then I will take you anywhere you want to go."

"Oh, you're good," I said, making him wink at me and reply,

"Yeah, I got that impression too when you were screaming my name and begging for more of my cock... *partner!"*

"I mean you're obviously a cocky bastard but you're a smooth cocky bastard... *partner!"* I added like he had done.

"Yeah, I know that too," he said over my lips before he kissed me again. I stood up and held out my hand ready to shake on it, making his lips twitch in amusement again as he looked down at my offering.

"Here's to our new partnership," I said, and this time he was no longer amused, but instead, he seemed enthralled by the idea. He took my hand and corrected in a way that sounded more like a promise...

"To the first of many."

CHAPTER NINETEEN

PERFECTION INTERRUPTED

A little time later and we found ourselves living our next slice of potential normality. We were back in our heart of the mountain and I had just made dinner, and considering this was all under Lucius' control in this void, it had been my famous chilli fries. However, as much as we pretended, the food wasn't real and as hungry as I felt, every swallow I made there was nothing that went down. But because neither of us wanted to kill the illusion we didn't address it.

We ended the night sat on the couch watching TV, and I couldn't help but notice that my Lego figure I had made him for his birthday was now as he said it would be. It was on a specially made stand, surrounded and kept safe by a glass box. Lucius soon noticed me staring at it because he whispered down to me,

"It is how the real one is kept."

"Really?" I asked, not even trying to hide how happy this made me.

"Yes, I had it made… *despite you leaving me.*" He said

this last part on a growl at the memory and it was one I wisely chose not to comment on, as I knew it was still a sore spot with Lucius. But then he surprised me by adding,

"Your father was certainly surprised by the sight of it."

"My father?! You mean he was here… I mean there… I mean wherever the real place is?" He laughed at that and said,

"Yes, I believe that time working together to try and find you was the only good thing to come out of your little, what we shall call, misguided adventure." Hearing this gave me even more hope.

"It was?"

"Let's just say that we came to an understanding and agreed on a point that mattered most to me," he said with a grin as if remembering it for himself.

"Which was?" I asked. I felt him pull me close from where he was sat behind me on the couch, before he told me,

"That you now belonged to me, as I had claimed you as my Queen." I smiled big and looked over my shoulder at him, before commenting dryly,

"Oh, I bet he just loved that." He laughed and said,

"There might have been an F word or two."

Not long after this and a bit more teasing on the fact my father had no choice but to deal with the idea that we were together, I lay back and snuggled further into his arms. We continued to watch TV and of course, he picked something he would know, and we had already seen. Which was the first episode of discovery, something that made me smile as it took me back to the first time we'd ever done this together. It also made me giggle to myself at the parts of the episode that were hazy, and he obviously hadn't remembered too well. However, the action scenes played out with surprising clarity making me tease him on the fact.

"I can see what bits you were focused on." He squeezed my sides playfully before whispering to me,

"I could play something else." Then suddenly the screen showed a very erotic image of a woman being fucked over a desk with her head thrown back in ecstasy as she came, screaming out in ecstasy.

"I think you'll find this one is being played out with a lot more clarity, for the sight is burned to my memories," Lucius whispered to me just as her neck was taut, muscles straining, and her dark hair fanned out around her. It took me a moment to realise what I was seeing, but the moment Lucius' name was released from her lips I recognised it. I suddenly bolted from his arms and stood in front of the TV with my arms out trying to block the image.

"Oh, my Gods! Turn it off, turn it off!" I shouted in my utter embarrassment, making Lucius burst out laughing, to the point where he found it hard to stop.

"What's the matter, sweetheart, surely you're not embarrassed by the sight?" he mocked in jest when he controlled himself enough.

"'Course I am not, now turn it off!" I demanded with a stomp of my foot, and he watched the action, making his lips twitch as if it was all so very amusing to him. Then he got off the couch and walked to me, tilting my head back so he could kiss me, and all the while the sounds of us making love echoed around the large open space.

"You are perfection, *my perfection,*" he told me before spinning me around, so I had no other option than to face the TV. I tried to turn my face away, but he collared my throat, which I was starting to think was his kink, then he used his thumb on the bottom of my chin which forced me to look. Then he whispered,

"Open your eyes, I want to share with you that perfection that I see… look how beautiful you are… fucking stunning as you take my cock so well… like fucking a goddess… this is my Heaven and I want to share it with you, *please.*" With that one word whispered at the end, then I could do little to deny him. Because it wasn't often that I heard it from him, and I would class as him bringing out the big guns. So, I did as he asked and opened my eyes, and it was like watching some virtual porn video from a headset, as he would look down seeing our connection for himself, the way his cock would disappear inside me, stretching me around his girth. Then he would go faster, and my moans would get louder, and louder, with my hands scratching at the wood of his desk, trying to find something there to hold onto.

There was no denying the erotic sight was turning me on, especially not when he snaked a hand down my body and discovered this for himself. He slipped his hand in the waistband of my jeans, before his fingers parted the soft folds of my sex and found me dripping with need.

Then he whispered behind me,

"*I've always wanted to fuck you standing up and facing a mirror so you could watch yourself getting my cock… looks like I found something better.*" I shuddered against him and he started to rid me of my clothes, for I don't know how many times in how many hours, I just knew it was a lot of sex in a short space of time. I was starting to think that my King missed me.

Then, when I was naked in his arms, still stood up and watching us both on the screen, he bent me over a little and reared up inside of me. I cried out at the same time the memory of me did and Lucius growled behind me, obviously enjoying the sound of echoed pleasure. After this he pulled my arms back so he could loop his arm through my bent elbows, using this as a way to hold me as he fucked me hard standing up. I came screaming his name, and the moment my legs were close to giving out, his other arm banded around my stomach, keeping me upright.

"Gods, just look at you, fucking perfect! And it is all mine! All mine to fuck when I desire, and by the Gods, woman, I fucking desire you, never another but you... *my fucking everything... my fucking world... now fall with me, for I want your release to be my own... COME NOW!*" he said, and his erotic words combined with the sound of us both coming on screen back in his office was all it took, that and the phenomenally large cock of his!

He held me even tighter, to the point I could barely breath out my release as I screamed, something that was drowned out by his animalistic roar behind me. Needless to say, that when we were finished, both on screen and off, I was gathered up in his arms, this time carried back to the couch instead of us both collapsing into his office chair.

It had been... *fucking perfection.*

After this sexual interlude, we went back to watching Discovery and snuggling on the couch, after he brought my clothes back to me of course... something I had to beg for much to his amusement, as he had been on a mission to keep me naked.

As for the episode, it continued on, but then a bit skipped suddenly to a place that had already played out. I turned ready to tease him about it. But when I found him asleep, I frowned, knowing this was strange as he rarely ever fell asleep before me. He must have been exhausted for this to happen and I thought it best to let him sleep in that case, knowing this whole experience must be taking its toll on his mind.

It also made me wonder how the screen continued to play it out, as if in his mind he was still dreaming it. But then my answer came when the image started to lose clarity. As first it started by blurring around the edges, and then people would disappear from the scene completely. I naively smiled to myself thinking that Lucius was trying to hold on to the image for as long as possible until it was obvious that heavy sleep was kicking in.

But then something more started to happen, after the screen became distorted altogether, losing all colour before turning to a grainy black and white image. At first it looked like an old photograph, but then that's when I sucked in a startled breath the moment I recognised the castle. I wondered if this was Lucius' memories when he was trying to get inside?

I squinted my eyes as I saw something in one of the windows, so as gently as I could, I got off the couch without waking him, and walked towards the TV. Then I crouched down a little trying to see in the distance and make out what it was. That's when I recognised the thing moving along the windowpane as numbers started to appear. It came to me that it was an image of me writing my message to Lucius in my blood. I looked down at my hand to see a large plaster on it now, one Lucius had envisioned to replace the blood-stained dirty piece of cloth I had used. I wondered if this was something in Lucius' memories too, but then I suddenly remembered back to that moment. I had looked down hoping to find him there and had been disappointed when coming up empty... no one had been down there. Which now made me question, how was this part of his memories?

I soon found out the answer and unfortunately, I did so

too late. A figure emerged from on the battlements on the other side of the castle in view of what I was doing at the window. Then, as if it was all being filmed by a camera, it zoomed in on the figure of the King, who was now waving a finger at me, telling me I was in trouble.

Then suddenly he jumped from the top of the castle and fell, making me suck in a breath as he landed with a thud in a broken heap on the floor. I couldn't understand what I had just witnessed, for whose memories were these? In fact, who was this King, as he may have been dressed like one, but it wasn't the same King that had spent his time chasing me around his nightmare world of horrors.

I had no answers and I was only left to watch as the vision continued to play out. The angle of the image panned out suddenly, showing the black and white picture of the castle once more. It was like watching a mixture of the two, an old flickering movie and an old black and white picture held up in front of the lens.

But I didn't dare take my eyes off that broken heap on the floor and at first, I thought my eyes were betraying me the second I saw a flicker of movement among the twisted limbs. But then it moved again and again and then unexpectedly, it was coming towards the screen, walking backwards like a crab but as if it was still trying to fix itself with every step. Doing so until it became that of a man once more. The figure twisted like an insect before finally it stood tall as this new unknown King was whole once more. After which he abruptly started to run and I in turn started to shift backwards, first falling on my ass and then scooting backwards the closer to the screen he got. In my panic, I started shaking my head, but my voice seemed trapped, unable to call for help. I couldn't speak, I couldn't call out, as I was too frozen with fear. Then this other King reached the lens and started to push himself through into Lucius' void. I knew then the reason was because Lucius was asleep and had lost control.

"Lucius," I whispered at first, but he didn't hear me, and I knew I had to make myself louder, the next time shouting his name,

"Lucius!" I turned to look back at him, barely allowing myself enough time to take my eyes from the frightening King, who now looked more like a zombie, as his face was decayed and hanging from his bones as if rotting to grey lifeless flesh. A dead King that started to drag himself into this world.

"Lucius, wake up!" I shouted again, now scooting backwards and scrambling to my feet before rushing over to him. Then I started shaking him, screaming down at him,

"Wake up, wake up, WAKE UP AND HELP ME!" I ended this in a scream the second I felt myself being grabbed from behind. A hand had shackled my ankle and yanked hard enough that I fell first into his lap and then onto the floor. The Wraith Master was using this broken dead King to try and drag me back to his prison of a void. I saw myself being pulled back further and further away from Lucius, and as I reached out a hand to him, I screamed,

"LUCIUS, SAVE ME!" I tried to kick out, but the action seemed useless, I ended up twisting round with my leg still painfully in the broken King's grasp, now seeing the back of him as we got closer and closer to the TV screen. Then I heard my saviour.

"Hey, Asshole!" I suddenly saw the figure turn around, someone who had just turned back into the Wraith Master. Then, just as his head looked up, I saw Lucius swinging something in his direction that could have been a mace. It was heavy enough and big enough that it sent the King flying back into the TV and instead of it smashing, Lucius created a portal at the last moment. This sucked him inside back to being a part of his own Hellish void. Then Lucius moved past me and quickly motioned his hand over it, sealing it up to prevent the Wraith Master from getting through again.

I lowered my face to the floor and tried to breathe. Then, when I felt hands on me, I screamed, the fear of him getting me again overwhelming my senses, until I felt myself being scooped up in a pair of strong arms and heard a voice I knew speaking in my ear.

"Ssshh, I've got you, you're safe now… safe in my arms." Lucius started trying to comfort me when I was clawing at him, in a desperate attempt to hold on and never let go. I wondered if it was the first time Lucius had ever seen me this scared, for the fear was currently making my whole body shake against him. Because, unlike Lucius, I had no power here and my biggest nightmare was the inability to be able to defend myself.

All of my father's doubts at being unable to match the supernaturals in his world when it came to a fight, had now rooted themselves as extra insecurities to be entwined into these new fears. The result had made me terrified in this place because I knew that the King's power was too overwhelming, and without Lucius here now as my saviour, I would be at the mercy of that King once more.

"I can't… I can't go back there… I just can't go back there, Lucius. Please keep me safe… please, I can't go back to that nightmare, I won't survive it," I said as the tears ran freely down my cheeks, and he cupped my face, now holding me to him. I was tucked into his lap with his knees up and his arms around me cocooning me in safety. Yet I still clung on, as any moment something could rip me from his clutches, from the protection of his arms.

"Come now, I have you, you are safe," Lucius said, after

giving me a moment to cry and no doubt finding it difficult to hear.

"But I wasn't… what happened, the King… he got through and…"

"I'm so sorry, Amelia. I must have fallen asleep, I must have given in," Lucius said in a pained way as if he had let me down and was chastising himself for it.

"Are you okay?" I asked, making him scoff as if my concern for him was solely misplaced as he obviously took the blame for this.

"As much as it fucking pains me to admit, being in the Fae realm, far from my own, and keeping up this alternative version of your void, it is taking it out of me," he said whilst gritting his teeth.

I hated seeing his struggles, but I knew it was more difficult for Lucius to admit it, as admitting weakness was not something that came easy to any King. I snuggled myself closer to him, burying my face in his neck and trying to slow my heartrate and the shudders that still shook my body from my tears. I so badly wanted to be strong for him but right now it was so difficult. Especially with the fear growing inside me like a sickness. Because I knew as well as Lucius did that there was only so long he could keep this up.

"What are we going to do?" I asked, my tone saying it all when I felt him kiss my head, before whispering against it,

"Keep holding on, Amelia, don't let go."

I wish I could have listened to him and done as he asked, but it was as if something inside me had changed and I knew it was after watching myself die. Because it made it more real, more of a possibility of it happening again. It often made me wonder why, when you were younger, you were so carefree that you would take more risks with your life, taking more chances to be adventurous. Whether it was cliff diving or jumping out of a plane, going on the highest rollercoasters, or speeding down the road on the back of a motorcycle. Whatever it was, you took more risks when you were younger, yet you had your entire life ahead of you. Why was that? Why was it that humans only grew cautious as they got older, for the fear that our lives would end sooner than we wanted them to? It was a backwards mentality for sure, but I could kind of understand it.

I, too, had gone through everything to get to this point with the view that I would survive it all. With the view that I could face things head on, using my intelligence and my knowledge of martial arts and weapons training. Gods, but even dumb fucking luck, like Lucius had said, had managed to aid me. But now that confidence had been tainted because I couldn't get it out of my mind how vulnerable I was in this place. That I was not as indestructible as I thought I was. That being the daughter of a Draven didn't necessarily mean that I could face anything and survive it. The power of Lucius' blood wasn't always going to save me.

I hated to feel weak and fragile and above all a simple mortal, but in that moment, I had never felt so scared of losing my life. In fact, I don't think that I had ever felt more connected to the human world, and right then, with just one look at the tears rolling down my face and me shaking like a leaf in Lucius' hold,

Well…

He knew it too.

CHAPTER TWENTY

IN PLAIN SIGHT

I felt so bad for Lucius, as you could see that he was struggling to hold on to his control over the void as time went on. I had even offered him my blood but then he reminded me that unless he drank the blood from my actual body, then it would only be symbolic, just as it had been in the mattress shop… admittedly not a sentence I ever thought my mind would form.

I had been about to ask why he didn't go back into the real world to do this but quickly stopped that train of thought when he said that he wasn't prepared to weaken me further by chancing it, as in his mind my body was already too fragile. Explaining how he hadn't had any success in getting me to keep down food, or much water for that matter. He told me that he believed this was down to the infection that was slowly travelling down my arm. However, I had just been happy it still kept away from my heart and from the looks of things, I wasn't the only one.

As for the rest of our time, this was spent together in a simpler setting with us both lying in a modest bed and wrapped in each other's arms. I had scolded him on trying to give me too much in the beginning, but he assured me he hadn't 'wasted' his power like I believed. It was just the time that was spent physically being there that had drained him, something that would have had the same effect had he not created such an elaborate void to protect me in.

But it broke my heart to see him looking so tired, and I felt so helpless, knowing I could do nothing to help him. Also knowing it was because he was trying to keep me safe didn't help with the guilt I felt. Yet, despite my guilt, I also saw it for what it was, and it filled me with so much pride. Because it was so heroic and beautiful, and his love for me filled me with so much joy, I found tears in my eyes as I looked at him. With the both of us lying on our sides, keeping that connection with our gaze. His hand rested by my hip with his fingers drawing lazy circles against my skin.

He was once again dressed as he once had been in the field, and I was now in comfy black sweatpants with a wide grey waist band and a big grey sweater that was warm and cosy. But despite this comfort, I still needed to point out the obvious.

"I think we need to talk about…" He stopped me by leaning into me and kissing the rest of that sentence from my lips.

"Don't go there, sweetheart," he told me gently and when I opened my mouth to say more, he swept on in there and deepened the kiss. Yet it was not enough to take away the question of inevitability, because we both knew what had to happen. At some point Lucius would have no choice but to go back in hopes of him discovering a way to break whatever this connection was. And we both knew what that also meant, he wouldn't just be leaving me, *he would be leaving me vulnerable.*

Of course, Lucius had tried to reassure me everything would be okay, but it was difficult after what I had been through when trapped inside this void without him. I just wished I had more control, but so far all I had managed to do was write four numbers in blood on a window. In fact, I hated this feeling of being so helpless, as I just wasn't used to it. I wasn't used to feeling weak or scared. And more than anything, I wanted to be strong for Lucius. I already knew that he didn't want to leave me, it was the very last thing he wanted to do, which was why he would be feeling guilty about it. But I just wasn't strong enough not to let my emotions show.

"It will be fine, sweetheart, I promise you," he said, making me lower my face so he wouldn't see the doubt plainly written all over it. Of course, he saw it anyway.

"You don't believe me?" he asked, lifting my chin up so he could gain my eyes.

"It's not that I don't believe you, I just don't know how it's going to work." This was when he ran the backs of his fingers down my cheek and long my neck before telling me,

"I have an idea, but you have to trust me that it will work," he said after putting his forehead to mine and cupping my cheek. To which I didn't answer him the way he wanted me to, but instead I gave him a tender look.

"You look so tired, honey," I whispered, framing his face with my hands and he leant his weight into my palm, a weight of both my life and his own was something I felt in that moment…

The weight of our future being the heaviest of all.

"I confess, I feel as if I could sleep for a week, but only if I had you by my side." I gave him a small smile in return wishing I could promise such a thing, yet once again, my face said it all.

"It will happen again, you need to believe in that," he said, gently reprimanding me, and I felt so guilty as I knew showing him how worried I was, wasn't exactly helping. But it was just so hard to fake an optimistic outlook. So, in the end, to give him something, I nodded, knowing I couldn't give him anymore.

But then the moment Lucius tensed in my arms I knew something was happening back in the real world and it only took a moment later before the dread washed over me as I too knew what it meant. Lucius would have no choice but to leave me, which also meant leaving me to the mercy of the mad King.

"I know that look and I won't let it happen," Lucius said as if reading my mind, or more like reading the look of alarm on my face, one that was easy to read in my body language alone, especially when every muscle seemed to tense all at once.

"So, this idea of yours, it doesn't by any chance include a tower that nobody can get to and me growing my hair so that you could climb up it when you come to recue me... does it?" I questioned, trying to make light of it with a joke. Lucius smirked and then tapped my nose telling me,

"There's the funny girl I love."

"Yeah, well let's just hope she's still here by the time you get back and not in one of those crazy Wraith cells... wait, what's that look for?" I asked, referring to the knowing grin on Lucius' face.

"You trust me, yes," he said, and it wasn't a question but more like a reaffirming statement, reminding me of all the reasons that I should.

"I'm almost afraid to say yes, but I do so, *yes.*" At this he looked touched, and gave me a warm look in return before telling me,

"My plan is to hide you in plain sight and in the very last place he would expect to find you." I held my breath, unable to breathe for a moment already fearing this plan before he had said it. Which was why I opened my mouth at the ready to call him crazy, something he stopped quickly when placing a finger to my lips.

"Just hear me out, okay, my power here is limited, and will last longer if I use what we already have of his world." Alright so with him saying it like that, then yeah, it kind of made sense.

Now all I had to do was kick my logical mind into gear and override the part that was controlled by fear. It was such a foreign concept for me, considering all the things that I had been through. Yet, every single one, my mind had viewed as more of a challenge and had accepted it as a do or die situation. I had simply acted and focused on the power of saving my own skin and what I needed to do to achieve that. I had never been totally overruled by fear before and have it freeze me helpless, making me useless to do anything more than to plead and beg to survive it. I'd always taken my survival into my own hands, relying on my own strength to get through it. But just knowing that Lucius was leaving me, and the King was out there somewhere looking for me, hunting for me, well, it was enough to have me feeling helpless once more.

Which was when I started to wonder something, knowing that the longer I had been trapped in the void, the worse this fear had grown. Something that in itself was understandable, yet despite this it still felt so out of character. Which was why I asked,

"Do you think this poison, this dark essence of the Wraith Master, do you think it could have anything to do with my fear?" I asked Lucius, making him raise a brow in surprise.

"What do you mean?"

"I mean the longer it's been inside me, the way it had spread, do you think it may have... I don't know, maybe had the power to make my fear spread, to make it grow and control my emotions?" I asked, almost praying that it did and I would get my backbone back as soon as this shit was over with!

"I don't know, but it is possible... why do you ask?"

"Because it doesn't feel like me. I mean, ask yourself, when have you really known me to be afraid of anything?" I asked him, and I could see for myself the cogs turning as he thought back.

"You make a good point there," he admitted, and I sighed in relief that I wasn't just grasping at straws and trying to make excuses for feeling and acting like a coward.

"I will enquire about it once the Oracle has been found," Lucius told me, obviously thinking that my theory bore weight.

"Do you think they found this Oracle of Light then?" Lucius pulled back a little and ran a frustrated hand through his hair, then turned back to me and said,

"Gods, but I fucking hope so!"

"But what if they haven't, or what if they did and she can't help... what if she doesn't know anything about Wraiths or..." it was at this point Lucius had hit his limit, and he proved this by hooking a hand behind my neck and pulling me to his lips as a way to reassure me. But it was also something else that I feared it to be... *his goodbye.*

And now it was time for mine, the one I never had the chance to tell him the last time I... *I died.*

"I need to tell you something, Lucius."

"If this is your, 'I love you and goodbye' speech, then no," he said firmly, and I released a sigh grabbing hold of the material at his chest and pulled him back to me, stopping him from turning away.,

"I know you don't want to hear this, but you got to say your goodbye and you may not know this, but I saw everything just before my heart stopped beating. I heard how much you loved me and how much you didn't want to let me go," I confessed, as the memories of it all were making my words come out as barely above a whisper. At this his eyes widened in shock, speechless that that I had witnessed all that had happened. I saw him swallow the hard lump of emotion down before closing his eyes as if the painful memory was replaying itself in his mind's eye.

So, like all of those times he had done it to me, I placed my fingertips to his chin, applied enough pressure to raise his face up and told him softly,

"*Lucius, look at me.*" Then I watched him open his beautiful grey blue eyes of steel, and seeing them so full of emotion, well it almost broke my heart all over again.

"You had your goodbye, now please let me have mine." At this, he finally conceded with a silent nod of his head before producing a bench for us to sit on in what could have been any empty park in the world. Then, taking my hand he sat us both down, and in turn I took a deep breath, about to tell him the hardest thing I had ever said in my entire life.

Every word of it the truth of my feelings...

"Ever since I met you, I had never wanted anything so much in all my life than to be yours. It pushed me to the verge of obsession and despite that day at the museum trying to fight it, my walls came crashing down the first time I saw you there."

"*Sweetheart,*" he said, taking my hand in his and kissing the back of it, his eyes never leaving my own as he took in every word.

"I knew you were meant to be mine, Lucius, I just knew it! And every second I spent with you after that only solidified the idea. I… I… just want you to know that despite everything that happened since that moment, all the craziness, the kidnappings, fighting rogues, witch's, the whole lot of them, I want you to know, I don't regret a single second of it, because even if it brought me only one moment like this with you, then it was all worth it."

"Amelia, Gods, please…" I ignored him and shifted closer so I could frame his face with my hands, before I told him in a desperate tender tone, needing him to understand my heart, *one he owned,*

"Because you are worth a thousand moments of pain and fear and fighting, for just a single one where I get to call you mine. So, if this is our last moment together, then I want you to know that my only regret is that I didn't get more."

"More," he whispered back in agreement, putting his forehead to mine as we shared this moment.

"I would never regret coming to Hell and back for you, my soul mate, keeper of my heart… I love you more today than I did yesterday, and I will love you more tomorrow than I do right now, for it will never stop growing. And if I am lucky enough that if I have to leave this world today, that I do so with the tiniest shred of my soul left… *for that will be enough to never forget how much I love you,"* I said with the tears streaming down my face and I wasn't the only one, as when Lucius crushed his lips to mine…

Our goodbye kiss tasted of both of our tears.

After our kiss had finished, one I knew would have deepened into something further had Lucius had enough energy left, it was time for his plan.

"I won't be gone long, I promise you," he said, again trying to reassure me. Then he pulled me into his body and kissed me gently, this time it was quick and fleeting because we both knew that given the chance, we would have made it into something more... anything to stay together just that little bit longer.

But he was being called back to reality and I had never been so scared for our future. So unsure... *So terrified.*

"I need to tell you, if the worst happens, everyone I love, Pip, Adam my aunties, my uncles, Ella, my friends... Gods, my parents... Lucius, please tell my parents that I love them and that I am sorry for everything I ever put them through," I said with fresh tears falling.

"It won't come to that, Amelia, I won't let it... but just for your peace of mind then I will promise you I will tell them," he said, making me nod in reply and instead of forming the words, most of which we both knew had been said, I found myself holding onto him as though my life depended on it... *Which it did.*

It also meant by the time I opened my eyes, I soon realised what Lucius had planned and I sucked in a frightened breath the moment I saw where I was.

"Lucius, I can't... I can't do this, I just can't!" I hissed, grabbing him to me in a desperate way and fearing I would never have the strength to let go. Because now I found myself in one of the same cages that the King and Wraith Master had imprisoned his warrior souls in.

"I will be masking this cell to make it look as if it is just another one of the wraiths trapped here," he told me.

"But what if he discovers me, what if he sees that it's not one of them. You only have so much power here and..." he quickly cut me off before he allowed fear to make me hysterical. He gripped the tops of my arms and said firmly,

"Hey, listen to me now, you are my girl... my brave girl, you're a Draven, Amelia Draven who never stays down. You never stop fighting, you never give up... you hear me?" I took in his words and kept a hold of them as if they gave me the strength I needed to do this. So, I nodded once, my gaze of determination telling him that I understood.

"Now, I will be as quick as I can, and I know how much power I have left before it will end," he told me.

"But how will I know how long that is?" I asked, knowing this would be important.

"I will leave you with a timer and if the worst happens and I do not get back here in time, then before the timer runs out, I want you to open the door and run," he said, and I swallowed hard at the idea.

"But..." he gripped me tighter, and said again in a desperate tone,

"I want you to run, Amelia, and I want you to keep running. Keep running for as long as possible and don't let him find you... promise me!" I released a deep breath and told him,

"I promise."

"That's my brave girl," he said, kissing my forehead.

"How will you find me if I do?" I asked, having a bad feeling about all of this.

"Now that I have been here, I am connected to you, so trust me when I say, I will find you. I promise, I will come back for you, Amelia, and I will find you... just stay strong... stay safe... *and continue to be brave for me,*" he whispered with his forehead to mine before kissing me sweetly one last time, and unfortunately having no choice but to leave me to my fate.

Leaving me to my fate after I watched the painful sight of him disappearing before me, mouthing silently five words,

"I love you, my Khuba."

CHAPTER TWENTY-ONE

LUCIUS

A KING'S DARK HEART

The moment I returned back to reality, I wanted to go back. I hated leaving her, but more than that, the struggle came from seeing how scared she was... she had been utterly terrified. And she had been right, pointing it out as strange herself, for it wasn't something I was used to seeing. No, for I had always admired and marvelled at the strength of her heart and mind. Yet this time, I knew it was different.

Their joint void had tapped into some deep-rooted fear inside her and I agreed that the longer the Wraith's dark essence was infecting her, that her fear would only get worse. Because just thinking back to the way that she had clung to me, not wanting to let me go, it had broken my heart to witness it. Even worse, knowing that I had no other choice but to let her go.

Yet, I had tried in vain to hide from her my own

weakness, for being in that void for as long I had done, well towards the end it had been pushing the limitations of my strength. I knew that it would have only been a matter of time when I would have been a useless entity and cast from the Wraith Master's void. So I knew how important this time was. I knew that everything relied on coming back here and discovering what could be done to get her out of that place. To break the connection.

So, without any other choice I had to leave her, which was undoubtedly one of the hardest things I'd ever had to do in my entire existence. But then when she had begun to tell me her goodbyes, at first, I didn't think I had the strength to listen. In fact, I had tried to stop her from doing so, before realising that I had no right. I had no right to deny her that privilege, no matter how much I hated the thought of her believing her need to say it. Her words, however, would stay with me forever and the love she had for me would keep me fighting until the very last breath I possessed. I would never stop fighting for her, but in order to do that, I first had to leave, and I fucking hated myself for it!

But the moment I had heard the voice in my head telling me to come back, I knew I had no choice, for our time was running out. I knew the second I opened my eyes and took a deep breath as the feeling nearly overwhelmed me after being away from reality for so long. Then after sitting up and shaking the dizziness from my mind, I looked straight down at my girl. I then hissed when I looked at her arm to see that the infection had spread even further.

"Fuck!" I hissed when it now looked to not only be further down her arm but now spreading back towards her heart, as if it had nowhere else to go.

"It is getting worse, my Lord," Carn'reau said before throwing me a wet cloth to clean myself with, first using it to scrub down my face and then unashamedly wiping where I had spilled my seed. Then instead of wasting anymore precious energy, for my girl needed it more, I got up from the bed and changed into a set of fresh clothes that had been provided for me. The dark grey tunic and trousers matched my deadly mood.

Because the moment I had opened my eyes, I had only wished to see one thing and that was this damn Oracle of Light. Meaning that the only words I wanted to hear out of anyone's mouth was that they'd found her and that she knew a way to save my girl.

Needless to say, my temperament was classed as both murderous and tense as I snapped,

"There had better be something else I want to hear, Carn'reau." He nodded and then wasted no time telling me,

"We found the Oracle."

"Thank the Gods," I uttered, closing my eyes for a second.

"Actually, ye kin thank three Scotsman fur that one," Trice McBain said as he walked inside the room, looking a little worse for wear than when he first started on his journey. Damn, but it looked as if he had been in a battle himself, telling me his journey and task had not been an easy one. I didn't even know how long it had been, as I had lost all sense of time in the void. The bitter taste of the Wraith Master, now in control once more, was one that threatened my demon to lose control. However, I knew I needed that strength, and he did too, so my demon stayed dormant... *for now.*

But my decision to hide Amelia there sat in my gut like a fucking poisonous lead weight, despite knowing it was the only choice I had. Yet hiding her in plain sight as one of his own still took a lot of power and my energy was waning. But it was the only one that I knew could last for any length of time, one that would soon dwindle down to nothing. I could already feel my hands starting to shake as I had split my mind into two places. And for what many considered in me as possessing the most powerful mind control, this was saying a lot. Hence the reason why I snapped,

"Have her brought to me at once!" Trice opened his mouth ready to say something that would have made my blood boil, however he took one look at me, and quickly realised something was different. And I hated to admit it, as nobody ever wanted to look weak in front of others, but I knew in that moment that was exactly what he saw. But, instead of homing in on it like a wild animal getting the scent of dying prey, he looked to Amelia's sleeping form and surmised quickly,

"Ye made it through." His shock was warranted, along with the wide eyes of Auberon, who had also joined us and looked as if he could barely believe that I had achieved this. As for Carn'reau, well, he knew all too well of my powers and had not been surprised.

"I'm trying to keep her safe, but time is not on our side," I gritted out through clenched teeth, and was just thankful it was a frustration Trice understood. "Have her brought here at once, I don't give a shit if she's tired or hungry or whatever the fuck else, I WANT HER HERE NOW!"

I never thought I would admit it but, in that moment, I was thankful that Trice had formed a connection with Amelia and therefore felt my sense of urgency, now being his own. As he walked past me to the door and roared out the same order to his brothers, now telling them of our urgency.

So, as I waited, I leant down to my girl, brushing back her hair with shaky fingers and whispering to her in hopes that she could hear me.

"We found her, sweetheart, by the Gods we found her.

Not long now and I will be back with you, stay strong and just hang on a little longer," I said hearing the waiver in my voice, knowing she wasn't the only one who needed to stay strong.

It was a strange feeling, as if my mind was being torn in two, when all I would have needed was just five minutes to break away from the void and replenish some of my energy in the real world. It was like needing to heal something that would have come easy to me naturally. But in the void, it wasn't my body that needed that healing, it was my mind... *a mind that desperately needed regenerating.*

As soon as I heard footsteps approaching, I kissed her forehead once before sitting back up, not trusting myself to stand. Vern entered first, then a woman behind him that was only seen by the halo of green foliage stuck in her hair. Gryph was then seen behind her, as if preventing her from running, or fearing that she would try, which told me that she had tried to once or twice before.

"I take it you're the reason I am here, rendering my life forfeit, for your disposal," spoke a haughty voice that almost had a regal hint to it, despite her words coming out rough and raw. It was as if it had been years since she had spoken a word to anyone. I felt my fingers curl into a fist before swallowing down the stream of profanities that I wanted to hurl her way. However, Vern stepped out of the way and showed me the result of her attack from the King's uncle.

She was blind.

It was in that moment I recognised her fear. Why she had the right to be so pissed off, for what did she owe us but nothing, least of all her life. Because her blindness was no doubt something that had been done to her before delivering what Haleth, this evil uncle, had believed at the time was the fatal blow. How she had survived, I had no knowledge but at a guess I would say it had something to do with the earth of this realm. One even I could tell she was connected to, even without all the green shit in her hair.

Speaking of which, she looked like a wild woman, half possessed by the forest. Slices in her skin had been wound with roots from a tree and moss was seen growing beneath, replacing her flesh. She wore a robe in a Grecian style, gathered at her shoulders in knots.

I wondered if this had been what she had been wearing when attacked? As it looked as if the forest had taken her body and healed it itself, breathing new life into the Oracle. For she looked near consumed by it, with vines, moss, grass, you name it, as the whole dress was covered in it. Maybe when she had fallen to the ground and bled into the soil, all she had needed to do was whisper some incantation to their Earth Goddess, asking her to heal her. Perhaps this is how she managed to hide all of these years, as I had been told that the Oracles of this realm were more like witches in my own.

As for healing, the only thing that hadn't been healed had been her eyes, as they had obviously been cut out of the sockets, an injury she had hidden with the headpiece she wore. Great massive antlers wrapped in vines gave it height, along with dried flowers entwined with ivy, sticks, twigs, and the Gods only knew what else. Because, at this point, I wouldn't have been surprised if some fucking woodland animal had popped his head up out of there. In fact, if my girl had seen her, there would no doubt have been a muttered joke or two whispered in my ear.

The finishing touch to this headpiece was the skull of some animal that was being used as part of a mask, covering over half her face. A dried blood-soaked strip of material was bound across the animal's skull where its eyes should have been, along with hers. Her pale white skin matched that of her hair, that looked more like matted wool hanging down either side of her face like dead albino snakes.

She was a wild woman to be sure, and no doubt the product of survival of the fittest, for it was clear she had embraced the land and used every part of it to maintain that survival. The King, Auberon, looked beyond shocked as if he couldn't believe he was looking at the same woman he once knew. As just the sight of her was playing out the tragedy of her life, one that no doubt had begun with a life of great privilege and status amongst his world.

But right then I cared little about her past or admittedly, all the wrong doings that had been done to her. No, right then all I cared about was the wrongdoings that had been done to my Chosen One. Meaning that I fucking prayed like never before that this strange creature before me now held the key to unlocking my girl from that prison void.

Which is why I told her,

"You have my word you will be protected, Oracle of Light." At this she looked towards the King and snapped,

"I am the light of nothing, for your uncle extinguished it. No, now you will call me Elswyth, for I am an elf of the forest, resurrected by the great Goddess Fjörgyn of the Earth." This was when I lost my patience snapping,

"I don't give a fuck what we call you, I only care for the life I want you to save." Then I looked down at my girl, knowing her gaze did the same.

"Ah a Chosen One to a Vampire King, some even say with the power to save us all... yes, I've heard of you." At this she surprised me, and I must have let it be known on my features as it made her smirk, something that was unnerving when not being able to see her eyes.

"I wasn't an Oracle for nothing and as the oldest entity in the room, I have seen my fair share of prophecies come and go." At this I wanted to point out that she may have been an Oracle, but she certainly wasn't fated with the sight enough to know that she would lose her eyes. Thankfully, I restrained myself just in time as I needed her to help me, not to piss her off enough to refuse.

"I may be blind from power, but it does not mean I cannot see and detect the disdain of your doubt in your mind, for you stink of it," she said, obviously reading my thoughts.

"Then if this is true you will also know that half of my mind is currently elsewhere trying to keep my Chosen One safe, and that…"

"Time is of the essence, yes I know, it always is," she said in an almost bold tone but if she hadn't held my Chosen One's life in her hands, then in that moment I would have got up and strangled her, shaky hands be damned. Instead, I was forced to admit,

"I need your help."

"But of course you do, in fact, I'm surprised it took you as long as it did to find the secrets I left for your father," she said looking to both Carn'reau and King Auberon, making me wonder how she knew who was here or not.

"I may be blind but I still have the gift of recognising auras. Unsurprisingly, vampire, yours is black, very much like the cloud of fear that is slowly consuming the entirety of your Chosen One." Needless to say, this made me growl for I cared little about the insult and more about what was happening to my girl.

"That's great, witch… this will then be the part where you tell me how the fuck I get rid of that fucking cloud and you do so quickly enough before it consumes her completely!" I snapped, making her chuckle,

"I like you, vampire, you have spirit… back when I was

an Oracle of this place, no one dared speak to me like you just did, it is quite refreshing."

"Well, I'll happily oblige in throwing all manner of insults and profanities your way as long as in payment you just tell me how to save my girl."

"The light of your soul, is something we all need and right now yours is the only one that's keeping her alive… in fact, it's what brought her back in the first place." On hearing this it surprised me, so much so that I didn't have it in me to throw back some sarcastic remark in return, I was too dumbfounded.

"The only reason I came here and prevented my creatures from ripping apart your three Barbarians, was when they spoke of the love you have for this girl. She is one I have been dreaming of for years, the light may have gone out but the Fates… well, the Fates never really want to shut up," she said, tapping her head amongst all the foliage that her skull was somewhere hidden inside.

"You've been dreaming of her, of this moment?" I asked desperate to know.

"I have, for the Eye of Janus does not only speak to you. For I was awakened long before your girl ever graced it with her touch and then became its new Guardian." Fuck! This was something I hadn't known, for if the Eye had chosen her as its new Guardian, then my girl had just placed an even bigger target on her back than I believed. It also made sense as to why the witch had wanted her, because it would have made any of their plans to take over my people before killing them impossible without use of the Eye. They needed someone to control the power of the Eye, something Amelia had undoubtedly proven she could do after using it to destroy the Harpies… something this estranged brother of mine, had lain witness to.

Fuck!

"You know then of what I saw, what the Eye of Janus showed me when I touched it?" I questioned knowing I only had this single opportunity to do so.

"I do, which is why I now put to you a choice. Save the girl and there's no guarantee you will save your people. But if you sacrifice the one you love, then the prophecy will be null, an empty void to fill with an unknown future. A future you will rewrite and one that will only be in the favour of your people, for to stop the infection, Tartarus needs what you stole from its own heart of darkness," she told me and to me it was not a choice, for I would have sacrificed everything for Amelia.

"I wish to save the girl, now tell me how," I said without a moment's thought and from the grin she gave me in return, it told me that she knew that this would be my choice, making me question why she even bothered to ask it in the first place. Had she simply been entitled to do so, by some connection to the Fates, bound by them and her duty. Making me wonder…

Had this been a fucking test of my faith?!

"Very well. The Wraith Master was once a King driven by greed and the need to consume as much land as he could. The realm of Hyperborea was once divided, and ruled by two brothers, Theron, and Phalaris. However, Hyperborea fell to ruin when King Theron set his sights on ruling that of his brother's half of the realm. This was after a great banquette was held and in witnessing that of his wife's attention on his brother Phalaris, Theron became enraged and jealous," she said, and as much as I knew parts of her story were no doubt important, I knew I didn't exactly have the time for them.

"Please tell me there is an end to this story," I snapped, making her smirk before she walked over to Amelia and the

Wraith, who was still lay beside her, still unconscious and being kept that way.

"A darkness took hold of his heart and he kept his wife locked away to prevent her leaving him, despite her bearing him two sons. Once his brother discovered this news, he set out with his vast army, one far greater than his brother in order to save the Queen who he had fallen in love with. He knew his brother had no hope of defeating him and planned to take control of the rest of the realm, this being for the good of the people. Then he planned to marry his brother's wife, making her his Queen instead. But it didn't happen this way."

"Of course, fucking not," I muttered wryly, as she picked up Amelia's arm and ran her finger down the line of infection.

"He made a deal with a dark entity, a devil in hiding that no one knows of. For it is said that those who discover its name will have the power to summon it. Then, when it is summoned, it will grant you a wish, yet the price is high, for it wants the light left in a person's heart. The last of what they love as a sacrifice. Only then does he grant them the power of the Wraith of Fire."

"Then how is something like that ever to be beaten?" I asked, gritting my teeth.

"It is simple, for this fire can be stolen," she said, making me suck in a breath, instantly putting my nerves on edge.

"And just how do you suppose I do something like that?!" I snapped, making her say,

"Who said anything about you stealing it." Then she looked down at Amelia's sleeping form and indicated just who she was referring to.

"Oh, no, no fucking way!" I barked back at her, before she pointed out,

"What choice do you have here, Vampire, besides, I told you to choose your fate, and this, I am afraid, is it."

"But what if I…"

"Only the one connected to the Wraith Master can steal his power. For his darkness is already inside her." I looked horror stricken at what she was saying, with my gaze going first to the Wraith and then to my girl.

"I cannot let her become like that, I couldn't do that to her," I told her, feeling as if it was now as hopeless as I fucking feared!

"But who is to say that she would?"

"What do you mean?" I asked, barely hanging on to any hope left, but it was enough to ask all the same.

"No one who had summoned this devil has done so with kindness in their heart. They do so for greed or driven by hatred. Their hearts are already black, and they do not fight what they are given. They embrace the darkness. I do not believe this describes your Chosen One."

"Fuck no!" I said, instantly making her grin.

"I didn't think so," she said pushing back some of Amelia's hair in a loving manner, the way a mother would to her child.

"Then there is hope… hope that she will beat the darkness when it is given to her… hope that she can control the Wraith's fire," she said, making me release a pained breath at the thought of what could potentially happen. But what fucking options did I have left!?

None.

This was it. This was all I had, and I fucking knew it!

So, with a heavy sigh I asked,

"What must she do?"

"She must do to him what he did to gain his darkness."

"And whit wis that?" This question came from Trice. She

looked to him as if knowing exactly which of the brothers that question had come from and said,

"He ate the heart of his wife and his two children."

"Bugger me!" Gryph hissed, and Vern the posh twat said,

"Oh dear, that's jolly unfortunate." Something I wisely chose to ignore.

"It is why in his own void he relives the Hell of his actions, that is, when he is not walking the earth as the ruler of souls he condemned to the same life as he," she added.

"Condemned how?" I asked, knowing this would no doubt be important.

"Once he had the power he needed, he knew as a Wraith Master to command an army that could not be killed also meant there was not a war that he could not win. So then, by sending his men into battle, one they had no hope of winning he knew once dead, he would have the power to resurrect them into his Wraiths."

"And with this great power, how is it he's not controlling all realms?" King Auberon asked.

"Because the deal he made with this devil was to grant him this one victory. After that, like the devil who granted him this darkness, he would only ever be able to rise after he was summoned. He may be a Wraith Master, but he is far from free."

"And Amelia, what will become of her if she manages to do as you suggest, does that mean she will be tied to that same fate?" I asked, needing to know before I put her through any of this.

"No, I do not believe so, for I think it will simply sever the tie to the devil's deal, for he didn't make it with her," she replied, making me snap,

"You *think*?!"

"Nothing in life is certain, Vampire, but you yourself

should know this better than anyone," she said making her point, and causing me to rake a shaky hand through my hair in frustration.

"So, this uncle of yours, this is how he'd managed to call upon this Wraith Master and use him against you?" I said looking to Auberon and Carn'reau, but it was once again this Elswyth who answered.

"Ah now, who said anything about the uncle?" The moment she said it she surprised everyone, making me growl at the implications of that. Of course, Trice said it first,

"The witch, sae that wis her plan a' alang, however she didnae expect Amelia tae be 'ere 'n' git caught in th' crossfire."

"And what needs to be done?" I demanded, knowing that there were other times we could discuss who was behind summoning the Wraith Master and now was not one of them.

However, it was at this point that Elswyth said something I was not expecting. Fuck, but no one in the room was expecting what the answer would be, and as for the consequences, then I had no idea of what they could be.

I only knew of the horror still left to come…

"She has to consume his heart."

CHAPTER TWENTY-TWO

AMELIA

AS THE BLOOD SAND FALLS

I knew I needed to stop watching as the sand fell but it was difficult, as with each black grain that slid down into the bottom tear shaped piece of the hourglass, it represented even more time slipping away. As for my timer of death, it was simple in its design, filled with black sand and encased in a simple wooden frame of three black carved pillars holding the glass in place. The whole thing was about the size of my foot, and it had appeared the moment Lucius had left. In truth, I don't know how long I had been staring at it, but I knew it was long enough when the sight of it started to blur.

Of course, it was better than the alternative, as the only other thing for me to look at was my haunting surroundings. However, after so long even I had to admit I was getting used to the sight of tortured souls. And I also had to admit that Lucius had been right hiding me in plain sight, as it had worked so far. Especially when I looked down at my own hand and found it was the same as all the other wraiths imprisoned.

But naturally, it was strange looking at yourself and seeing something different, and unsurprisingly at first it startled me enough that my back hit the back of the glass cage. This made it bang, which in turn made all the wraiths in front of me, raise their heads as one. I had muttered a whispered sorry that got no response in return. But, when Lucius had said that he would keep me hidden from view I had no idea his plan was to make me appear as one of them. Yes, granted, it was a genius plan and one I couldn't exactly complain about so far.

Yet I looked to the rest of the wraiths who took in the sight of me, and I could just tell that they knew I was the intruder. I was the one that had infiltrated their world of misery and the longer I remained in that cell, the more I couldn't help but feel sorry for them. I wished I had the power to release them, to help them gain some peace. Because there were thousands of them locked away in such a way, I knew this was only mirroring a truth. Because the King's void wasn't a real place, yet I knew deep down to the very core of me that this place existed somewhere else, and all of these souls were just waiting. Waiting for the day that someone was strong enough to defeat their master and release them.

In that moment I wished so much to have been strong enough to do that, and it made me wonder what would happen if I ever managed to take control of this void and release them, would it have a similar effect on the reality wherever they were kept?

At one point I had even tried talking to one, someone I had named Trevor. In my boredom, I had even created a back story for him, imagining him as someone who lived in his mother's basement just waiting for the day to meet a nice girl and be able to afford to move out. Poor Trevor. Of course, he could have also been some weirdo living in that basement after first killing his mother, burying her in the garden and spending the rest of his days pretending to be a girl online that was into cosplay and stalking famous people.

Yes, this unfortunately had been what had become of my stir-crazy mind. But then, after trying to communicate with Trevor, the old image of a soldier simply shook his head at me, either telling me he didn't understand or perhaps that he couldn't even speak. But then I also wondered if it was another reason, like could he be warning me silently that if I was heard, the King might come back.

So, I took it for the latter and remained silent just in case. I was left wondering whether this Oracle would ever be found and if they somehow managed to bring me back to life, would she be able to help me in this private quest of mine in freeing these poor souls?

"One thing at a time, Fae," I muttered to myself, barely a whisper heard. Besides, we already had so much going on, like discovering who this man was that was supposedly Lucius' other brother? And as for the witch, who seemed to be working for him, what was her purpose in all this, and was she the girl that I had seen with all that power? The girl that had been forced to watch her mother being burned at the stake?

Did her past have anything to do with my future?

There were still so many questions left unanswered that my brain actually hurt. But as time went on and as the sand continued to fall, those questions were soon left forgotten and replaced by panic, and I started to lose my nerve as every noise I heard had me questioning if the King was back.

Lucius had told me that if he wasn't back in time then I needed to get out of there and run. To run and to keep running until he found me. I had to trust in that plan, which was why, as the sand was getting closer and closer to the centre, ready to make its way down to the bottom, I knew my time was running out, I soon had to make a decision. Lucius had made the cell so it could be opened from the inside, yet I knew that as soon as the King arrived, he would no doubt have ideas. Like having the power to make this cell into whatever he chose it to be. A tomb buried in some crypt. Or a coffin about to be lowered into the earth. Hell, he could just seal it closed and fill it full of water if he chose to. He could have just stood there and watched as it drowned me or worse, fill it with fire and watch me burn.

Gods, but it was so fucking frightening, it was almost as if these horrific ideas were being planted in my mind! Because this was how I'd spent my last ten minutes, thinking over and over of all the ways that I could die. Which was why, the moment I knew I had to get out of there, I reached for the lock and found my hand was flickering in and out of being that of a wraith and human flesh.

I knew then that Lucius' power was coming to an end and if I didn't leave now, I may never get another chance to. But then I froze with my hand over the latch when I heard a strange clicking sound. I looked up to see that it was the wraith, the one I duped as Trevor and had been trying to speak to. Well, now he shook his head before nodding to one side, telling me something was coming. This was when my heart started pounding against my chest. Gods, but it was so powerful I almost worried that it could be heard by every being in the room.

My hands began to shake and as I lifted them up, I could see myself changing back with the rest of my body flickering between that of a terrified human girl, and a wraith just like everyone else. I knew then I had blown it. My time to escape had been lost. I knew it when I heard footsteps as they grew nearer and with it came the angry sounds of a frustrated King.

"Where is she?!" the King demanded before hammering what sounded like a fist against the glass doors in anger. A strange hissing sound came from those he terrorised with his anger.

"I know you have seen her, she cannot help you, for I am your master! Now tell me where the girl is!" It was at this moment I wondered whether they would give me away, yet as he came into view, I stood just like the rest of them after quickly hiding the hourglass behind my feet so he wouldn't see it. The long floating material that encased each wraith like a blanket of death was one I had seen doing the same to my very form.

I just prayed it continued to do so for a little longer.

"I cannot feel your white Knight in my realm, the intruder that wishes me dead. Well, he cannot save you now," the King said, taunting me just before I watched as he appeared, now walking down the centre aisle and straight past my cell. I was too afraid to even take a breath, just praying that he didn't look too closely my way, as I knew the moment the last of the sand fell, then I would turn back into the girl that was at his mercy.

I swallowed hard before releasing the faintest sigh of relief when he continued walking to the end of the room. I knew then that he would have nowhere to go other than to turn and start walking down another aisle. Then, as soon as he did, this would be my chance to escape. So, I waited until enough time had passed. However, because the King had stopped taunting me, it also meant that silence had swept over the space and it was deafening enough so when the last of the sand fell, the glass cracked.

I turned suddenly and looked as it fell and rolled along the floor. A slight sound that in everyday life would have gone by unnoticed but like the cracking of the twig in a silent forest, it echoed, sounding far louder than it ever should. I gasped before slapping my hands over my lips, feeling my own skin and making me look down to see I was back. Which meant only one thing, *there was no more hiding left for me.*

My time had run out.

And with it my last chance.

Because the King had heard me, I knew this when I heard his hurried footsteps getting closer. This, along with the sound of his madness. His sinister laughter was a sound that clawed along my nerves and this, combined with my panicked breathing and the pounding of my heart, well it made a potent song of death on the horizon. But I needed to know if I still had a chance, so I stepped forward a little and grabbed for the handle, but as soon as I did, it suddenly disappeared meaning I was locked inside.

"*No!*" I hissed in panic.

"Oh no you don't, not before I've had your heart!" the King taunted, his insanity a high-pitched cackle as though as he was playing his favourite game. It was in this moment that the wraiths surrounding me started to go crazy in their cages as if they were trying to help in some way. It was as if they were trying to mask where I was.

"I will find you, you cannot keep hiding from me!" Again the wraiths were trying to mask the sound of my panicked breaths, as if they somehow knew that I possessed the power to help them, yet if their King got to me first, then they too had lost all hope. I wondered how I knew this and whether they were projecting their feelings in some way. I picked up the hourglass thinking that I may be able to use it as a weapon of sorts, seeing as my option to run was taken from me. But then I watched as it started to change in my hand and the simple black frame suddenly became the haunting figure of a metal Reaper. A statue with its wings spread backwards holding the glass in place. Inside I saw something moving, so I looked closer to see a small figure of myself. I was desperately trying to swim up to the surface of the sand, one that was now filling with blood from the bottom. The sight of myself drowning in it as I lost the fight to escape had me crying out in horror. Then as I screamed, I dropped the hourglass. It smashed on the floor, instantly oozing blood, and when I looked down at my hands I saw that they too were covered. I wondered why when I felt the agonising pain in my shoulder making me scream. I looked to the side to see blood was gushing from the open wound. I knew then that King was doing this to me in order to find which cell I was in.

And with that scream… *now he knew.*

He had found me.

Suddenly he was right there in front of me, and I fell backwards trying to get further away from him.

"No! No! Please!" I don't know why I begged as it was clearly what he enjoyed hearing, if that sadistic grin was anything to go by. He pulled a knife from inside his jacket, and I could see that it was the same one that had been used to cut out the hearts of his family. It was still stained with his heinous crimes.

"I will have your heart, girl, and as soon as I do, this ends. You will die and I will live on, the eternal darkness was promised to me!" The King smiled, obviously now knowing for sure that this was the way to ensure his life continued.

"Come on, Lucius, please, please find me!" I shouted as the door started to open and the King raised up his blade ready to come down on me and like a coward, I lowered to the floor, slipping on my own blood, then I prayed to the only one that mattered.

"Lucius, I will always love you... wait... that's it," I muttered this last part looking up at him.

"If you consume my heart, it will be one full of love, not darkness, so ask yourself... what will that do to you and your army?" It was enough doubt planted that it made the King pause before he could strike. His frown told me he was questioning his actions and my words.

"My wife loved me, my children..." I had to think quickly.

"But how could they have loved you, if when you consumed their hearts, it darkened your soul?" I asked, continuing to feed him that doubt, that fear just like he had done with me. He started shaking his head as if he didn't want to believe me.

"What if they hated you, and it was that hatred you consumed, the hatred they felt for you is what created you... is what you are. That rage burning inside you and your bitterness is fuelling it..." I said over and over.

"Stop it!" he demanded but I continued on, feeling for the first-time power in the void. Because it wasn't a blade I needed to cut him deep, it the weapon of doubt... my own weapon of fear to use against him.

"Your wife was scared of you, wasn't she... she didn't love you...?"

"No, no, I'm not listening!" he said, shaking his head more violently now and using a hand to hit himself with as if trying to rid himself of the voices.

"She wished you'd died, she wanted the army to win so she may escape you! So she may take your children and run to the other side declaring her loyalty to your enemies!" I snapped, now getting back to my feet and with it, feeling my strength returning to me. He continued to shake his head as if my words weren't possible and then I knew I had to drive home one last doubt, the biggest of them all.

"In fact, ask yourself… wasn't she the one who contacted your enemy, the King she truly did love. The one who promised to save her from this terrible life and upon your death, make her his Queen!" I said, piecing this together from the things I had seen.

"I killed my brother! I threw him from the top of my castle after he witnessed what had become of my whore of a wife! I laughed at his grief, and when his blade ran straight through me, he knew then what I had become. Then I made him watch as his precious army fell one by one. My army of death could not be beaten!" the King said, gaining back some power by shocking me with the horror of it all.

"And now… YOU WILL BE NEXT!" he roared in his rage before erupting into his true form, and I staggered back at the terrifying sight. Then the flash of crimson I saw above me was the blade coming down to take yet another heart that hated him. I couldn't help but whisper his name as I only thought of him.

"Lucius."

Then, as it continued to come down upon me I closed my eyes and thought of nothing but his face, needing it to be the last thing I saw in my mind's eye.

The face of the man I loved.

However, an overwhelming sinking feeling washed over me and suddenly I felt as if I was falling. I opened my eyes to see that I was, as in literally falling through the floor! I fell fast enough that I managed to escape the blade as it came down above me. Because it made impact, but it was too late. I had made it through, and the floor that had once been beneath me had suddenly become glass above me.

The tip of the blade making it crack, one that should have been embedded into my heart. Then the glass shattered and the illusion above me vanished.

Then I continued to fall, until finally…

Love caught me.

CHAPTER TWENTY-THREE

LUCIUS

HEART OF DARKNESS CONSUMED

The moment she landed in my arms, I finally took a breath of relief. One so profound I had to force myself to remain standing. I had been longer in the real world than I wanted, and fucking cursed myself for it when I realised. Because once we had formed a plan, I knew that for it to work, I would need my strength to achieve the main aspect of it. This meant that I had no choice... *I needed some time to replenish what I had lost.*

Elswyth had told me the only way for the infection to stop was for her to be fed his heart. Of course, I had no problem with this, and I had quickly held out my hand demanding a blade from my general.

"Blade, now." The order had snapped out of me like a piece of high-tension wire had been cut. However, the Oracle smirked and told me there was far more to it than that, which her words would soon confirm.

"As heart-warming as it is to see how quickly you are willing to kill in order to save your Chosen One, there is a little more to it than that I am afraid," she said, making me grit my teeth and force out,

"Explain!"

"Cutting out his heart and force feeding it to her will not work for she will only reject it," Elswyth said, making me growl in frustration before snapping,

"Then what, I can't exactly choke her on it?!"

"It must be symbolically done at the same time it is done in the real world." The moment the meaning of her words fully penetrated, I closed my eyes and scrubbed my hand down my face. Then I pushed back all my hair with a little shake of my head, as if I was trying to take in what she was telling me.

"Tell me you're not seriously saying that you want me to go back to her in the void and force her to eat the heart of a King she is fucking terrified of?!" My anger was clear to see as I felt my eyes turn demonic.

"If you cannot get her to eat it in the void, then she will not accept it in the real world," Elswyth said laying it out in black and white, and fucking crimson, as there was nothing left for me to say but hiss a curse.

"Fuck!"

"The King gained his powers by consuming the hearts of those he loved and in doing so, he also sacrificed the lives and souls of his people. She is infected with that darkness that clings to her and it has locked her mind to his. The only way to defeat that darkness is by consuming it herself," Elswyth said again, hammering home my reality… *I had no other choices here.*

"And whit will it mak' her?" Trice asked, and I growled.

"I don't give a shit what it will make her, as long as she

survives, anything after that is a problem we will face once she is awake and breathing!" I snapped, already making up my mind.

"You dinnae give a shit whit it wull dae tae her!?" he bellowed and if I'd had the strength, I would have choked him whilst giving him my answer!

"Like I said, it is a problem I will face when it happens, but I would rather have a problem to deal with when she is back to the land of the fucking living, than have no problem to face and being left with a body to bury... now do you fucking get me, shifter!" I growled, and as painful as my words were to say, let alone think, they were strong enough to get the point across.

Because it was true, there was a risk of what it could do to Amelia, but it was a risk I was willing to take in order to save her life, for that was all that mattered in this moment. Which was why I knew that I would have to have enough strength, so that when I went back into their void, I could fight. So, I could find this fucking King and cut out the bastard's heart myself! This, unfortunately, before forcing my Chosen One to eat it.

Fuck!

Gods give me fucking strength to do this.

And speaking about strength, by the time I got back into her void, I cursed myself because I knew her time had already come to an end. So, I did the only thing that I knew I could do, not wanting to waste a second or play my hand too soon to the Wraith Master by letting him know something demonic was coming for him.

So, I had positioned myself in a place beneath her and dissolved the floor so she would slip through and I could catch her. Which was precisely what I did and from the look of things, just in fucking time!

"Lucius!" My name came from her lips like a prayer had been answered and I held her to me, cradling her head and absorbing every breath her body made. Amelia had never been the type to be over-emotional, as no matter what she went through, she simply accepted it and moved on with such determination, it often left me astounded at her strength. Yet, being here in this place and knowing what I now knew of the Wraith, of the infection and their connection, it all made sense. As Amelia had been right, the longer she was locked to this place, the more her fear would consume her.

Which was why I knew it was pushing her to her limits. Something I would soon be adding to and boy, didn't I just feel like the bastard for doing it. But for now, I held her to me, and gave her the time she needed to calm down. I don't think I had seen her cry so much in such a short space of time. Her fear was nearly overwhelming. A fear that on anyone else would have left me feeling hungry but coming from her, it only left me feeling sickened and angry that anyone had made her feel this way.

Oh, but I was going to enjoy killing the sick bastard, wanting first to ram that crown he didn't deserve up his ass! However, making Amelia eat his heart was something I knew was going to be harder than Elswyth had said.

But I wasn't about to fuck this up and after hearing the reasons why, I now knew how important it was for Amelia's mind to watch as the King died at my hand. So she then could feel empowered enough to take back control and she could beat the darkness when she would have to consume it.

And, well, if she didn't enjoy the sight of me ripping his heart out for her and gifting it to her on a platter, then I knew who fucking would! I just wished I had been the one forced to eat it as I would have pulled up a chair and tucked right in without a moment's hesitation. But Amelia was not like me, as the taste of flesh didn't exactly come natural to her. And consuming the blood of your Chosen One was not like consuming the blood of anyone else. As it was not the blood she had a thirst for, it was the connection it created. It was having our souls entwined by the Fates themselves, and drinking from each other was more like drinking from an elixir of that love. Something that tasted as if it had been sent from Heaven, despite the Hell in which I was born.

It was the purity of our connection that tasted so sweet.

This I could attest to, as I had tasted enough blood in my time to know that nothing tasted like Amelia's, *nothing even came close.*

"I am here, I'm here now," I told her, knowing how close she had come to being taken and I was just thankful that I had been able to keep my promise, despite how close it had come. But now I was back and this time I felt strong. This time I knew what was needed to be done to put an end to this once and for all.

And end it would, for that was my fucking vow!

"Did you find her, the Oracle?!" she asked me desperately once she'd got control of her emotions.

"I did," I answered, instantly wanting to ease her worry, and her sigh of relief was one I felt down to her bones as her body relaxed into me. In fact, her relief was so pliable I couldn't help but feel guilty knowing that I would soon have to take it away again, when I had no choice but to confess exactly how we were to beat this. Unfortunately, it came sooner than I hoped.

"And did she say there was a way, did she tell you what we needed to do?" she asked in a rush of questions, and had I not felt the weight of what needed to be done resting on my shoulders, I would have laughed at her eager curiosity peeking through. Not that I could blame her, for she wanted this to be over just as much as I did.

"There is a way," I told her softly.

"Oh, thank the Gods," she replied in a breathy release of words. Again, the guilt rode me hard.

"I...I..." I found my words failing me, wondering how the hell I was supposed to tell her what needed to be done, just praying she didn't ask me about the possible consequences that could transpire from what we were about to do.

"What is it, oh God... it's something awful, isn't it?" she said assuming as much.

"I'm not going to lie, Amelia, this is not going to be easy for you," I confessed, making her beautiful eyes widen, a reaction that was only the beginning.

"What is it, what do I have to do, Lucius, *tell me?"* she begged.

"Something needs to happen simultaneously in this void and in reality," I said, starting with the easy stuff like a fucking coward!

"Okay..." she said, shaking her head as if she didn't understand what was so bad.

"I will have Trice at the ready and when I give him the word, he will kill the Wraith Master that lies next to you and at the same time, I will kill the King, and then we will both remove his heart at the same time and..." I winced, swallowing hard as if the words wouldn't come out, making me look away. My reaction was enough to tell her the rest.

"And? oh God no, please... please don't tell me what I think you're going to say," she said, making every muscle in my body tense, forcing me to look back at her. I cupped a hand to her cheek, trying to offer her some comfort through my touch. Then like many times before, I used my thumb to raise her chin, so she was looking at me. Then I promised her,

"I will be with you, it will be alright Amelia... I will be with you... you won't be doing this alone," I said, and before she could back out, I took her hand knowing we didn't any time left to talk about it. This was it. This was what was happening. I admit that I was pleased when she allowed me to lead her from this blank void of a room I had created, because Elswyth had told me where the King would be.

I had to go back to the start.

Back to where this darkness had truly begun.

But as soon as the door I produced opened and she saw what was beyond it, she froze, creating a tension on my arm as she tried to pull back. The fear there in her eyes broke my heart.

"Come, Amelia, trust me... trust me, my love, this is the only way," I told her as soothingly as I could, making my voice gentle and coaxing. Thankfully, she allowed me to get her moving once more, but I dare not let go of her arm, fearing she would bolt and run from me this time. So, with my grip unyielding, I walked her into the room and across the threshold, back into the King's past.

The grand banqueting hall no doubt remained very similar to how it had been that day, other than the line of wraiths that stood along the walls, dressed as servants. I very much doubted that the King had wanted an audience as he slaughtered his family and ate their hearts the day it happened.

The cry of horror behind me made me tense and grit my teeth. As, despite all the horror I myself had caused throughout my years, even I was sickened by the sight. Three slumped forms lay folded at the waist as if asleep on the table. It was why I pulled Amelia closer to me, demanding,

"Eyes on me, sweetheart." I allowed that authoritative tone to emphasise my words, being thankful when it worked. As it was effective enough so that she tore her eyes from the painful sight of the family's death. Then I told her softly,

"They're sleeping." Of course, it was a lie, one she might have known. But it was also one she wanted to believe in, so she nodded, allowing that lie to weave around her tender heart. I tightened my hand around hers and led her further into the room, making sure she was behind me and protected. I had the power to make the family disappear, which would have made it easier for my girl to witness. However, I was hoping to use the sight to my advantage, for what Amelia was about to do, as I hoped revenge and justice would be enough of a driving force, enough motivation for her to accomplish this difficult task that faced her.

It was certainly going to make killing him a more pleasurable experience for me, knowing what the sick bastard had done. My only regret was not being able to take the time to make him suffer.

Speaking of which, at the head of the table playing out his own part, was the mad King acting now as if we hadn't even interrupted his gluttonous consumption, which was his punishment to relive over and over again.

"This was how I found him before," Amelia informed me quietly, making me growl, one I directed solely at the cause of my Chosen One's pain. I fucking hated, utterly despised and was sickened by the fact that Amelia had been forced to witness this alone the first time. I just wanted to get my girl home, knowing now how close she was to needing that slither of normality. One I had taken her away from since the very first moment I stepped into that museum. A guilt I quickly rid myself of, as now was not the time to be thinking of the past. As it was hardly helpful in that moment, and neither was

punishing myself for it, because no doubt there would be enough for that later, especially with what I had planned after this.

What I knew I had to do.

But first, came the horror.

"Time for this nightmare to come to an end, my love," I told her the moment I felt her hands creeping onto my shirt, with the front of her plastered against my back as if I was her shield. The one that could stop anything from harming her. I had to say, the feeling only spurred me on, and I was arrogant enough to know how much I enjoyed the idea of being her hero.

However, I couldn't cut out his heart with her clinging to my back, so I turned and forced her gaze to mine and away from the King, who still didn't seem to notice us standing there. No, he just continued his gluttonous crimes, cutting into the hearts on his silver platter as if every bite was drawing him closer to his ultimate goal. What he didn't know was that with every bite he took, he ultimately lost a piece of his soul to an eternity of darkness. One I just prayed didn't have the power to turn my girl the same way. My only hope was that she would be the light that had the power to defeat the hatred and rage that had created the Wraith Master in the first place.

"Stay here, this won't take me long." Her fearful eyes reminded me of a doll, one so breakable and so fragile, I almost expected her skin to start cracking. Fuck me... I didn't know what it was about her but whenever I saw her unshed tears veil over her sapphire blue eyes, by the Gods, it was stunning and had the power to render me breathless! I kissed her forehead and turned my back on her, ignoring the swell of guilt when I had to pull away from the hold she had on me, feeling the tightness of my shirt before it loosened, knowing that her grip hadn't been enough to keep me there.

After all, I was a vampire on a mission, and wanted to get the fuck on with it so I could get her the Hell out of this fucked up memory! So I stormed my way over to the King, cutting the distance with long, determined strides. Then, as soon as I was close enough, I picked up the discarded dagger that I knew he had used on his family and just as his face looked up at me, there was the tiniest spark of sadness there as he said,

"Is it time… time to finally die?"

"Yes, and let me show you how a real King does it!" I thundered before grabbing his hair, wrenching his head back and pinning him to the chair. Then I looked up and shouted,

"NOW TRICE!" Then I stabbed the dagger into his chest, being sure not to pierce his heart in case I needed it still beating when I ripped it from his chest. His eyes widened as if shocked, before they left mine to look down at his own dagger sticking out of his chest. I wondered in that brief moment if his own wife had done the same thing, that shocked expression as if never believing it could be true. But then something unexpected happened, and it started when I called Amelia over.

"Come here, my Khuba," I said, hating the way she stood there trembling. So, I held my hand out to her and assured her,

"It's alright, I'm here and we're in this together." And then, because I didn't want to voice it too loud but still wanted her to know my meaning, I silently mouthed, *'be brave'*.

At this she nodded, and, in that moment, I had never been more fucking proud of her. But I needed that connection, so when she put her hand in mine, I pulled her to me, knowing that the hardest part was yet to come, *for both of us.*

I turned back to the King, ready to cut his beating heart from his chest when he started laughing. His madness consumed him, but then he started whispering a word and blood gurgled in the back of his throat before being pushed up his throat. I didn't quite catch what he had said, so I leaned in closer, and that was when I had my answer as to who had sent him. Something, I didn't think to care about, because I thought it would make no difference.

However, I was wrong.

It made all the difference in the world. As the name he uttered was one I thought I had forgotten. One I had not heard uttered in over 2000 years. One that now made me feel as though that blade was in my own fucking chest and my heart was about to get ripped out.

"The witch, Dalene, she is coming for you."

The name of the witch was none other than…

My wife.

CHAPTER TWENTY-FOUR

CHOKED HEARTS

N o.

No, it couldn't be.

I just couldn't fucking believe it! First, I questioned whether he had the ability to access my own mind and he had somehow plucked that ancient name from the oldest of my memories, one buried under a 2000-year-old layer of dust. My reaction was instant as I staggered back a step and Amelia didn't miss it.

"Lucius, what is it… what's wrong?" I shook my head, telling her no… but from my mouth came silence as I was trying to form the words, but nothing would come to me. It was impossible.

It was fucking impossible!

I could barely believe it, no… this was a trick. A way of disarming me, it must have been. There was no way she could have survived all of this time. It wasn't possible, despite the things I remembered seeing. The things I questioned, even when I walked the Earth as nothing more than a mortal man!

I scrubbed a hand down my face and I was forced to

disregard the panic in Amelia's tone as she asked me if I was alright. Instead, I ignored her completely, stepping back up to the King. Then I grabbed a fistful of his tunic, coming close to rattle him to death, never mind the blade sticking out of his tainted flesh.

"Where did you hear that name, tell me!? TELL ME!" I roared down at him, feeling Amelia flinch next to me. Yet the mad King merely laughed, before he looked up at me and smiled through blood-soaked teeth, and then he confirmed,

"She is your witch, then she comes to claim what you took from her. THEY WILL CLAIM IT ALL, MY WIFE; YOUR W...!" at this instant I took over, and I knew I had to silence him before he finished that sentence! My anger couldn't take anymore as I ripped the blade from his chest, before stabbing it through the other side cutting off his words. Then I sickeningly started to carve his heart from his cavity, ignoring the gagging sounds from Amelia, as she no doubt vomited, making me wonder if she did in the real world. However, my rage could not be contained as it was all consuming. A small voice in the back of my mind told me that I should have made him suffer, made it last longer so I have might have gained more information from him. However, in my selfishness I couldn't chance Amelia hearing exactly who she was.

Who the witch was to me.

Because it was one thing keeping a brother from her, but a wife... I knew she would never forgive that. I then thought of what happened the last time she had mistakenly heard something, she had felt betrayed enough to run from me and managed to hide herself away for months. I might have been able to chance that in the human realm, but down here, no fucking way I could chance it! So, I hid my shame by ending the King's life, making it so that he never said one more word to my Chosen One.

So that he never fucking mentioned that cursed name to me again!

I didn't realise, but by the time I had finished carving his heart out in my rage, I had changed. meaning that when I reached inside his chest to grab the still beating heart and rip it out, I did so with the hand of a Titan. Then shamefully, I dropped that heart on a nearby plate and in my demonic tone growled,

"Eat it!"

It was the first time I chanced to look at her since my discovery and now she looked utterly petrified, and it had nothing to do with the dead King but all to do with me. I was ashamed. I had now become the stuff of her nightmares, yet I couldn't be tamed, not this time. She started to shake her head, tears streaming down her face.

"I can't," she told me, and my demon bellowed, needing this to be over,

"Eat it!" She flinched, and I hated it, hated knowing I was fucking this up! Knowing it was because of what I was, the heart of my guilt had turned me into this monster version of myself. It was the same fear I had seen from her in my throne room that day. When she had been forced to play the part of my sex slave and I had been forced to play the master.

But this was no stage, and this was no play we were forced to act out. It was just me and her surrounded by death, surrounded by the evidence of how dangerous love was. What it pushed dark hearts to do.

"Lucius, please." Fuck me, but those eyes. Those stunning blue eyes, now swimming in her tears. I tried to hold on to their beauty for as long as I could but as the tears continued to spill over them, now knowing that I was the

cause, well it only managed to fuel my rage even more. So, I tore my gaze away, and pulled out a chair, something that echoed along the floor as I felt it splinter under my grip.

"Sit down and eat the fucking heart!" I said, more dangerously this time, which was when she started shaking her head and taking her first step away from me. I growled, knowing time was of the essence here and this was the only way to save her. So, I stormed over to her the second she turned around now running from me. But she had no chance as I caught her in no time, easily snagging her around the waist. Then I lifted her up, hoisting her feet off the floor so she could run no more. She started to fight in my hold, but it was useless. Like this, my true demon form, I was taller, wider, and much stronger than she was used to. This meant she was tiny in my hold, almost like a child struggling against an adult. and yet the guilt continued to fuel my demon.

I only released her when I sat her down in the chair in front of the heart, one now overflowing with blood. Then I placed my gauntleted hand on her shoulder and held her there.

"Let me go, I can't do this!" She started to cry, and I felt like an utter bastard. Since hearing that name, something inside of me had snapped and trying to get the man I was back was proving difficult. Then when she didn't move, I picked up the heart and held it to her mouth knowing I had to be cruel to be kind. Then I told her,

"If you do not eat it, I will force it down you, do you understand, little one?" I almost didn't recognise the voice that came out of my lips, for the threat came straight from my demon, one that didn't understand why she was being so stubborn. But then as if she was blind to what I was, she raised her hand and covered my demonic one, the one I'd covered in a gauntlet to no longer expose her to the chance of being tainted by Tartarus. Her touch was enough to reach my demon's softer side. And as for her eyes, well they belonged to the man she fell in love with. The Vampire who owned her heart.

Her tears were mine.

"Please, please, there must be another way, please, *my Khuba.*" When she whispered this last part, it shattered me. Suddenly the hand she was holding was that of a man, because she had managed to push back the demon in me and bring forth the man that was worthy of the claim. I swallowed down the bile that threatened to burn like acid as I deserved. I then leaned down, kissed the top of her head and told her,

"Forgive me, forgive me, my love."

Then, because it was for her own good, I took control over her mind and manipulated it for the first time and now...

Taking complete control.

CHAPTER TWENTY-FIVE

AMELIA

A SLICE OF NORMALITY

I woke up in my bed, and as it was a sight my mind was so used to seeing, my subconscious found nothing startling. My room was as it always was, a few clothes thrown casually around, some littering the floor after missing my hamper. A small dresser and two bedside cabinets, where there was a pot of face cream I hadn't bothered to screw the lid on properly. A glass of water half consumed, and my glasses that I reached for in my lazy state, missing the first-time round and knocking a book to the floor. I picked it up remembering I hadn't read it in a while. In fact, it was a distinct book that had been helping me with some recently discovered Minoan pottery that had been brought into the museum. The pots themselves are used as a tool for dating the Minoan civilization.

I then spotted my dress from last night on the floor at the

side of my bed, as if it had just been peeled from my skin. Now why that memory stuck I don't know. Then I spotted only one of my black heels, and a quick look back to the bedside table and I noticed that on the glass was red lipstick marks, that's when I knew it was the morning after the gala.

This made me grin, because memories of what happened that night started to infiltrate the fog a few glasses of champagne had managed to create. Meaning, that when I got up, I wasn't surprised to find myself naked, and a ridiculously girly and happy giggle escaped.

Yet, instead of going to the bathroom and spending an hour getting ready in case what I found outside that door was actually true, I spent ten minutes in the bathroom. Ten minutes which consisted of feverishly brushing my teeth after having a large morning pee, spraying myself with a bit of scented moisturiser, so I wouldn't make it obvious with full on perfume. Then I brushed and tied my hair up into a messy bun, hoping it looked natural. I also found a cute pair of candy striped pyjama shorts, that made a little bit of sneaky bum cheek pop out and say hello. I then added a white vest top to match, that had 'Sweet as Candy' written across my breasts in a rainbow of pastel colours. They were what I hoped were understated sexy in a 'I'm not trying too hard' but still, mainly cute type of way.

Once done, I then walked out, pushing my glasses up my nose and stepping into my girly, yet geeky living room, and it was there, after a quick scan of my very small living space, that I found the glorious sight of who I hoped pretty soon to be able to call my boyfriend.

"Lucius." His name came out in a breathy whisper. He had stayed the night. Lucius, Vampire King, who I thought hated me, had stayed the freakin' night in my little flat in Twickenham, and after nothing short of taking me on a date!

I confess to being surprised at finding him there at the gala after not seeing him for so long. And I most definitely didn't want to admit to him, but he had given me the night of my life. We had left the gala early, and he'd taken me to dinner, and then we talked about so much, it seemed as if he had wanted to know everything about me. He had asked about my work, my social life or lack of, and then he apologised for not seeing me sooner. I had been gobsmacked. Gone was that cocky arrogant asshole that I'd last seen in his club in Germany, and in his place was a kind and generous, gentleman. One that was playfully flirty and a total contradiction to what he had been the last time I'd seen him. Of course, a lot of the past still weighed heavily on my mind, but I couldn't help but be pulled in by him. But I just couldn't help it, not when he had been so warm and even affectionate towards me. Not when he constantly seemed to be touching me whenever he could, making my belly flip every time or my heart race.

In fact, I hadn't had a chance against him, because you didn't just fall in love with a man, being that on the verge of obsession, and ever really forget them, no matter how much you tried. The memory of what could have been, would plague you every now and again and it was simple things really that made you remember them. They reminded you that they were somewhere in the world and you would question whether they ever thought of you. You always tried to move on, but you knew deep down that if they ever came back into your life, it would be near impossible for it not to affect you. And as for Lucius, who I had always considered my Chosen One and soul mate, I had always held on to this dream version of Lucius. Dreamed of the real one that I would have found that night when turning up to his club all that time ago.

Now that dream had come true.

Which meant I would have been a fool to ignore it, and seeing him there at my kitchen counter like he belonged in my space, I was just glad that I hadn't listened to my doubts. I was just glad I'd listened to my heart.

"Good morning, beautiful," he said, making me blush, still not used to being complemented by such a man. Because if there was one being in this room that held all the beauty, well, it didn't feel like me but more like the Adonis of perfection now stood looking at me, wearing a pair of jeans and nothing else. I briefly wondered where he had got those jeans from, considering last night, he had been wearing a suit, but something strange clouded over my mind at that point and when I looked back at him, he wasn't wearing jeans at all but the suit trousers he had been wearing.

I must have got it wrong.

Yes, that was it.

"You alright, sweetheart?" he asked, with a raised eyebrow questioning my actions as I took my glasses off and cleaned them quickly.

"Yeah, sorry, I'm not really a morning person as you can tell," I said with a nervous laugh at myself.

"Well, you were sleeping pretty heavily, and I know after last night you must have needed it," he said, winking and making me giggle. Because that's when last night came to me in flashes like an erotic film was being played out. A compilation of the best bits playing now like some pornographic best-selling blockbuster. I could even hear the commentary, that well known movie voice telling the audience how many times this man had made me come. It was definitely Oscar worthy.

"My Amelia, I do believe you're blushing," he commented, making me blush even more. His gaze homed in on it in seconds before he said,

"Come here and tell me why." Gods, but why did his voice have to be so luring like that, I felt as if I was being caught by some magical net before being pulled in. I wracked my sex infused brain, trying to think of something witty to say in return, but unfortunately my girly bits wouldn't quite help me out and they fluttered, reminding me of what he did to me last night. Because after first making love to me and taking my virginity in the most beautiful of ways, he healed me and then took me the way he wanted to take me. And Gods almighty, it was raw and rough and so fucking beautiful!

"Oh no, if I come anywhere near you, you will corrupt me again," I decided to say when it finally came to me, especially when he raised his brow again, only this time it was done in a cocky way. But before my eyes could track his movements, he was suddenly stood in front of me and taking my face in his hands.

"Word of warning, pet, when a Vampire has claimed his Fated mate, then nothing comes between them, *not even you,*" he said in a stern yet gentle way, and before I could question it, he kissed me. Not just a slight morning kiss as a way of greeting his girlfriend for the first time in the day, but a full, deep and passionate kiss that had the power to curl my toes. My hands instantly circled his wrists just so I could hold on as he had tipped my head back and brought me up to my tiptoes. Gods, but my heart felt like it was going to explode! Both from the amazing kiss and from hearing his admission of claiming me as his own.

It felt like a dream.

"Mmm, sweet indeed. Now, come and sit down, for you must be hungry," he said, after ending the kiss in a soft and sweet way by continuing to lay gentle kisses along my lips, jawline and down my neck. This was before he led me over to sit at the counter, and suddenly that's when I realised there was something cooking on the stove. I remember my eyes widening in surprise,

"Don't tell me you cook?" I asked, and I didn't know why I was so shocked.

"I'm over 2000 years old, sweetheart, and I don't exactly keep a housekeeper on retainer," he said after leaving me stood next to the stool so he could go back to attending the food.

"Meaning?"

"Meaning, I clean my own shit and I cook my own food," Lucius said, being as blunt as ever and making me burst out laughing, and he grinned because of it, one that reached his eyes as he took in the sight of my hilarity.

"I'm glad to hear that no one wipes your ass for you, handsome," I said, teasing him about the use of his words and surprising even myself for being so brave. But when he rolled his eyes, that grin of his didn't hide anything.

"Now, sit your ass down, my funny girl." I gave him a salute and took a seat on one of my kitchen stools in front of my little island. The smell was a bit strange, and it made me wonder if it was steak. If it was, then it was a bit of a weird breakfast choice... although, what did I know, he was a Vampire after all.

"You know, my favourite cereal is in the cupboard, I would have been happy with that to save you all the trouble."

"What can I say, I wanted to impress," he said shrugging his shoulders, then raising his spatula in the air slightly before turning back around and using it in the frying pan to flip something over.

"So, what culinary delights do you have in store for me?" I asked, making him turn back to me and tap his nose, telling me,

"Oh no, this is a surprise, you'll have to guess."

"Well, aren't you just the international man of mystery, and speaking of international, you never got round to telling me how long you're going to be in town for?" I asked, feeling a little bit embarrassed and possibly coming off a little bit needy but hoping not. I mean I had just lost my virginity to who I considered my Chosen One and after what he had confessed to feeling for me last night, then I was kind of hoping he was planning to stick around. He smirked at me and I felt my cheeks heat before I started backtracking,

"I mean it's not massively important at this point, I just wanted to know how many dates I had on the horizon before you have to go back to Germany, is all." At this, his smirk turned into a full out grin, and after leaving whatever was cooking in the frying pan, he came over to my side of the counter. He turned my stool around, so my back was to the kitchen. Then his large hands rested on the countertop, caging me in.

I swear I stopped breathing. Actually, I know I did because he leant his face closer and whispered,

"Breathe for me, Pet." I released my breath that very moment, feeling my cheeks flame in embarrassment because he knew what having him so close did to me. Gods, but I needed to get a hold of myself. But then when he stepped into me, all my little pep talk went flying out the damn window. Especially when he gave me a pointed look, one that looked both authoritative and demanding. It was also one he gave me because I obviously wasn't giving him what he wanted and after not understanding what this was, his gaze softened before his hands took over. He gripped my knees and applied a little pressure before they were opening for him to step into the space created. I sucked in startled breath when I felt the hard length of his erection against me, a sound

he obviously enjoyed hearing, if his knowing grin was anything to go by.

Then he framed my neck and used both of his thumbs to tilt my chin back, so I had no choice but to look up at him. It was a possessive and dominating hold, and once again it was one that had my girly bits fluttering with just the memory. His hand circled my throat, holding me in his grasp as he thrust his cock inside me over and over again. I had thought I was going to come undone and literally unravel at the seams, it had felt so good.

But right now, he was clearly focused on what I had asked him, wanting to know how long he would be here.

"Tell me, sweetheart, is this you asking me not to go or you telling me that you would miss me if I did?" he asked me in a cocky, knowing tone that, coming from anyone else would have been annoying, given the circumstances. But on him it was more playful, and sexy in that self-assured way, as if he would have been happy if this had been the case, so I shrugged my shoulders playfully in return and teased,

"Maybe or maybe I just want to know how much birth control I'm going to need." Then I winked at him and he burst out laughing. It was a beautiful sight, and one I couldn't help but sigh at in a dreamy way. One he missed due to laughing, thank the Gods.

"Thankfully, none, because nothing could stop me from spilling my seed deep inside you, this sweet, no longer virginal pussy that I own and is mine for the taking." His sexual words drew out another spasm and I found myself whispering,

"Then maybe you should, you know, *take what's yours again.*" At this he growled playfully, before whispering over my lips,

"My Kitten, you tease me," and then he kissed me and

once again. It was long and deep, and by the Gods it had me ready to throw myself at him. But then he pulled away and told me,

"Not until after you've eaten, sweetheart, after all, I need you to keep up your strength, especially for what I have planned." I shivered in response to this, and his knowing grin was all primal, in a sexual satisfied way as if he knew what he did to me, and of course, after last night, he most certainly did... *intimately.*

"As for how long I'm here, well, then long enough to convince you to come back with me," he said in an assured way that told me he wasn't joking.

"You want me to come to Germany, to Munich... *with you?*" I questioned, surprised, as he started to walk away back to his side of the kitchen and back to his culinary delight.

"Of course, I do, what did you think, that I would be content with a one-night stand?" he asked incredulously.

"I... well... honestly, I didn't know what to think... this is all still kinda new to me here, Lucius," I admitted, letting my head fall forward into my hands before pushing back my hair and raising my eyes to look at him again.

"I understand that, sweetheart, but thinking that I would come back here, claim my Chosen One, and then walk away again would be the total opposite of what you should be thinking." I swallowed hard and shook my head a little as if asking myself if all of this was real. Like I had said, it felt too much like a dream, too much like a living fantasy and everything I'd ever wanted now coming true.

"So, you've claimed me?" I asked, my voice nearly high-pitched and strained, telling him that I could barely believe this was happening, despite his playful words earlier.

"Yes, sweetheart, I have claimed you, my Chosen One,

and something I should have done a long time ago." Hearing him admit that was like a soothing balm caressing my soul, one that had been fragile for so long since his words of dismissal that night. But then with just one sentence, it was as if it instantly healed all the damage made and I didn't give a damn at how weak that made me!

But again, I had to be sure,

"And you want me to move to Germany with you?" I had to ask again.

"Correct me if I'm wrong, but you were ready to do it the first time you came to me." I blushed at this, embarrassed by the thought. Because what had I been thinking nearly throwing myself at him like that?

"I see I hurt you deeply, Amelia, and I can only apologise and spend my lifetime making it up to you. Starting with you moving to Germany with me," he said, and I found the tips of my fingers in my mouth, biting on them as was my habit. He homed in on the action and a soft tender look overtook his features, making him instantly look years younger.

"What about my parents?" I asked.

"I'll admit they're not bad, but I think they might get in the way moving in with us," he joked, making me give him one of those looks, that said 'ha ha', silently.

"Look, Amelia, I'm crass, and say shit as it is, as I see it, and now will be no different when I tell you I don't give a fuck about your parents. I don't give a fuck what anyone thinks, all I care about is how you think and how you feel." Well, this I couldn't argue with, and neither did I want to.

"Now, enough of this talk, we will figure out the details as we have all the time on our hands to do so. But first I want you to eat your breakfast and every last bite at that."

"Every last bite, eh?" I asked as he put the plate in front

of me and leaned over it, to get closer and whisper like my life depended on it...

"Every. Last. Bite."

CHAPTER
TWENTY-SIX

GOODBYES HURT

"*Every. Last. Bite.*"

"That's a large plateful of food, Lucius," I informed him, as it was.

"Every last bite or you will hurt my feelings," he said, making me laugh. I took the fork he held out to me, before stabbing it into a piece of meat and then I popped into my mouth, purposely chewing on it to show him that I was eating. His grin was one I couldn't decipher this time.

It was chewy and had a strange flavour to it, but then when I started to think too much about it, scrunching up my nose in distaste, it started to change. It began to taste and feel more like steak, one that had been dipped in garlic butter, the way I liked it.

"You know this is pretty good, actually." Lucius gave me a strange look and then told me,

"It's good for you."

"Yeah, steak is good for me?" I asked with the disbelief evident in my tone.

"Need to get all the iron in you as possible," he replied with a wink.

"Ha, I knew there was an ulterior motive." At this, the look he gave me was a strange one, as if he almost looked guilty about something but he quickly shook it off. But then a thunderclap sounded, making me jump before suddenly the Heavens opened as they say. The rain started to lash against my window as storm clouds overhead made it slightly darker.

"Well, I guess that means a day inside then," I commented, trying to break the ice that had frosted over our conversation suddenly. But then, the moment I didn't have anything in my mouth, he nodded down at the plate prompting me to eat once more. Wow, he really did want to take care of me, and obviously feeding me was all part and parcel of that. Was that who I was right now, his human pet to take care of? Because I had to say the thought made me want to giggle. But then, knowing Lucius, if I admitted as much, the conversation would return into us going shopping to buy a sexy collar and lead. Mmm, could be fun. This thought had me squirming on my stool, now asking myself if Lucius had managed to create a sexual monster in me.

"So, tell me, what would be your ideal date from start to finish?" I asked, again trying to get the conversation started once more, as Lucius had gone quiet and strangely, he seemed unsure.

"I wonder why you ask that now?" he said in a knowing tone that made me laugh.

"Hey, I'm not fishing for you to take me out on a date, but you've got to entertain me some way, considering I'm going to have my mouth full…" he groaned at this as if remembering last night, and I laughed before amending,

"…with your delicious food, of course. If I'm going to be busy then talk to me," I asked, and again he watched me put another piece of steak in my mouth and I had never known anyone so interested in watching me eat before. He even seemed to relax with the more I ate and kept his gaze on my plate.

"Well, knowing what I know of you, I could tell you what your perfect date would be," he said as if he was so sure he would be right. As if we had been together for months and already knew each other intimately.

"Oh really, now this is going to be interesting, considering you don't actually know that much about me," I said speaking my thoughts, and he laughed at this in a way that made it seem as though it was a ridiculous notion.

"Trust me, sweetheart, I know a lot more about you than you think," he said as if this should have been obvious, which it clearly wasn't considering this was only really the second time I had spoken to him for longer than just a few words. Our other times were fleeting moments at best, and not ones I considered as conversation. So that begged the question... just how did he know me if this was true?

"You seem very confident," I said before popping in another piece of meat.

"Alright, I will play by telling you what your perfect date would be, one that would probably consist of a museum or a manor house somewhere in the country. Perhaps a picnic, but one only if it included sprinkled Donuts with bacon on top, and then in the evening we would probably finish off lying on that couch over there after just consuming your famous chilli fries. Then I would run my fingers through your hair as we watched your favourite show, perhaps Star Trek Discovery, or maybe even a Star Wars' movie... so, how am I doing so far, sweetheart?" he asked when my mouth literally fell open in shock.

"How… how could you… do you know all of that, how could you possibly?" I stammered out the question.

"I will tell you after you've finished your breakfast," he told me nodding down to it again.

"Seriously, you expect me to eat after all of that, I mean that was a bombshell and a half!"

"Amelia, please just eat it for me, okay?" he pleaded softly, and I found this was a weird reaction. It also made me look down at my plate, seeing that my steak looked a lot bloodier than I was used to eating. I found myself shaking my head the moment that bloody steak turned more well cooked and instead of being covered in blood was soaked in garlic butter again. The doubt then cleared from my head as if it had never been there.

"Seriously, have you been stalking me?" I asked before he nodded down to my plate, and I rolled my eyes but took another bite seeing that I'd consumed over half of it at least.

"I will tell you this much, I have known you are my Chosen One for as long as you have and despite not handling things well back in Germany, the fact of who you were to me and the importance of that, did not change," he said, making me frown in confusion.

"And what does that mean exactly?" I asked then took another bite.

"It means I take care of what I own," he stated firmly and looked down to the plate as if this held some hidden meaning.

"Of what you own?" I asked shocked, and again he nodded down to my plate and I took another bite which seemed to appease him.

"You are mine, Amelia, you always have been, and I protect what is mine, always. But it goes further than that, it would be like protecting my own heart. I need you to be safe and I confess that when I wasn't here to do it myself, I would have others make sure that your safety was a priority," he said stunning me to silence for the moment, as it was like hearing the confessions of a guilty man who didn't think he had done anything wrong.

"I can't believe I'm hearing this," I muttered breaking the silence.

"Eat and I will tell you more," he said.

"Seriously, what is it with you and getting me to…?" I stopped the moment his stern look told me to.

"I'm telling you to eat because I care for your well-being, and the importance of keeping you safe is all that matters to me… I need to keep you…" he paused a moment as if struggling with his words and I wanted to question why. But then he continued, after swallowing hard as if pushing down a memory. No, not just pushing it down, but forcing it down as if it was a physical entity.

"*Fit and healthy…* I want you staying strong, and I also know that mortals definitely need food for that to happen," he said, making me realise how seriously he was taking this feeding me. His need to care for me obviously ran deep within him and as much as it made me feel cherished, it also made me question all the things that he wasn't saying. But then I took another bite and I saw that he reacted physically to this, instantly relaxing his shoulders, and taking a breath. It made me realise that this wasn't just something serious to him, it was something he needed, and I couldn't help but question why?

He seemed to get be getting more agitated as the time went on, more concerned and worried, as if this was all stressing him out. I had only three pieces left, and I tested it by putting my fork down and telling him,

"I'm full and I honestly could not eat another…"

"*No!*" he snapped suddenly. But then he saw the way I

flinched and forced himself to take a breath before trying again.

"Please, Amelia, please… just do this for me and finish."

"Why is this so important to you, it's just three little bites, Lucius?" I saw him tense again and release a frustrated sigh. It was as if he was trying to think of a reason and I almost felt sorry for him. I expected him to get angry again but instead he took a different approach.

"What if I told you that this was something symbolic to my memories and meant a great deal to me, would you finish it then?" he asked, making me sit back a little as if startled.

"Symbolic how?" He ran a hand through his hair, that I was starting to come to recognise as a frustrated gesture, and one my own father used to do on many occasions when dealing with my mother.

"There was a time long ago the Fates once told me, they prophesised the life of my Chosen One would become mine once more, even after my mistakes that I had made, if she would eat the first meal I had ever made anyone," he said shocking me.

"This is the first meal you've ever made anyone?" I asked, feeling touched by this confession and he nodded. So, I grabbed the plate and pulled it back to me. Then to prove how much I cared about him and his feelings, I started eating once more, something that definitely made him happy. He even breathed a sigh of relief and one I could now understand, considering what he just told me about the Fates.

This was symbolic and clearly meant the start of something new and I wanted to give him that.

"Thank you, you have no idea how much this means to me," he said, as he started walking over to my side just as I had one last bite to consume.

"I'm glad it means so much to you, even if I do find it a

little confusing. But hey, it was a good steak, maybe next time you wanna put something with it, like a potato or something other than just meat... I know you're clearly a carnivore, but still." At this he laughed, and he took my fork off me which held the last piece. Then he held it out for me to take, and his eyes focused solely on that last piece as it disappeared in my mouth. Then his intense gaze didn't leave me as he watched me chew it, and then when I swallowed it, he released a held breath and closed his eyes as if some unknown emotion was washing over him.

"Ta da, mission accomplished, and symbolic gesture made. Now maybe a cup of... wait, Lucius, I feel ..." I never finished that as the world started to spin and then Lucius stepped up to me. He caught me before I fell off the stool, and pulled me close to him before picking me up. He then held me to him, with not a single ounce of panic in his eyes, as if he knew what was happening. As if he'd had a hand in it.

I knew I was right the moment he whispered,

"I know, sweetheart, just hold on, it will all be over soon I promise, just hold on for me."

"You... you did this...?" I whispered back making him nod, telling me that yes, he had. But I didn't understand what it was exactly and was about to ask what he was talking about when suddenly my head fell back, and my eyes closed. Then I started to feel sick to my stomach with the food just lying there like lead that had been thrown into an empty well. And all the while his voice echoed around me trying to soothe me.

"Just hold on... just hold on, Amelia... *hold on to me."* He knew what was happening and I opened my mouth again to try and ask him, but nothing came out. Then suddenly this world started to fade away, as if it had all been make believe. I knew that even without opening my eyes and seeing it for myself what this had all been. That's when I started to realise as the memory started flooding back to me,

It had all been a lie.

"Lies." The one and only word I managed to get out, and this time he wasn't telling me to hold on, he was whispering something else to me.

"I'm sorry, I'm so sorry, sweetheart... I had no choice." The guilt was easy to hear in those words as he meant it, but it was too late. Because suddenly I found myself plunged back into the reality of my life. And it wasn't some cute fairy tale ending. It wasn't waking up one day and realising the man I had loved all these years suddenly loved me back. It wasn't my perfect night at the gala or my perfect morning... it had all been make believe. An elaborate ruse, a slice of a fantasy I got to live through, and my price paid...

The heart of darkness I had consumed.

I knew that the moment I opened my eyes and saw the empty bloody plate on a table I recognised. I got up out of the chair and staggered backwards, seeing for myself Lucius as he reached out for me, and I screamed,

"Don't touch me!"

Gods, I hated how hurt he looked, but in that moment, no one was more hurt than I was. He had lied and manipulated me into eating that heart, and the logical part of me told me that he had no choice. I knew that even before he started telling me,

"I had no choice, Amelia... please, please believe me, love, I had no choice as we were running out of time and..." I held up a hand to stop him before that hand went to my mouth and that's when I felt it. That's when I felt the change start to happen and the warmth curl inside my belly replacing the sickness that had once been there.

"Amelia, what's happening, tell me, tell me what's

wrong!?" he asked but, in that moment, I couldn't answer him as I felt the change wash over me. I knew then, that very moment, the possibility of what would happen to me after I'd eaten that heart. One so full of hatred and darkness, consumed by a bitter greed. Because my thoughts of why he had done what he had done were true. Those insecurities I decided to play on while being trapped in the cell with him, were real.

I looked at my hands and I saw the lines on my palm, ones people used to read a person's future. Well, now there was only one thing my future was telling me,

I was becoming that same darkness.

Because those lines were now black, with it spreading underneath my skin and I made a fist with my hand. It was the darkness that had the power to consume me, and I couldn't let Lucius see this.

I didn't want him to see me fail.

Because if I wasn't strong enough to push it back and contain it, then I knew what I would become. I looked up at him, feeling my eyes already changing, and his face said it all as he watched it happen. Yet he remained strong, telling me,

"It's alright, Amelia, I am here, and we will deal with this together," he said, and a lump formed in my throat at his desperate words. But I knew that with all this raw emotion, what I needed to do. I needed to use it. I needed to feed from it, from the love I felt for the man in front of me. I needed to use it like a weapon again this thing.

But I also knew that we couldn't do this together like he thought. Because this was all on me, and having him here in front of me confused things. Because I didn't want to rely on him to get me through this, not like I had done since I was first locked to this place. Begging for him to come and save me.

Well, no more.

No, now it was time to save myself.

I staggered back to the table and when I felt my face start to change further, I picked up a clean platter and saw for myself my reflection. My eyes had turned completely black with tears running down my face in long dark streaks. My face was white as snow and my lips black with the blood in my veins now replaced with something else... something dark and deadly. My hair floated around me and a cloak appeared telling me only one thing...

I was turning into the Wraith Master.

I was running out of time.

"Gods, Amelia... please, fight it... we can fight it..."

"No!" I said, after I turned back to Lucius and he saw what I had become. But despite what was happening now, I no longer blamed him for what he had done, as he had done it to save my life. He had created a beautiful lie and if that had been my last moment to ever remember, then it was the best one.

Which is why I told him,

"You have done all you could... now it's my turn... I love you, remember that Lucius... remember that, no matter what happens next, please just remember that one thing... *I love you...*"

He started shaking his head as if he knew what was coming. As if he knew there was only one option left for me, and it was one that didn't include him.

Which was why he reached out to me knowing now I was the new Wraith Master, and that meant one thing.

I now had the power in this void. *The power over him.*

"No, Amelia, please don't do this... don't..." he said but it didn't matter, it was already happening. Because this castle was mine now, along with its madness.

One that if I had any hope of surviving, I had to do it alone.

So, as I made the man I loved disappear, I did so with more black tears streaming down my dead eyes.

"NO! AMELIA NO!" he shouted as the last of him disappeared, and with it what I knew could have been my last...

"Goodbye, Lucius."

CHAPTER TWENTY-SEVEN

FRACTURED HEART

"NO!" I bellowed the moment I was forced back into the real world, turning quickly to see Amelia remained deathly still on the bed.

"FUCK!" I roared as it looked as if she was still dead, and my anger erupted over with such a powerful rage that, had she not been lying there next to me, I would have let everything left inside of me succumb to my demon!

Yet it did not and only because I could feel that she was still alive, and I knew my anger would be useless against her will. I had already tried to keep hold of my place inside the void, one she now controlled, but she had forced me from it and wouldn't let me return. I was once again back to being fucking useless!

I could see the remains of blood around her lips, where Trice had done his job and forced her to eat the heart, doing so at the same time that I had been manipulating her mind into believing she was eating a steak. It had been the hardest thing to try and get her to believe, as the longer the fake memory went on, the more my control started to slip. I did everything in my power to get her to eat it and seeing now that the poison had completely left her body, I knew it had been the right thing to do.

And that sight alone gave me hope, because what I had seen of her before I left, she had been changing into the Wraith Master. So, I had to wonder how it wasn't affecting her body here? Was she controlling it or was this supposed to be the way of things? Gods in fucking Hell, but I cursed myself for not knowing the answers!

The last time I was left to feel this way was when she had first stepped into Hell after I begged her not to! Why she continued to believe that she could do things alone was fucking beyond me, but I just knew that I was back to being stuck somewhere between being furious, worried, and hurt that she had done this to me again!

It felt as though everything I had done up to this point had all been for fucking nothing if she was to let herself die now… for why would she give up now… it made no fucking sense! No sense at all, for her to give in to the darkness now! I had believed with everything in me that she had the power to beat it back. She had too much goodness in her, so much light and love in her heart, so much strength. But then when she had turned to me, I had seen it for myself. I had seen what she was becoming, and it broke my fucking heart. The moment I had seen that light in her soul diminish to darkness.

Gods… I begged for it not to be true.

As for the one who had done this to her, the fucking cause of it all, there he was. The hollow shell of who had once been the Wraith Master but was no more. Not with his dark heart now missing. It was nothing more than a sickening reminder of what had happened, and I let my rage take over.

"FUCKER!" I roared before lifting his body from the bed, so he was nowhere near her. Then I couldn't help it, but I started to tear into him, punching my demonic fist into his face before the entire thing caved in under my hand and became mangled flesh and bone. Then I dragged his remains away from the bed just in case what I did next managed to touch her.

My lost, sleeping Princess.

"AAAHHH!" I bellowed, my fury now igniting my demonic hand as I set his whole fucking body alight, knowing I couldn't stand it any longer. I needed to watch as his body turned to ash and nothing was left of him but dust. Then, once I was done, I staggered back until the back of my legs hit the bed and I let myself fall onto it, now sitting at its edge like a fucking desperate man. I looked down at my hands, sullied by death and destruction, now asking myself if I was ever worthy.

Is that why she had sent me away?

Had she not trusted me? Had she not thought that I could have helped her through it or was it that she didn't think I would have accepted her if she didn't have the strength to beat it back...

Is that what she thought?

Because she would have been wrong, I would have accepted her no matter what, fuck she could have become the most evil being alive and I think I would have fucking accepted it, just so I got to keep her... and I didn't care what that made me, for we both could have become lost to... *to darkness together.*

But first, I needed to try. I needed to convince her to hold on, to hold on to her humanity and not let what she was now

293

becoming to take control of her. Because the light in her soul was worth saving, and if it was in my power to achieve this then I wouldn't give up, even if she had, for she deserved nothing less than me giving it my all.

Because, in reality, I had been living like a ghost for 2000 years. A mere shell of what I was supposed to be, until she came along, and I felt as though I had taken my first mortal breath once more after a millennia of solitude. Lifetime after lifetime of servitude to a race that had been thrust upon me. I was a heartless King who had learned what it truly meant to have his heart beat for the first time whenever she was near. A heart that was now fucking breaking once more because of her actions.

Gods, I was so angry at her I wanted to scream down at her. I didn't even realise that I was doing just that, until I felt a hand grasp my shoulder. I was out of my mind with both worry and rage merging into one. I shrugged off the hand, turned and pushed whoever it was that was trying to hold me back. Then I covered her body with my own, my arms now holding my weight above her, so I could shout down at her face,

"How could you do that to me!? How dare you... how dare you do this to me again! Now let me back! I know you can hear me, LET ME BACK IN THERE!" I roared, making her shake beneath me, not through her own fear but because I myself was shaking. Because it was the first time I had wanted to call her every name under the sun, even though I would have meant none of them. I just wanted her to react to them... anything to tell me that she was alright. That she was still in there somewhere, in that fucking castle in a Wraith's void she now controlled!

I wanted her to come back and hit me, to fight me, throw every fucking profanity in my face and curse me to Hell and back! I deserved them all if I failed to save her! But there was not even a flinch, and in all honesty, I had no idea if the Amelia I loved was still in there fighting the darkness or not. I had no idea that if she ever did open her eyes, that they would be a pair I even recognised staring back at me. I had no idea what faced me, and was hopelessly left clinging on to the fact that it didn't matter as long as she was still breathing.

I didn't care how many people stared at me or witnessed my breakdown of emotions. But knowing how furious I was and how close to the edge my demon was, then it was little wonder why no one tried to restrain me again. Of course, everyone that would dare venture into this room knew that I would never hurt her... *no, evidently, she would only do that to herself.*

I snarled down at her like a wild animal, and in that moment, I despised her foolishness. How dare she say goodbye to me! How dare she throw me aside as if she had no more use for my help!

As if she no longer needed me.

No longer needed her hero!

I pushed away from the bed, no longer being able to even look at her. *I was too furious.* So, I turned my anger back on the room, now barking orders at people.

"I want every witch, every fucking healer, every Gods be damned sorcerer or elder, anyone with an ounce of fucking magic in this room, and I want them here right now! Bring back the Oracle, anyone strong of mind that can give me a fucking clue on what to do next and how to get back control of her mind!" I snapped with a roar of words.

"Erm, Lucius," King Auberon said, making me snarl at him.

"No, I don't want to fucking hear it! She cannot do this alone, do you understand...? She fucking needs me!"

"My Lord…" this time Carn'reau spoke, trying to appeal to me in some way but I was too fucking lost!

"Just do as I fucking order, NOW!" But it was at this point that Trice had clearly had enough, and was the only idiot brave enough to shout back at me.

"If ye shut th' fuck up 'n' turn aroond, ye wull see exactly why none o' that is needed!" I took a step closer to him ready to pummel my fist into his face when his words finally infiltrated my anger. I turned around just as Amelia sat up, shaking her head, before she shocked me to my core and said,

"Wow, that really didn't take me as long as I thought it would."

My heart stopped… *and then started to beat again!*

My Chosen One…

My girl…

My perfection… she was back.

"Amelia?" Her name came out as a whisper of disbelief, as if I was the one now being fooled. As if this was all an elaborate attack on my mind. But then her big blue eyes, the magnificence in them I instantly recognised, glazed over as tears filled them. I knew then, in that very moment, that no one could have recreated such a sight, because no one but I knew the beauty in them.

So, without another word, my feet took me over to her and before I knew it, I was taking her in my arms as if the whole thing was now a dream that she had created just for me. Here now in my arms again and this time for real. Just being able to feel the warmth of her soul against my skin and feel that heart beating for me once more against my own chest.

It was as if I had been the one to die and now found myself in Heaven, for this was all I ever wanted. Which was why I felt the same tears fill my own eyes as I held her to me, never wanting to let go…

Too afraid to ever let go.

I heard her little sob escape, telling me,

"I'm so sorry, Lucius… Gods, I'm so sorry I left you… can you ever forgive me?" In that moment all my anger, all my rage and fury, every last ounce of it evaporated in a second, and was replaced by utter relief. One so great it took my fucking breath away, and before anything else could come between us, I took her face in my hands and told her,

"Don't ever do that to me again, my heart… Gods, Amelia, it can't take it." Then I crushed my lips to hers and kissed her. I kissed her like it was the first time, like it was the last time and all the times in between. But mostly, I kissed her like it was the beginning of our future, be damned the Fates and their prophecies! It all meant nothing. It was sand falling between my fingers and water falling from the sky and sinking into the earth, before washing away any blood that may be spilled by my hands.

It meant nothing without her, for my entire world could slip away in a heartbeat, just as long as I was left with the girl in my arms right now. She was my everything, and that kiss was as powerful as they came.

She set my soul alight once more, giving me reason to breathe and giving my heart cause to beat.

"Amelia." I said her name like a prayer from my lips, one whispered against her wet tear-soaked skin. Her emotions being something for me to actually taste, a flavour I memorised and would never forget for as long as I was granted life.

"Does this mean you do forgive me then?" her soft voice asked, and the unsure, fearful tone broke my heart for a different reason. She feared my disappointment. She feared my hurt and my anger at her actions.

"Your heart beats, Amelia, that is all that is needed to gain my forgiveness," I told her honestly and she grabbed me to her and kissed me again, this time clinging to me as if she never wanted to let me go. After her sweet kiss, I admit, that I had no idea when the room emptied, nor did I have any idea how long our kisses had lasted and despite never wanting it to end, I knew there were far too many questions unanswered between us.

Besides, I wanted to make sure that my girl was okay, and even though kissing her was one sure way of finding that out, I also needed to know by looking in her eyes.

"Fuck, I was so worried," I admitted the second I pulled back only an inch from her lips.

"I know, I'm so sorry for that," she told me, and I felt her hand on my cheek after snaking in between us. It was one I covered with my own after first tilting my head and giving her more weight in her palm.

"I need to know what happened," I told her, and she nodded, understanding this need, for she would have been the same way. So, we separated enough to sit opposite each other. But even then, the space felt too great, and I had to lay my hand on her bent knee as she sat cross legged. She reminded me of a child about to tell a story, and I almost felt guilty because I saw how tired she looked. This, despite what seemed like endless days of sleep, that Hell, even I didn't know how long it has been anymore, easily losing all time and reality.

But yet we both needed this, her even more so when she suddenly said,

"Lucius, I have to tell you something." Her tone sounded both confessional and also worried. But as for me, then I knew as long as she was still my Amelia, I didn't care. However, Amelia did care, and this was enough to get me take it seriously and listen. Even if my hands would not stop from touching her and quite honestly, I didn't know if there was ever going to be a time that they would.

"Tell me everything, Amelia," I said, when it was clear she was waiting for me to help her start.

"There was already something in me that fought back," she said needing to blurt out this statement as if it were burning inside of her.

"What do you mean?" I asked confused by this.

"I'm sorry, I should probably start at the beginning," she said laughing it off as if she'd made a mistake, and the sound lightened my heart and eased my worry.

"After that last bite, when I started to feel strange, it was as if something was trying to consume me, and I guess it's easy to know what it was. The King had consumed hearts that he believed he owned, that he believed loved him, this from his wife especially. I could feel all those emotions, it was overwhelming. I felt as though I was drowning in them." I closed my eyes a few seconds longer, so I listened to her words and tried not to let the pain show how I felt at not being allowed to help her. However, my emotions must have been written there plain to see, because she quickly told me,

"I'm sorry I sent you away."

"Why did you?" I couldn't help but ask. At this she looked towards the window, the daylight now shining through and long passed the seemingly endless night. It was as if the rolling hills and mountains beyond the window frame held the answers she sought.

"I didn't want you to witness me fail," she whispered in a pained way and I was stunned.

"What?" I asked in disbelief.

"I didn't want your last memory of me, Lucius, to be some warped dark evil version of myself. I didn't want you to see me fail and I also didn't want you to witness it for another reason," she said, wincing at the memory of recent fears.

"What reason?" I asked, urging her on.

"If I failed, I only wanted one of us to feel that way as I knew if you had stayed to see it, then you would have held on to that guilt and made it your own, when it was only ever mine to possess. I didn't want that for you... or for that memory of me to be your last." I closed my eyes at this, letting her reasons wash over me and feeling the bitter sting instead of the soothing reasons I knew her words were trying to accomplish. But I didn't tell her this. That wouldn't have been fair, for there were no honourable reasons more profound than the ones she had given me. So instead, I told her,

"But you didn't fail."

"I know and it was thanks to you," she replied with a smile when seeing that her words had shocked me.

"Me?" She nudged me playfully with her elbow and said,

"Yeah, because it turns out that when your heart is already so full of love then it doesn't matter how much darkness you eat, all you have to do is hold onto that love and it overpowers everything." At this I couldn't help but grin, knowing now that this was the soothing balm that took away the pain her actions had inflicted. I grabbed her and pulled her to me, so overwhelmed by my feelings, I barely knew how to act other than that I had to hold her. I had to breathe her in, to embed my fingers in her hair, and hold in the memory for as long as possible.

"You beat back the darkness because you love me?" I questioned aloud, still amazed by the admission.

"Well, it wasn't all you, don't forget Star Trek and Lego, I love those things too you know." At this I burst out laughing, unable to help myself, then I muttered as I often did,

"There's my funny girl."

"Yep, and in real life too, how novel is that?" she joked, and again I laughed harder.

"Only you could make a joke out of spending days imprisoned in the mind of a mad King," I said with a shake of my head, but not in disbelief because this was my Amelia, and I knew that she would make anything serious into a joke if she could, just to lighten the mood.

"Yeah, well, I think we sure showed him... because correct me if I am wrong, that is his ash pile over there isn't it?" she said, nodding to where I had released my fury.

"It might have been a little overkill on my reawakening should we say."

"You mean you burnt the crap out of him and set his ass on fire?"

"Yeah, pretty much," I agreed making her laugh. Then she wrinkled her nose and said,

"Eww, please tell me you're not gonna start bringing your kills home as gifts, leaving them at my door like a cat." At this I threw my head back and roared with laughter, fuck my girl was funny! Then I told her with a playful wink,

"Sweetheart, right now if you start stroking me, I'll purr like a fucking kitten for you." It was at this that she threw her head back and burst out laughing and I marvelled at the sight, holding it to me like a gift.

"I'll have to remember that one, handsome," she said after some of her hilarity had run its course.

"In all seriousness and getting back to my dark tale of how I kicked Wraith ass... thank you very much... I also felt that I could beat it back because there was something I felt inside me, and I think it has something to do with the power I have back in Hell, the one that I unleashed at the harpies after touching the Eye." I nodded in understanding, already knowing there was something different about my girl since coming down to Hell. It was as if some dormant power had been awakened in her, and it often made me question if what I had taken from her was slowly being returned the more time we spent together. Being in Hell would certainly amplify this and speed it up.

After all, she had not completely been born human like Keira and Dom had first thought. There had been a power in her soul, one that should have been given the chance to bloom as she grew older. Yet it was one that I unintentionally had stolen, and now I wondered if with each exchange of blood, it wasn't only forming a connection, but it was also gifting something more in return.

But realistically, now was not the time to talk of such things, not after all she had endured. No, for now I wanted us just to have this moment of peace. Just to be given the time to bask in the happy glow of having my girl back, alive, and seemingly unscathed.

So, I pushed back the doubts and fears of what may come of this. I also pushed back the difficult conversations we needed to have at some point, or the new painful decisions I now had to make after hearing who the witch could be.

Because my fractured heart had just been healed and there was no way I was prepared to fracture hers with the truth of my past.

With the truth of…

My Wife.

CHAPTER TWENTY-EIGHT

AMELIA

WRAITH OF FIRE

The moment I had forced Lucius to leave the void I'd seen the heartbreak I had caused. But not only didn't I want him seeing if I failed, I also didn't want him seeing what I could potentially become in the process. The overwhelming feeling of darkness I could already feel as it had started to consume me before I had sent him back, and I hadn't been lying when I told Lucius that it had felt like I had been drowning in negative emotions. It was as if I was being held under water and forced to breathe in a flood of anxiety, depression, sorrow, bitterness, and jealousy. But, above all, a burning hatred! And I had been forced to bathe in it all the while trying to keep some semblance of who I was at the surface. Like being in a room full of hundreds of people all hurling abuse at you and trying not to let a single word penetrate your mind or feed your insecurities.

But as soon as Lucius had disappeared, I had finally allowed myself to fight without worrying about what he saw next, knowing this wasn't going to be pretty. I bent over double, holding my stomach as the pain radiated from within. Then, as I felt it start to burn, I crashed into one of the chairs, before throwing myself over the table, slapping my hands down in blood. I then looked down, bending over slightly as I fought to keep hold of it, so I could bury it deep. I panted like some wild beast was fighting to get out, one I couldn't allow yet. Maybe one day, but not yet…

Not yet.

"NO!" I roared, this time throwing my hand out in my need to dominate this darkness. I ended up hitting out at the dead King and instantly he burst into flames as if I had been the one with the power to do that. But this was all that was needed to shatter the last of his void and with it, the last of his painful bitter memories. His Hellish prison was not to become my own, and this castle was mine now. This void ruled by only one master and it didn't include any King.

"No, this mind is my own," I whispered to myself, trying to breathe through the immense power I could feel building within me. I looked up at the ceiling and closed my eyes before holding out my arms as if welcoming this new side of me. Instead of fighting the fear of what it could be, I now welcomed it, but only the parts I needed. It was as if there was a light buried so deep within me that it had been lost… lost for so long. Years lying in wait, biding its time. Its time to be reunited with my soul. A light that was now getting brighter, and this unleashed Wraith power was now feeding it and bringing it closer and closer to the surface, until it was no longer just a light…

But a raging fire.

One even I knew I needed to control… I needed to tame

it. So, I thought of Lucius, the centre of my world. The one who kept me anchored to my humanity, not because he was once human but because he loved me for who I was. And this worked. It didn't extinguish the fire, it just calmed it to gentle flames. Flames that would ignite with anger and then when it was no longer needed, be cooled by my love for Lucius. This was why, when I opened my eyes again, I found myself sat in the same beautiful setting that Lucius had created for me.

One from the memory he had gifted me with.

It had become my safe space.

I knew that, the moment I sat down amongst the crimson flowers and felt myself at peace. I lifted a hand to see as the black veins that once infected my skin now were retreating back, still at the ready to be called forth when needed. I hadn't just beaten the darkness, I had tamed it and moulded it into what I needed it to be.

"I did it," I whispered to myself in awe of what I had done. What I had achieved. A stolen power made into my very own and stored away like a weapon I might one day need. But then, looking out at the beautiful sight from Lucius' memories, I knew I didn't need to be here long, and I knew Lucius would be panicking, worried sick and out of his mind. It's just that coming here had made it easier to calm the storm.

But I did wonder at that humming of power I could now feel beneath my flesh. It was almost the same as how I had first felt in that meadow when I had erupted, hitting out at the McBain brothers and Lucius. It was something I usually only felt when my anger bubbled up, but now that I felt calm, I was amazed to feel it still there.

So, I did what anyone would do, *I tested it.*

I split it from the darkness I had consumed and contained in fire, and instead concentrated on the power that I knew had always been there. Then I held my arm out in front of me and focused on drawing the energy to my hand. It was like winding up a ball of wool tighter and tighter until it grew bigger and bigger, before I let it travel down my arm until it got to my palm. Then I felt it there like an object I could almost hold, something tangible and definitive.

I didn't know what I expected to see, but a ghost version of my own hand lifting away as if a piece of my soul was disconnecting somehow, hadn't been it. But seeing as it didn't feel wrong, and only as if this was meant to happen, I continued to try. Then when I threw it forward, letting it go, it shot forward and as it travelled it grew bigger and bigger. Then soon it wasn't a hand at all, but an invisible cloud of power that crashed through the land, distorting the void and shaking the world around me with the devastating force it created. I screamed in shock when I saw it ripped across the field, as if I had been a giant throwing an invisible boulder the size of a car.

"Holy shit!" I said in surprise and admittedly, with a nervous laugh. But then that wasn't it. Because I tried to draw it back to me but as soon as I did, it wouldn't stop. I saw it racing back towards me and I panicked, knowing that this might not have been a good idea.

"Oh shit!" I shouted this time as it came hurtling towards me, this invisible force that distorted everything behind it, so it wasn't completely see through. It grew in size and I didn't know how to stop it, other than to hold out my hands, close my eyes and brace myself for impact. Then, I was left with nothing more but to hope that it would be sucked back into me and not do to me what it had done to the landscape.

"Whoa!" I shouted as I caught it in my hand like I intended, but the force of it knocked me backwards until I landed on my bum with a whoosh of air expelled from my lungs at the impact. It was like being hit with a basketball in my chest after being thrown by some super elite athlete.

I rubbed my chest and muttered,

"Oww." But then I burst out laughing as I realised what I'd just done and I knew without a shadow of a doubt, that I was no longer just a mortal girl. I was no longer Lucius' human. I was something much more.

But with this came something else, something I didn't want to be, and that was a master to thousands. Which was why the next place I took myself to was back to the room of cells. Back to the Wraith who had tried to warn me the King was coming,

Back to the one I had named Trevor.

At the time it seemed as if he had tried to communicate with me, so it made sense to try him first and as it was no longer a place I feared, I found myself feeling empowered. I'd defeated the King with Lucius' help, and done to him what he had done to others, yet I had been stronger than him and not let that darkness consume me. I had morphed it into something more powerful, driven by a much more powerful emotion... *Love.*

But now there was one last thing I needed to do before I went home, back to the world of reality. So, I approached the cell and placed my hands on the glass door to get his attention. Then as soon as I touched the glass, I let my power hum beneath my palm and felt as it rippled through the cell. As soon as it touched the Wraith, it made his head snap up. He then made a series of clicking noises, shaking his head as if trying to communicate.

"Can you speak?" I questioned, making him shake his head telling me that he couldn't.

"But you can understand me?" At this he nodded, and I

was at least relieved to know that parts of this conversation could happen.

"I don't know if you know but I defeated your master, he will no longer be calling you to fight for him." He nodded again and then motioned to his heart as if telling me that he had felt this when it happened.

"I have to confess, I'm new to this and I don't exactly know what to do." At this he tilted his head to one side as if trying to understand what I was asking.

"I also speak without thinking sometimes," I added for no useful reason and again, he nodded, making me sigh.

"I want to release you all, to get you out of these cells, is that possible?" He nodded telling me yes it was before pointing to his heart as if telling me that this was where I held the power to do so.

"So, I just have to think it and it will happen?" This received another yes.

"But if I release you, it won't be releasing your actual souls, will it?" I asked, knowing this was the important part and I was right, as he shook his head telling me that no, it wouldn't.

"Because you're not really here, it's only the connection to you that is, as a way to control you, using this void," I said as if musing out loud and he told me this was right.

"Great, so is this a kind of, gotta find your resting place type of gig?" Again, he cocked his head to one side as if he didn't fully understand the question.

"Sorry, what I meant to say is, to free your souls I would have to find your resting place, in order to truly set you free… is this right?" Hearing this and understanding what I was trying to achieve meant something to him, as he told me that yes it would, he also told me so much more with his manner. Because he nodded and placed a ghostly hand to his heart, holding it there as if thankful. This told me that if such a thing was ever possible, I would be the saviour of their souls... *so many souls*, I thought looking up and down the line of cells.

"You know, this would be a lot easier if you could just tell me where that was." At this he made a clucking sound as if his tongue was hitting the roof of his mouth, most likely telling me he agreed. But then he reached up and pulled his hood back slightly, showing me exactly why he couldn't speak. The ghost like features we're almost rotted away, and I realised that clicking sound was him moving his jaw to the side with the bone that remained. This didn't frighten me, and I wasn't sure after this ordeal anything ever would again.

"Ah, I see that would be a problem, for a tongue, lips and actual vocal cords would help in speaking, eh?" At this he nodded.

"I will find a way, I promise once this is all over, I will make it my mission in life to free you all, but for now the very least I can do is give you a little bit of peace." Again, he placed a hand over his heart, one that was only half human and more ghostly than anything. His movements an echo, as they had been when I had fought them in the office. A trail of their movements following them everywhere.

"So just think it and it will happen you say." Again his palm made a motion with his heart and then he pointed to his mind telling me they were connected.

Wow, who knew Trevor would be so deep.

But then my new Wraith friend was right, what powered all of this was what was in my soul, and what made it more powerful was the need and want to do good by others. Not like the King who used them like weapons in an arsenal. Well, I'm sure I could have done the same thing but then who was to say that for every time I did, I wouldn't lose a piece of that good soul? Who was to say that every time I used them, I wouldn't have been falling deeper into the evil clutches of what created the Wraith Master in the first place?

No, I couldn't chance it.

I would never be like that tyrant and sully my soul like that!

So instead, I closed my eyes, put a hand to my heart and believed with everything in me that these souls deserved to be free. I imagined each and every cage disintegrating into nothing and leaving behind an army of lost souls. Then, when I knew the very last cell had faded into nothing, I finally opened my eyes, and a small shriek of shock left my lips when I was faced with it all.

Trevor, who I had been speaking to, stood at the front, and closest to me. However, the sight was most definitely a startling one to say the least and even more so when they started to move closer towards me. I couldn't help my reaction as I took a few quick steps back.

But then the unexpected happened, as before I had chance to doubt whether I'd made the right choice or not, each and every one of them lowered to a knee. It was like watching the essence of a wave as it hit the shore like a ghost of a memory. In fact, soon there was an ocean of Wraiths as far as I could see, all now bent at the knee as if I was there...

Well, *as if I was their Queen.*

They made a motion with their hands, that covered their faces before their palms found the floor in some sort of salute. That was when I fully understood this was them showing me their loyalty. It was them giving me their thanks for freeing them, no matter how symbolic it seemed. For the truth was they would never truly be free, not unless I made it happen.

"Okay, so you should probably all know now that I'm not

very Queen-like, but I vow to you all this promise. If it is in my power to do so, then I will find you all and free you. But until then, well this castle is yours... so, erm, go crazy and party all you want." At this the first one to look up at me was Trevor, my Wraith buddy. He nodded before putting his hand over his heart once more, then he bowed his head and I said,

"Until that time, I promise I will try and be a good Queen," and then I left, leaving behind the memory of the castle as if trying to leave them with a slice of a void I could hand over control to them. Yet the guilt of knowing that it was all just a symbolic gesture weighed heavily on me as I left. Because I meant every word of my vow, I wouldn't stop until I found a way.

Yet, when I walked away, something different happened and I looked down to see the scorch marks my footprints made, telling me that I wasn't just the new Wraith Master, I was...

The Wraith of Fire.

CHAPTER TWENTY-NINE

REMEMBERING

B ack in Lucius' arms. Gods, but it felt like Heaven and I would have believed it to be, had I not made absolutely sure that I was alive... trust me, I had checked... as in, *a lot!*

"You do know you can let me go and I'll come right back to you... right?" I commented in amusement after Lucius tensed the moment I tried to shift out of his hold, only so I could reach around to scratch my back. Because since I had made my way back to the land of the living, Lucius hadn't let me out of his sight. In fact, it went beyond this and seemed as if he also needed to be touching me. Not that I minded, I just knew there are certain things a girl likes to do on her own... like the three basic S's, although showering with him was always fun, especially the first time, I thought with a blush.

Speaking of which, I was also very aware there was one particular act we hadn't yet reacquainted ourselves with and well, on my part it wasn't through lack of trying. But Lucius seemed to be on a mission and I just hoped it didn't include celibacy, as it was starting to seem that way.

However, this mission did include getting me to eat and drink until I developed a little pot belly, something that looked strange on me, considering it was very obvious that I had lost weight. Something that was seen the moment I had finished eating and Lucius demanded that I bathe, and well, one stinky whiff of my pits and yeah, I had to agree with him, I had definitely smelled better.

The bathroom was very similar to the one I'd had in the room I had been given when I first arrived. This meant that I knew exactly what to do to fill up the unusual bathtub and well, if I thought to impress Lucius with my knowledge, I would have been wrong, because he seemed to be fixated on something else and whatever it was, it was worrying him, that much was clear. Because he became almost methodical in his actions. As if there was some sort of 'care for the girlfriend' checklist he was making his way through.

Something that only changed when I finally got out of my dress, one Lucius must have put me in when caring for his conked-out princess, someone he would have called his Sleeping Beauty. However, I was under no illusions with that one, as I often woke up to find drool on my pillow and no one in the memory of mortal beings ever looked sexy drooling… ever!

But as soon as he saw my ribs he frowned, now raking his eyes over every inch of me and I had to admit, it was taking a hit to my self-confidence. After this he stepped up to me and started running his hands down my shoulders, and then down my collar bone before down the side of my breasts and framing his hands on my ribcage. Then he ran them back down my sides before lowering to his knees to span my hip bones.

"Lucius, please, it is…" he stopped me when he snapped his head up and growled,

"Do not finish that sentence, for this is far from fine." It was at this point that I put my hands on my hips, despite being naked in front of him, and snapped back,

"Yes, well, it's a damn sight better than being dead!" Then I realised the cruelty of what I had said and covered my mouth with a hand as I gasped, and the second I saw the pain in his eyes I quickly apologised,

"Lucius, I am sorry, I didn't mean…"

"I knew exactly what you meant, Amelia," he said on a sigh before getting back to his feet and turning his back to me. I released a sigh myself and after shaking my head at myself, I admitted,

"I'm struggling with this, Lucius."

"You're not the only one," he said in return looking back over his shoulder at me, and the look he gave me made me reach for a towel and cover myself up, asking,

"Then does this make it better?" My tone said it all before I turned away and got into the bath, almost sighing at how nice it felt, despite feeling ashamed of the way I looked.

"Amelia." My name was a reprimand and a caress all at once. But then, when I looked his way, his eyes said it all. I must have looked so small sat in that tub with my knees up against my chest and I almost felt as fragile as I looked. Yet, after all that had happened, I knew I wasn't… I was a survivor.

"I don't like this any more than you do…" I said motioning down to my body, making Lucius frown. "Yet it is what it is, and I can't do anything to change that right now. So, I am sorry that every time you look at me you will be reminded of what happened. That will hopefully fade with time and well, with bacon topped donuts…" At this he scoffed a laugh, which I took as a good sign before I carried on.

"I didn't mean to snap but surely me being back here, being alive…" I felt him cupping my cheek and turning my face to his before finishing off that sentence,

"*It is everything to me.*" Then he kissed me swift and sweet before urging me forward so he could join me.

"Besides, a diet of Donuts and bacon doesn't sound too bad," I joked, making him nip at my neck and naturally it fell to one side in a submissive manner.

"My reaction was insensitive, for this I'm sorry," he said, and I nibbled on my fingertips trying to think of the best thing to say, and telling him,

"I'm only sorry that my actions were the ones that put you through all of this… again."

"This was hardly your fault, Amelia," he told me, and that felt nice not to be responsible for once.

"Lucius, can I ask you something?" He didn't reply but his silence implied that I could.

"You seem distracted and that's totally understandable considering what we've just both been through, but I wanted to ask, you would tell me if there was something important, wouldn't you?" At this I felt him tense behind me and because my back was flush against his chest, I couldn't have missed it even if I tried. But then he relaxed as if forcing himself to, before joking,

"I don't have any more brothers if that's what you're wondering." I laughed at this and said,

"It's usually the mother-in-law girlfriends worry about the most, although I think mine would have been lovely." At this he gave me a gentle squeeze to convey how he felt about this statement before telling me,

"Well, then consider yourself lucky, as Dariush is the only family I care about."

"But then again, the Devil is your father, so there is that,"

I said, and Lucius paused before letting out a humourless chuckle and remarked,

"You're not exactly one to talk here, sweetheart, not with your family tree." I laughed and said,

"Wow, family reunions are going to be fun, aren't they?"

"More like a fucking massacre, and you wonder why I don't want to celebrate Christmas," he said, running his hands up my arms and in no hurry to start the process of why we were actually in the tub in the first place, which of course was to clean our bodies.

"You know you're right, maybe a secluded cabin in the woods at Christmas time where no one can find us, is the way to go."

"Now you're fucking talking," he agreed on a growl.

"I still get a tree though and at least one present, that's the rule," I said teasing him and he leaned in closer, kissed the shell of my ear and whispered,

"Sweetheart, I'd buy you a whole jewellery store if that were the case." At this I looked back over my shoulder and said,

"Do I look like a diamonds type of girl to you?" At this he smirked and said,

"But of course, my mistake. I meant the entire Lego section of a toy shop." At this I grinned, patted him on the cheek and told him,

"Good boy, now that's better." To which he chuckled and this time it was because he found it funny.

"And talking of good boys, when are you gonna start washing me?" At this he raised his eyebrows in question, making me smirk as I wagged mine in return. Then, I turned fully, so I could plaster my front to his, squishing my breasts against his chest. Then I started kissing my way up his neck. His head went back against the rim as he let out a moan. I

looked at the scar by his neck that he had purposely left
unhealed. It was when I had 'claimed him' in the training
room that day before we had travelled back to Afterlife, and
the first time I had ever bitten him and taken his blood
without his help. He watched me kiss over it and gave me a
tender look. Then as I continued my way up, kissing, sucking,
and nibbling a pathway up his neck to his jaw and then across
his lips, I whispered,

"And when I say wash me, I actually mean... fuck me."
Hearing these last two words make him close his eyes and
groan.

"Amelia." Again that name wasn't said as a prayer this
time and more of a reprimand.

"Yes, Lucius," I said seductively. I was hoping it sounded
more like a sex kitten purring as I licked my lips, making his
jaw clench, telling me I achieved it. But then he took hold of
the top of my arms and pushed me back a little, so I was no
longer kissing him.

"It is too soon," he said but I was unconvinced and
showed him this by leaning close to him again, and telling
him against his skin,

"I disagree and clearly I'm not the only one," I added,
looking down the length of him to see the rock-hard cock I
could feel weighted in between us. However, when I snaked a
hand down there to take a hold of its steely length, he hissed,
sucking in air through his teeth before he shackled my wrist
and pulled me off him.

"No, Amelia," he said sternly, and this was when I
frowned and questioned,

"You're serious?"

"Unfortunately, yes and trust me, sweetheart, know that I
used all my will power when I said no."

"Why?" I watched as he swallowed hard as if forcing the reasons not to take me down.

"Because we do not know what toll the experience has taken on your body, other than the obvious signs," he added gritting his teeth.

"Oh, I get it," I said, turning back to face the other way giving him my back once more and trying to put space between us, something he prevented as soon as he banded an arm across my chest.

"I very much doubt that you do," he informed me.

"Hey, it's fine, you clearly have a type, and one with more meat on her bones." At this he growled angrily and tensed his arm, making me suck in a breath before he relaxed it.

"That is not fair, Amelia," he gritted out.

"Well, it's how you're making me feel, Lucius," I informed him, making him release a heavy sigh before he replied,

"I know what you're doing, you know."

"Yeah, what's that?"

"You're trying to provoke me by making me prove just how much I fucking want you!" he growled.

"Yeah, then prove it," I challenged.

"The rock-hard length of my cock that could pound nails into stone is proof enough," he pointed out, and I had to say as far as points go that was a pretty good one, but it still didn't get me what I wanted.

"Damn it, if I'd known I was going to get cockblocked, I'd have stayed in the void a little longer, maybe created myself a sex machine." At this he snarled against my neck and nipped my tender flesh in warning.

"And what do you know of sex machines, my little Virgin Princess?" he asked in that seductive tone of his that was doing nothing to cool my libido.

"Excuse me, once was a virgin! And plus, what's not to like, cock goes in, cock goes out and because it's a machine, that kind of indicates it can keep going unless there's a power cut," I said, making him grin against my neck.

"I also think you will find there is usually an operator behind that sex machine, and if you think I will let anything get in this tight cunt of yours other than my cock..." he warned me as he snaked a hand down my belly and after he cupped my sex, he then slid two fingers inside me, making me cry out as he finished his sentence,

"Or my hand, then you are mistaken." I moaned when he shifted his fingers inside me, now gripping onto my sex in the most primal of ways.

"Well, looks like I found a way to control my sex starved kitten after all. Now, hold still while wash you," he said, and I shifted against him making him tighten his hold, so I stopped.

"Ah, very obedient indeed," he hummed against my skin, licking his way up my neck and when he bit down to hold my flesh in between his teeth, I cried out. Then when he released me, I felt his pleased and knowing grin before kissing it better.

After this I was left in utter shock and in total need as he made good on his word and began to wash me. And the whole time he kept a firm hold of my pussy as if I was a pet of his. His fingers never once moved from inside me and I spent the whole time squirming in his hold. It was if I was his to control, and I had to say, that if they had only been to keep me still as he quenched the sexual thirst I had for him, then he failed... *miserably.*

Because every jerk of my body created by his hand caressing the washcloth over my skin, I also felt inside my core where he would not remove his fingers. Meaning that by the time he was finished I was a quivering mess, near begging him to let me come. It was a delicious, sexual torture, pure and simple. I was also amazed at how he did everything one handed, including washing my hair. Well, this was after first dumping flowers from a decorative glass holder so he could use this to rinse my hair free of the suds.

But again, that hand never moved.

Then, once we were finished, he shifted me forward before moving to his feet and bringing me up at the same time. I cried out as his fingers went deeper and the bastard chuckled! Then, to give me an easier time, he banded an arm around my waist as he lifted me the rest of the way, stepping out of the bath at the same time. Yet when he set me back on my feet he purposely went deeper again, this time making me hiss,

"Fuck," and I found myself gripping onto his arm for dear life. I wondered what his own reactions to my own were. He remained behind me so I couldn't see, but at least I hoped that hard cock between us said he was turned on and his restraint was closer to snapping.

He reached for the towel I had used and started drying me off, which was when I hit my limit and begging took the place of my moans.

"Please, oh Gods please, Lucius."

"Tell me what it is you want, sweetheart," he hummed in my ear making me want to snap back at him, only when he knew it too, his fingers fucked me faster. Meaning my words came out in a broken breathy way,

"You... know... what I... want."

"As do you, now give it to me, give me your fucking words," he demanded on a growl.

"Please, Lucius, please fuck me... please give me your cock and make me..." I begged unashamedly.

"Make you what, tell me?!" he demanded, and I knew he too was close to losing it.

"Make me forget," I whispered making him freeze solid behind me, then he asked with caution this time,

"Forget?" I released another breathy moan and told him honestly,

"Make me forget everything there ever was before you." It was at this point he had definitely hit his limit, as he removed his fingers, sucked them into his mouth and lifted me up in his arms.

"Damn you, woman, and your power over me and snapping my restraint, for I can never deny you my cock... fuck, I can never deny you anything!" Then he lowered me onto the bed as if I was the most delicate of beings and crawled over me.

"I won't make you forget, sweetheart, I will simply make you remember the only thing you need to... *now get ready to scream for me,"* he said, before impaling his length where his fingers had been and I did exactly that, I screamed his name.

"Lucius!"

Yet despite the most perfect intrusion, I still noticed that for Lucius, this was him being as gentle as possible with me, as after the first initial thrust, he took his time, slow and steady. And as I felt myself building, I found myself clawing at his back, begging him again,

"Harder, please... fuck me, give it to me harder, faster, I'm so close..."

"Easy, pet, there is no rush," he told me before taking hold of my wrists and pinning them above my head, so I had no choice but to go at his pace and it was maddening! As for Lucius, he seemed to be enjoying my desperation, my sexual struggles against him by trying to get him to go faster, begging him to fuck me harder. That sadistic grin never left his face and would only deepen every time I begged.

"I fucking love savouring you," he told me with an even slower drag of his cock, and the moment I tried to shift back down onto his length, he held onto my wrists tighter to prevent me from doing so.

"Behave or there are plenty of things in this room I could use to tie you up." At this warning I stopped trying to take back control and he knew the moment I relaxed, that I had submitted. His knowing grin of victory said he was pleased at my choice.

"That's my good girl, I love how addicted you are to me, how much you want it. I adore how I'm the only one that will ever get to see this side of you. Most of all, I fucking love how much you love me, for you have mine in return. *Now hold the fuck on as I give you what you want."* This was the only warning I received before he started pounding into me and I knew it was because he too was close, and he had dragged this out for as long as possible so that we would find sexual release together, and when we did, I finally understood why.

It was fucking beautiful.

Falling over the edge into euphoria together, there was no other intimacy like it, and as we both cried out, our release erupted from the both of us making me quiver around his cock and him spilling his seed into me.

Then, as he gathered me in his arms, with his length still hard and seated inside of me, we couldn't have been closer or more connected than we were in that moment.

And he was right,

He didn't make me forget…

He simply made me remember.

323

CHAPTER THIRTY

MEMORY LANE CHANGES

The day after it was still clear to me that something heavy still weighed on Lucius' mind and the closer it came to us leaving, the more distant he became. I had tried to talk to him about this, but he just shrugged off my worries as nothing more than an unsure future. He also didn't want to talk about this unknown brother of his, and he especially didn't want to talk about the witch, who he seemed to hold with nothing but hatred and utter disdain.

Of course, it wasn't hard to guess why, considering all she had done to us. But it was almost like he was keeping something from me, maybe a memory of the void that he had experienced when looking for me. I even wondered if he had been shown the same twisted memory of the witch when she was a little girl, one who had been made to watch as her mother was burned at the stake. At least this is what I had assumed had happened, because what else could that memory have been?

I would have even been worried that he felt differently about me now that I had possibly become something else, something I had explained in greater detail. Something I had strangely decided to do when stood looking up at Lucius with wide eyes as he blew some of 'Nero's all-seeing eye dust' in my eyes. Something he'd had Nero acquire for him before he left to come and get me, knowing that I most likely needed it. We had soon discovered I did after stubbing my toe on six things in a row. I was just surprised that it hadn't worn off sooner but then again, it hadn't been like I had been using my actual eyes in the void.

As for being worried about Lucius feeling any differently towards me, now that I wasn't strictly, 'his little mortal' anymore, they were unfounded as he had been sticking to me like we were joined at the hip. In fact, he became quite obsessive with it, never letting me out of his sight and keeping a hold of me and touching me at all times. I couldn't say I hated this or that after what happened, I didn't understand it, because I did. But let's just say I started to draw the line when it came to needing the bathroom, which was the only reprieve I got.

So, to say that his actions were confusing was a bit of an understatement. But then I had to keep reminding myself what watching the person you love dying in front of you could do to your soul. Which meant that instead of pressuring him to talk about it, I did what I knew he needed me to do, I gave him time. I let him keep me close and kept my hand in his without complaint. After all, when trapped in that void, it wasn't like he had found it easy, and I knew we all dealt with things in our own way so I had to respect that and hope that when the time came, he would open up to me and talk to me about it.

However, it became apparent something more was wrong when the Oracle requested to speak to me. There was a brief knock on our door and all she found was an angry vampire stood in her way. I found this surprising considering she had been the one to help us, but he flat out refused to let her come near me. This just made me question what was it that Lucius feared so much that she might tell me?

Well, at this rate I wondered what else could be in store for me, for surely there wasn't much left for a person to face and overcome... other than mutant hillbillies or an alien invasion. Yet, despite my asking what was wrong, Lucius was having none of it. Going so far as to take the Oracle out of the room into the hallway and close the door behind him. Now what they spoke of, I had no idea, but whatever it was, Lucius obviously didn't want me to hear and that in itself didn't bode well for me.

In fact, I came so close to pointing out all the bad things that happened by keeping things from each other. But then my mother's words in my head had stopped me. Because she told me that, although she regretted all that she had kept from my father during their time together before they got married, she realised that it was all fated. Every single moment of what they had been through had led them to an end destination, that I recently discovered meant my mother saving the world.

Which meant I was left unsure of how I felt, as I didn't know what to believe, what was in my gut or what I should be leaving for the Fates to decide. Were our lives already mapped out in front of us and we were just following the route that we had always been destined to take? Or did we have more control than that?

I had always liked to believe that we're in control of our own destiny but then if that was the case, how could I have believed that Lucius had been my Chosen One all of these years. In all honesty, my mind was a cluster fuck of emotions! I could have been asking myself these questions for hours on end and be no closer to an answer, or one that even came close to making sense. Because the simple matter was, each answer contradicted the next and simply left even more questions in its wake.

I understood not a single thing of the Fates or why they did the things that they did, or even whose side they were on. Because that would only leave me with one question left...

Had I truly been fated to die?

And speaking of things that were potentially fated, after Lucius and I had sex for the first time once back in the real world, I found myself needing to know another burning answer. I was well in the euphoric afterglow of sex and I had believed that Lucius would have probably been more inclined to answer me, being somewhat more pliable. So, whilst I had been lying next to him, I did so with my head against my palm and an elbow to the bed, I looked down at him.

"You have something to ask, sweetheart?" Lucius said, beating me to it and obviously sensing my gaze on him, despite having his eyes closed and an arm thrown over the top of his head.

"I might have."

"You always have," he amended making me huff.

"Ask, Amelia," he prompted after a moment of silence stretched between us.

"I wanted to ask, why did you plant that memory?" Now at this he removed his arm and opened his eyes to look at me.

"I thought that was obvious by now, as you didn't exactly look excited by the idea of having heart on the menu." I shook my head at the gruesome reminder and reworded my question.

"Yes, I know why you did it, and even though I was angry to begin with, I understand why in the end, but what I want to know is..."

"Why that particular memory?" he finished off for me and I nodded. He then released a heavy sigh before sitting up and dragging a hand across the back of his neck, now looking uncomfortable.

"I gave you that memory because for me, it was an easy one to create."

"What do you mean, why was that easy?" This was when he turned back to look at me and then he surprised the Hell out of me when he told me why.

"Because it's the way that I wished that night had gone."

"What?" I whispered.

"There is not much I regret in my life, Amelia, I know too much about the damn Fates for that to happen… and clearly between us there are moments that I have regretted, like in the way that I've hurt you. The way I pushed you away for years. but one single moment I regret where I knew I could have done things differently was the night of the gala," he told me, and again I was shocked by his admission.

"So that memory was one you wished had happened?" I asked desperate to know.

"When I saw you standing there that night, Gods, but how I wanted to step up to you, put an arm around your shoulders and prove to every single person in that room that you were mine. That I had claimed you as my own, and I fucking hated that I couldn't do that. That I had no right to it, not after the way I'd treated you," he said, looking both pained by the memory and annoyed at himself for causing it to play out the way it did. But then I reminded him,

"Yeah, I don't think that would have gone down particularly well and might have earned you a slap in the face."

"Well, we both know how that usually ends, so I don't think I would have minded," he teased.

"No offence, Lucius, but it didn't exactly seem like claiming me was in any way, shape or form, in your mind that night. If anything, you seem pissed off that you had to be there," I added giving him my side of things.

"I wasn't angry at you, I was angry at myself, by my actions and my refusal to take action. Knowing how I had treated you was the reason why I couldn't claim you as I wanted to and well, just seeing that guy coming on to you and I swear, I could have ripped his arms off and beaten him to death with them."

"Well, that would have got you noticed," I teased in return, making his lips quirk up.

"Indeed," he replied in a very Lucius kind of way before he continued.

"So, if there was ever a moment I could do over again, well clearly there would have been many, but that one… well, that was the real start of us and in all honesty, I felt like I couldn't have fucked it up any more than I did."

"So, what you're saying is that really you should have wined and dined me and charmed my panties off me, which granted would have easily been accomplished, because hello… sex in a suit…" I said, pausing to wave a hand up and down his body making him smirk.

"And then after said first time sexathon for this girl, you would have cooked me breakfast in the morning?"

"Yes, that is what I am saying… *Sweet as Candy,"* he said, reminding me of what he conjured up for me to wear, making me wonder if I should have been suspicious of it being the only thing there for me *to wear.*

"Do you even know how to cook steak?" I joked and he gave me a look that said what his words followed.

"I didn't lie when I told you that I was over 2000 years old and in that time, I have managed to fend for myself quite easily." I smirked at this, but it turned into a grin when he added,

"That being said, I'm not exactly a souffle kinda guy, so don't get excited." At this I laughed.

"Damn and I'm such a souffle kind of girl too," I said, swinging my arm out across my stomach in one of those, oh shucks moments.

"Who are you kidding, sweetheart, you're a doughnuts and bacon type of girl and that's just plain weird." Now at this I feigned being offended.

"Erm, says the guy who bites me during sex and drinks my blood... hello, I think society wouldn't class me as the weirdo here." His lips twitched before he admitted,

"I would say good point, but considering humans have an unhealthy obsession with vampires, I would say most of the female population would call that hot." Damn him, he'd made another good point!

"Yeah, well maybe in movies and books, women will be flicking the bean to the thought, but trust me, in reality you try to bite someone and suck on their blood, they're calling the cops and that's a mood killer for anyone." At this he threw his head back and howled with laughter. Then he pulled me close to him and buried his face in my neck before pretending to bite me, then when he had finished making me giggle, he pointed out,

"I don't remember you complaining, sweetheart."

"Yeah, well after the first time, they just thought it was a prank caller, so I gave up." His chuckle was once again buried in my skin.

"So, that memory you planted, is how you wished it had gone?" I asked again.

"Well, if it had, then I wouldn't have needed to shout at

you for not locking your door quick enough," he said reminding me of that night.

"Yeah, that was definitely a buzzkill... ha, get it... buzz... okay so granted, it's a Pip joke." He ignored this and said,

"No, a buzzkill would have been you being there when they came to ransack it." Jeez, just mentioning it was a buzzkill.

"Well, considering we now know that I was being stalked every day of my life thanks to the 'Lucius squad', then I doubt that would have happened," I threw back, making his lips twitch again.

"Yes, well clearly I wasn't able to keep you safe everywhere you went, like the museum for example."

"You did keep me safe; you took a bullet for me, remember?" I reminded him, wondering how we managed to go back so far down memory lane... oh yeah, I asked.

"Oh, how could I forget, for after my initial rage at the ones who nearly took you from me before I could even claim you, it was the first glimpse I got of the damage you were capable of inflicting," he said, making me wag my brows at him as I said,

"You were impressed, huh?" He rolled his eyes before telling me,

"Admittedly your father taught you well, yes, but I think my memory was more focused on the way you adorably wanted to protect the artefacts or when you suggested we interrogate the guy and that I should use my fangs to do so. I didn't know whether to burst out laughing or just snap the guy's neck quicker, just so I could kiss you senseless." I smirked at this and said,

"Yeah, that probably wouldn't have been the most romantic first kiss for us, doing so over a dead body...

although it would have probably been quite fitting, considering how bloody and often gruesome our relationship followed on after that point," I teased, making him nip at me playfully.

"Yes, unfortunately it has been anything but conventional, to say the least."

"Lucius, you live in a castle in the middle of a hollowed-out mountain, just how conventional did you expect our relationship to ever be?" I asked laughing, making him raise a brow at me.

"Come on, with my upbringing it wasn't exactly like I didn't know what I was getting into," I said, wiggling closer to him and teasing him with little pinches up his sides. But he rolled suddenly and slipped me beneath him, then he pushed my hair back and held it there framing the sides of my head.

"So, giving up normality and convention was easy for you? Remember that mortal life you desperately sought out, do not think me fool enough not to remember that you once lived in a flat in Twickenham, for fuck sake," he growled, and I released a heavy sigh before telling him,

"Yes, and ask yourself why I did that, Lucius. I was ready to move and study in Germany for you. I came to Transfusion that night and practically laid it out on a platter for you. Who do you think turned me towards that mortality? After you saved me... after... after the factory and that car journey home, the one where I spent in your arms, who do you think I spent my time waiting for?" At this his gaze softened and he ran the backs of his fingers down my cheek as he said tenderly,

"You were sixteen, my beauty."

"Yes, but I wasn't sixteen forever, Lucius, and I waited for you a lot longer than a year," I told him, and for a very small moment he bit his bottom lip before releasing it in a regrettable sigh.

"It was for the best, Amelia, surely you see that now, surely you see how brutal my world can be. Gods, Amelia, you saw how I had to treat you in my throne room. I'm a King in Hell, a ruler of brutal souls and yet, despite that rule I still had to treat you like my damn sex slave."

"Well, there are worse things to be treated as where you're concerned," I said winking at him, but when he didn't take my teasing bait I conceded,

"Okay, so I understand what you're saying, and yes at the tender age of my teenage years, your world would have been a shock, but you should also try and remember my upbringing. I'm not like my mother, you know, I may have been technically born mortal, but I wasn't exactly brought up like one... I could kick a guy's ass at the age of five." At this he too conceded,

"I know that." But the way he said it was more to do with the mention of being compared to my mother.

"I don't mean it like that," I said.

"Then I suggest you get to the point of what you do mean, before this conversation takes a very dramatic turn, one you will not like," he warned, making me snap back,

"Now who's being sensitive about my mother, because it isn't me?" His look said it all.

"I just mean that my mother wasn't just born a mortal, she was raised that way. Other than seeing demons she thought was all in her head, she had no idea of your world, no idea of my father's. Yet when she discovered it all, did she crumble? Did she run away in fear? Did she find out what my father was and get on the next flight and spend the rest of her life hiding from him? No, she didn't, because she was in love with him." He released a sigh and looked the other way before I cupped his cheek and forced him back to me, so he was looking in my eyes when I told him,

"Because love doesn't make you weak, Lucius, it makes you strong and I am no exception to that rule. So why you think I would be, is beyond me."

"Amelia, you are the strongest person I've ever known, but this is only something I have discovered since knowing you after that point in the museum. Yes, you are my Chosen One, something I knew from the very first moment I laid eyes on you. Something that was carved in my heart the moment I rescued you from that old factory. But, Amelia, you must understand, I didn't know you. I didn't know of your passion, of your loyalty and your strength, but most of all I didn't know what was in your heart and the lengths you would go to, to protect it, to protect those you hold dear inside it," he said placing his palm over my heart, one that beat again because of him. I released a loved-up sigh this time.

"Okay, so that all sounded pretty good," I admitted, after wiping away a stray tear his words had manged to pull to the surface.

"Like I said, my regret was a missed opportunity, a missed opportunity to make you mine the right way," he said referring back to the night of the gala.

"Then that, honey, is all the answer I will ever need," I said in return before kissing him, a kiss that developed into the passion and strength of heart that he spoke of, because I wasn't wrong, and he would never realise it to the fullest extent of what I knew in my soul.

Because in love there was the strength to defy even death, and the love I had for Lucius was...

The strongest of all.

CHAPTER THIRTY-ONE

WITCH SECRETS MATTER?

After this chat, it wasn't long before Lucius was making plans for us to leave and again, he did all of this without leaving my side. He also refused to take any meetings in the King's office, stating firmly that he never wanted to step foot in that place ever again. I didn't need to ask to know why this was, as I felt the same way. Yet, I knew for Lucius it was definitely more painful. In fact, I think if the room had been in his own castle, then he would have burned it to the ground without a second's thought. And like I said, I didn't blame him as it would have been like visiting a graveyard, and reading a headstone belonging to someone that was still alive but had also once been buried there.

But since my return I had spent most of my time locked in a room with Lucius and I was most definitely going a little stir crazy. Meaning that when he announced we were getting ready to leave, well, I was more than ready for it. Despite knowing that I was most likely just swapping this room for one with a higher view and one of a never-ending storm that could kill anything it touched… yep, I was talking about Lucius' tower. One I was assured that now the hex had been removed, there would be no way for anyone to get to me there. But then I remember joking, saying,

"And not even a family member?" His reaction to this was not what I expected as I had only been teasing him.

"What makes you say that!" he snapped making me jerk back a little before putting my hands up in surrender, telling him,

"Hey, don't shoot, okay, I was just joking." I watched him visibly relax a moment and again it reminded me back to that day when he had to force himself to relax.

But then came the last day when we were about to leave, and something different happened. It was the first time Lucius had been forced to leave me as there was word that a rider had arrived seeking counsel with Lucius. He looked so torn that I offered,

"I can come with you if that makes you feel better."

"No!" he snapped and again it was so unlike Lucius, this erratic reaction to things, it had me questioning if he was losing his mind over worry for me. But straight away he seemed to recognise that he had snapped at me for no reason, making him walk over to me. Once there, he captured my face in his hold and said to me,

"I'm sorry, I have been on edge and just want to get back to my own fucking realm, away from this cursed place." This I could understand, as let's just say it was never going to hold good memories for us. Although, to be fair, there weren't many of those left anyway as something bad seemed to happen no matter where we were.

"I get it, it's fine," I told him, making him release a heavy sigh before giving me a sweet kiss and telling me,

"When did I get so lucky to have such an understanding Queen?"

"You mean girlfriend or *eternal life partner*, because the last time I checked, sweetheart, I wasn't standing in front of a minister with you next to me," I said teasing him about the past.

"Not yet, *eternal life partner*," he teased back. "Gods, I am never going to live that one down, am I?" he asked, making me smirk, roll on my heels and say,

"Nope, not a chance," to which he groaned in jest before telling me,

"I won't be long, and I will have the McBain brothers stationed outside your door, no one is to gain entrance, Amelia, do you understand?"

"Hey, I'm not the one worrying here," was my answer to his utter paranoia.

"Right," was his clipped reply. Then he kissed me again and stormed out of the door. I soon heard him barking orders, relaying to them what he had told me. However, the McBain brothers obviously didn't find a certain person a threat and I had to say I wasn't surprised as to why.

"Vena!" I shouted the moment my friend walked through the door running to embrace her. I had seen her since I'd come back, and unsurprisingly it had been an emotional reunion. But one under the watchful gaze of my new 24-hour bodyguard.

"I never thought I would catch you alone, how have you been since being locked away in here like his prisoner?"

"I'm not his prisoner," I said incredulously as her question had surprised me.

"Well, that's the rumour going around, and not surprising considering how crazy he's been," she said with a little shake of her head, which now have me questioning what else Lucius had been up to.

"What do you mean?"

"He's had my brother triple the guards surrounding this place, it has become a fortress." Okay, so this wasn't surprising, and I found myself relaxing a little.

"I don't know why or what he's worried about, it's not like the Wraith Master can come back." Vena shuddered at this as if terrified at the thought. I wisely refrained from telling her that wouldn't happen, considering *I was* the Wraith Master. Although, granted this wasn't something I was going to start introducing myself as in a hurry.

"I don't know either, other than it has something to do with this witch."

"What about the witch?" I asked, wondering now if this was what Lucius had been so weird about.

"I don't think I should be telling you this," Vena admitted, now looking nervous and shooting a little look over her shoulder as if she half expected Lucius to be stood there with his hands on his hips, ready to say a growly boo to her.

"But you're going to because you're my friend, right?" I said, nodding and prompting her to do the same.

"Yes?" It came out like a question and I laughed.

"It's fine, Lucius and I don't keep secrets," I said trying to reassure her, because clearly, *we did.*

"I overheard my brother when he was giving orders to his men."

"And those orders were?" I asked in what I hoped was an enticing tone.

"That the witch might try another attack, so to triple the guard." At this my mouth dropped, before asking,

"Another attack, what are you talking about?" Her hands

flew to her mouth and her purple hair flew all around the place as if completely untameable.

"Oh dear, I fear you don't know."

"Vena, tell me, please." I pleaded this time as I knew she was the only one around here who would give in.

"The Wraith Master, he wasn't sent by our uncle after all... *he was sent by the witch.*" At this my legs gave out and I sat back down on the bed, thankful there was something beneath me. I didn't know what was more shocking, the fact that the witch had gone to such lengths to reach me here or that Lucius hadn't told me. As for this new information, then it was of little wonder why he was so tense and why he had been paranoid. I stopped myself in time from dropping the F bomb. Instead, I went with a Vena classic.

"Pisspots!"

"I am sorry," Vena said in a small voice.

"No, don't be sorry, I hate being kept in the dark, although I don't know why he didn't tell me himself," I admitted, feeling embarrassed that he wouldn't tell me, and Vena knew that we obviously did keep things from each other. *Or at least, he did.*

"Maybe it's the same reason he won't let the Oracle see you, even though she is desperate to," Vena suggested.

"I know she came here to try and speak to me but I'm not sure why she is desperate," I admitted.

"I have a confession," she whispered, leaning closer and a waft of something minty and sweet she had obviously been eating drifted in front of my nose.

"Go on," I urged.

"I promised her I would get a message to you, it is about your future." I tensed, not knowing whether I had the strength to listen to this or not.

"She said... gosh, I hope I get this right..."

341

"Just take your time," I told her as she looked to the door and back at me. Then finally she said,

"I fear we do not have much of that left." No, she was probably right about that.

"I confess I was confused at what it all meant but she told me to tell you that she would be here waiting for you when the time came for you to complete your mission, for you to free the souls... like I said I didn't quite understand it myself, but she assured me you would." ...erm yeah, *I most definitely did.*

"Was that everything?" I asked.

"No, not exactly."

"What else?" Seriously, I loved Vena, but this was like pulling teeth!

"She told me to tell you not to trust what you think you know, that even the Vampire King should not trust what he thinks he knows either, although that seems a bit cryptic to me, as all anyone can believe is what they think they know... right?" I smiled at how innocent, sweet and naïve she was. I hoped she never had to endure even a small slice of what I had to for love. I hoped it came easy to her when the time came. she deserved to be happy.

"Oh, and one more thing, she told me to tell you, that a sacrifice for love isn't always given with a life, whatever that means. Don't you just wish these Oracles would talk normally and say what they actually mean, it would make life a lot easier," she said adding her personal thoughts, and I had to say that I agreed with her. They took frustration to a whole other level.

"It certainly would," I agreed but then there was a knock on the door, and she jumped up quickly.

"Oh, that's my cue to leave, I didn't ask them, but they said that they would warn me when he was coming back." I understood her fear of Lucius, as he had been like an angry jungle cat snarling at everyone, and I doubted that Vena would have been the exception. I squeezed her hand then she ran to the door slipping out of it, and I confess to being curious as to what her reaction would be when coming across Trice. However, I hadn't had chance to ask her anything about it and that saddened me. But then, in that moment, I also couldn't help but think about everything that she had told me, both about the witch and also what the Oracle had said. That when I was ready, she would be here waiting. Well, I hope she wasn't holding her breath on that one as who knew when this threat on Vampires would be over!

I also found that I had to make the decision on whether or not to confront Lucius on the fact that he had been keeping this from me. Or I knew that I could just let it go for the time being, as in all honesty I think arguing about it was probably the worst thing I could do.

So instead, I forced myself to do nothing, and Lucius was preparing for us to leave, I knew I had made the right decision. Because Lucius was anxious enough and now, I wasn't surprised seeing as he was obviously worried about the possibility of another attack or retaliation of some kind.

As for our journey, we waited for the first of the nights to fall, telling me it had been six days since the Wraith Master tried to take my life. But, as Lucius was pulling me through the Palace, I asked him,

"Can you at least let me say goodbye?" He had been ready to argue, I know this, but when he saw my beseeching eyes, his gaze softened, and he nodded. However, it was strange because I had a sense that everyone around me was keeping something from me too, but everyone was too afraid to speak freely. I shook off the unnerving feeling I had and said goodbye to King Auberon, joking with him that I bet he was glad to see the back of us. He scoffed back a laugh and replied,

"It is unmistakable that you most certainly know how to bring excitement to a Kingdom, yet I am most pleased to see you well, for it was not an experience anyone who witnessed such would get over anytime soon... *a few in particular.*" He said this last part when leaning down to grant me a quick kiss on my cheek and whispering in my ear. Then, when he raised back to his full height, he looked towards first Trice and then to Lucius, telling me which two he had been talking about.

In fact, I had come close a few times to arguing with Lucius over my being able to speak to Trice, something that I held back only out of guilt for Lucius. Because I knew how difficult this was on him and I was trying so hard not to make things worse, especially after what I had snapped at him before taking a bath that first day.

So, no matter how upsetting it was being kept from speaking with him, I also know Lucius was my first priority, meaning I tried to understand this from his point of view, and other than being able to grant Trice a few nods of my head and a whispered, 'I am okay', I hadn't been able to say anything more to him. Thankfully, he had understood this as I think it was clear to everyone that Lucius was dealing with this the only way he knew how...

As an overprotective King.

My next goodbye came to a tearful Vena, who feared she would never see me again, and I had to say I held the same fear.

"I wish you didn't have to leave me, for I'll never find another person who understands me better."

"Oh, I have an idea one will," I said looking towards Trice, and the moment she followed my gaze she blushed and shook her head.

"I owe you so much, Vena, I would never have survived this without you, you have been my rock when I was searching for him, you really don't know of the strength you hold. But promise me something… Never change who you are, for you are perfect and you should never let anyone make you feel any less than that. So, promise me you will never change, and I will be happy knowing that I have a friend here who is perfect just the way she is." By the end of this she had tears streaming down her face and I pulled her to me to give her a hug, squeezing her tight.

"Amelia, it is time, my love," Lucius said, gently reminding me that we had to go. So, I let go of my friend, saying yet another painful goodbye, for my time here seemed to be full of them. The sight of Vena standing next to her brother as he put his arm around her, doing so to comfort her in her loss, was the last thing I saw before the doors to the throne room were closed behind me. Carn'reau was escorting us with his men to the portal that was closest to Lucius' realm, along with the McBain brothers taking point, ahead of the small army. And as soon as I was outside, I took in a deep breath, as it was the first chance I'd had to go outside.

And as I breathed in the fresh night air, I was left hoping that for once,

This journey ahead would not result in…

Utter disaster.

EPILOGUE

LUCIUS

I wanted to curse myself!

Every single moment I had spent with her these last days had been like some bittersweet torture. For I knew what I was keeping from her and I had come so close... so fucking close to telling her. But I couldn't. It was too dangerous.

Gods, but I couldn't fucking believe it! I could not believe this cruel twist of fate, it was barely even fathomable. Just her name was one I forbade myself from saying for fear it would end up as acid in my mouth!

My fucking wife!

Now, what deal that treacherous bitch had made with whatever demon she had been worshipping at the time of her death, was anyone's guess! But it was starting to look like it had something to do with this unknown fucking brother of mine, and that was something I needed to get to the bottom of. And well, there was only one fucker alive that knew the details to that one!

Of course, it also looked like a two-thousand-year-old

history was coming back to try and destroy me for a second time! Of course, she had managed to get me killed the first time, but clearly that hadn't been enough for her!

Fuck, but that woman had taken everything from me!

She had taken... *Gods*... but I could even think it. It was too fucking painful. But then again... *burying your own child wasn't ever going to be anything but painful.*

But one who had died at the hands of your wife... no, the only thing as painful as that was watching as my Chosen One had died in my arms.

And now, I had experienced both.

This was why I hadn't told her. Why I hadn't told her any of this. I couldn't risk it happening again. I couldn't risk losing her, and now I was faced with a past decision I had to make for a second time. Because now I knew there was only one place safe for her, and I knew that after hearing that fucking name... well,

It wasn't with me.

No, I was only ever going to be the cause!

I was the fucking curse!

Not any Tree of Souls.

Which was why I had been planning, and when my brother turned up at the King's castle and told me of the news, my decision became final. It was one I made there and then. So, I had sent him to get the people I needed to make this exchange happen. For them to be ready for her. And as much as it pained me to allow Amelia to believe this journey was one that led back to my realm, back to my tower, that was not the case.

Because this was where we would be parting ways.

My life for hers, so that she may live. It was the only way.

So, as we rode on with my arms around her, I tried not to think of the end.

Of the inevitable.

I tried not to think of who would be there waiting for her when we arrived.

And as for me,

I was headed to only one place…

My Father's Realm.

ABOUT THE AUTHOR

Stephanie Hudson has dreamed of being a writer ever since her obsession with reading books at an early age. What first became a quest to overcome the boundaries set against her in the form of dyslexia has turned into a life's dream. She first started writing in the form of poetry and soon found a taste for horror and romance. Afterlife is her first book in the series of twelve, with the story of Keira and Draven becoming ever more complicated in a world that sets them miles apart.

When not writing, Stephanie enjoys spending time with her loving family and friends, chatting for hours with her biggest fan, her sister Cathy who is utterly obsessed with one gorgeous Dominic Draven. And of course, spending as much time with her supportive partner and personal muse, Blake who is there for her no matter what.

Author's words.

My love and devotion is to all my wonderful fans that keep me going into the wee hours of the night but foremost to my wonderful daughter Ava...who yes, is named after a cool, kick-ass, Demonic bird and my sons, Jack, who is a little hero and Baby Halen, who yes, keeps me up at night but it's okay because he is named after a Guitar legend!

Keep updated with all new release news & more on my website
www.afterlifesaga.com
Never miss out, sign up to the
mailing list at the website.

Also, please feel free to join myself and other Dravenites on my Facebook group
Afterlife Saga Official Fan
Interact with me and other fans. Can't wait to see you there!

 facebook.com/AfterlifeSaga
twitter.com/afterlifesaga
instagram.com/theafterlifesaga

ACKNOWLEDGEMENTS

Well first and foremost my love goes out to all the people who deserve the most thanks and are the wonderful people that keep me going day to day. But most importantly they are the ones that allow me to continue living out my dreams and keep writing my stories for the world to hopefully enjoy… These people are of course YOU! Words will never be able to express the full amount of love I have for you guys. Your support is never ending. Your trust in me and the story is never failing. But more than that, your love for me and all who you consider your 'Afterlife family' is to be commended, treasured and admired. Thank you just doesn't seem enough, so one day I hope to meet you all and buy you all a drink! ;)

To my family… To my amazing mother, who has believed in me from the very beginning and doesn't believe that something great should be hidden from the world. I would like to thank you for all the hard work you put into my books and the endless hours spent caring about my words and making sure it is the best it can be for everyone to enjoy. You make Afterlife shine. To my wonderful crazy father who is and always has been my hero in life. Your strength astonishes me, even to this day and the love and care you hold for your family is a gift you give to the Hudson name. And last but not least, to the man that I consider my soul mate. The man who taught me about real love and makes me not only want to be a better person but makes me feel I am too. The amount of support you have given me since we met has been incredible and the greatest feeling was finding out you wanted to spend the rest of your life with me when you asked me to marry you.

All my love to my dear husband and my own personal Draven... Mr Blake Hudson.

Another personal thank you goes to my dear friend Caroline Fairbairn and her wonderful family that have embraced my brand of crazy into their lives and given it a hug when most needed.

For their friendship I will forever be eternally grateful.

I would also like to mention Claire Boyle my wonderful PA, who without a doubt, keeps me sane and constantly smiling through all the chaos which is my life ;) And a loving mention goes to Lisa Jane for always giving me a giggle and scaring me to death with all her count down pictures lol ;)

Thank you for all your hard work and devotion to the saga and myself. And always going that extra mile, pushing Afterlife into the spotlight you think it deserves. Basically helping me achieve my secret goal of world domination one day...evil laugh time... Mwahaha! Joking of course ;)

As before, a big shout has to go to all my wonderful fans who make it their mission to spread the Afterlife word and always go the extra mile. I love you all x

ALSO BY
STEPHANIE HUDSON

Afterlife Saga

A Brooding King, A Girl running from her past. What happens when the two collide?

Transfusion Saga

What happens when an ordinary human girl comes face to face with the cruel Vampire King who dismissed her seven years ago?

Transfusion - Book 1

Venom of God - Book 2

Blood of Kings - Book 3

Rise of Ashes - Book 4

Map of Sorrows - Book 5

Tree of Souls - Book 6

Kingdoms of Hell – Book 7

Eyes of Crimson - Book 8

Roots of Rage - Book 9

Heart of Darkness - Book 10

Wraith of Fire - Book 11

Afterlife Chronicles: (Young Adult Series)

The Glass Dagger – Book 1

The Hells Ring – Book 2

Stephanie Hudson and Blake Hudson

The Devil in Me

OTHER WORKS
BY
HUDSON INDIE INK

Paranormal Romance/Urban Fantasy

Sloane Murphy

Xen Randell

C. L. Monaghan

Sci-fi/Fantasy

Brandon Ellis

Devin Hanson

Crime/Action

Blake Hudson

Mike Gomes

Contemporary Romance

Gemma Weir

Elodie Colt

Ann B. Harrison

Lightning Source UK Ltd.
Milton Keynes UK
UKHW041515210521
384127UK00002B/428

9 781913 904845